SHARON SHORT's SENSATIONAL JOSIE TOADFERN STAIN-BUSTING MYSTERIES ARE . . .

"Hilarious!"
Carolyn Hart

"Delicious!"
Earlene Fowler

"Good clean fun!"
Mary Kay Andrews

"Many cozies use up all their cleverness in their titles, but Sharon Short's books about stain-removal expert Josie Toadfern of Paradise, Ohio, save a lot of smarts for character and plot."
Chicago Tribune

"Josie makes a charming heroine . . . You'll be hungry for more Josie adventures."
Romantic Times Bookclub Magazine

"Cunning, with cleaning tips galore and a simply wonderful domestic goddess on the scene."
Mystery Scene

SHARON SHORT

A STAIN-BUSTING MYSTERY

Murder Unfolds

AVON BOOKS

An Imprint of HarperCollinsPublishers

This is a work of fiction. Names, characters, places, and incidents are products of the author's imagination or are used fictitiously and are not to be construed as real. Any resemblance to actual events, locales, organizations, or persons, living or dead, is entirely coincidental.

AVON BOOKS
An Imprint of HarperCollins*Publishers*
10 East 53rd Street
New York, New York 10022-5299

Copyright © 2007 by Sharon Short
ISBN: 978-0-06-079327-2
ISBN-10: 0-06-079327-9
www.avonmystery.com

First Avon Books paperback printing: March 2007

Avon Trademark Reg. U.S. Pat. Off. and in Other Countries, Marca Registrada, Hecho en U.S.A.
HarperCollins® is a registered trademark of HarperCollins Publishers.

Printed in the U.S.A.

10 9 8 7 6 5 4 3 2 1

This one is for Janice Short,
my wonderful mother-in-law,
and a good friend, too.

Acknowledgments

It's been said by far wiser writers than I that an author never really creates a book alone, but with the support of a team. I can avow that this is true . . . even when some team members do not know they are part of the team.

To wit: the entire town of Port Clinton, Ohio. Little did the good people of this town know that on December 31, 2005, in the Great Walleye Drop crowd, there lurked a writer. Yes, dear Port Clinton-ites, I was the one who kept glancing around and jotting notes, just so I could use your fair city and your wonderful celebration for this novel.

Readers, take note: all the nice things I've written about Port Clinton and its citizenry are true. The not-so-nice stuff and people, I made up. And I changed the occasional establishment name, to protect the innocent and the future of their enterprise, and rearranged parts of the town for my own purposes.

The Great Walleye Drop as described is very close to what actually happens, although again for plot purposes, I did take a few liberties. No, I'm not saying which details I changed. I think anyone who gets the opportunity to attend The Great Walleye Drop should take it, and figure out those details for themselves. (Although I have to say, the bit about the Elvis impersonator being an excellent singer is really true.)

Some team members go above and beyond for the author. This is always true about team Short: David, Katherine, and Gwen. But this time, my husband and daughters really went the extra mile . . . or miles . . . all the way to Port Clinton.

I'll always cherish the memory of my daughters going from mumbling "our buddies get to go to Florida for the holiday!" to getting caught up in the spirit of The Great Walleye Drop, linking arms with my husband and me, and swaying as we all crooned along with "Elvis" to "Dixie." How cool is that for a pair of adolescents?

Thank you, Janice Short, for dog-sitting ain't-nothin'-but-a-hound-dog Cosmo, so we could go to the Great Walleye Drop.

Thank you, Ellen Geiger and Sarah Durand, for trusting me on this one.

Thank you, Mary Tom Watts and Crystal Echols, for the candle-wax removal tip.

Thank you, Judy DaPolito and Katrina Kittle, for writerly coffee chats and lunches.

And thank you readers! You are a part of my team, too, and the emails and notes you send me saying "keep writing!" mean more to me than you'll ever know.

Murder Unfolds

1

"We're gonna die," Cherry Feinster said, although her words didn't come out that smoothly. Her teeth were chattering, which was no surprise since we were on a small, leaking houseboat on Lake Erie. At about two-thirty a.m. On New Year's Day.

"You want your last words to be a statement of the obvious?" Sally Toadfern said, also stuttering. If we'd known we were going to be kidnapped and then forced aboard a boat on a stormy winter night, I'm sure we'd have all bundled up in extra scarves and gloves.

Cherry and Sally had every reason to think we were doomed to young deaths, either due to hypothermia if we managed to stay on the boat, or from drowning when the ice storm pitched our boat over and then tossed us into the freezing—and in some parts frozen—Lake Erie.

And it wasn't as if anyone would come along and find us, even after the ice storm blew over. Fishing charters and ferries stop running on Lake Erie in late November, and they don't start up again until March.

By then, we'd be walleye bait at the bottom of the lake.

Except, I wasn't about to let that happen. I'm Josie Toadfern, owner of Toadfern's Laundromat and the best stain-removal expert in Paradise, Ohio. Or in Mason County. Maybe even in all of . . .

We hit something hard. Ice chunk? Pier? Land? In the dark, it was impossible to tell.

Sally, my cousin and one of my two best friends—the other being Cherry, who was now crying and hiccupping—started humming the "My Heart Will Go On" theme song from the movie, *Titanic*.

"Stop that," I chattered. Sally and Cherry were tied to each other, back to back, ankles bound. They'd been kidnapped first.

I'd been kidnapped second.

I was bound at my ankles and wrists, my wrists in front of me, which gave me a little hope, because if I could get to something sharp, I'd have an easier time cutting through the rope tying my wrists.

I also felt a bit of hope because I wasn't bound to anything, although Sally and Cherry were tied to the anchored legs of the dinette table. I'd been brought onboard last, and there hadn't been anything to quickly bind me to. So our captor had just whacked me in the head, knocking me out for the second time that night.

When I'd finally come to, I'd tried chewing on the rope around my wrists. Two gnaws told me that was going to be impossible. So I started to butt-scoot toward the tackle box I knew was just outside the cabin. Butt-scooting was a painfully slow inch-by-inch process, given the cold, the listing of the boat, and the fact I was bound.

Still, my plan was get to the box, pray that it wasn't locked, that I could open it, and then find something sharp like a fishing knife that I could use to cut my bindings, and then free Cherry and Sally.

I hadn't thought beyond that, but I was lucky to have come up with any plan at all, given our situation: the leaking boat, the icy water, and Sally's persistent humming/chattering of the *Titanic* theme song.

At least our captors had left our mouths uncovered, since our screams wouldn't get the attention of anything other than a few frigid walleye, trout, and salmon, so we could talk. Of course, I'd hoped our talk would be about getting out of our predicament.

But Sally was intent on trying to use humor to lighten our last minutes on earth. Well, on lake.

"Sorry," she said. "Since you don't like Celine Dion, how about the old Gordon Lightfoot tune about the *Edmund Fit-fit-fitzgerald*—"

"Th-that freighter went down on L-lake Superior," I said, surprising myself with the recollection.

"Then how about the th-theme from *G-G-Gilligan's Island*," Cherry stuttered. "At least they ended up on a w-w-arm island."

We'd been left without any light, and since it was the middle of the night and there was an ice storm, we didn't even have a glow of moonlight.

Thud. This time, I went skidding across the floor. I used the momentum to butt-scoot even faster, and finally hit the edge of the cabin door with my leg. Eager now, I scooted my way out. As soon as I was outside the cabin, icy rain lashed my face.

I slowed, hoping to find the tackle box with my legs or arms, before going over the edge of the boat.

Finally, I bumped into the box. I struggled, but soon used my bound hands to lever the lid open.

With my teeth, I pulled the glove off my right hand. I knew I'd risk cutting myself, feeling around for a knife that way, but I also knew it would be harder to find with a gloved hand.

Carefully, I pushed my hands into the top of the box, feeling around and drawing back when at last something sharp stabbed into the side of my hand.

But the pain was wonderful because it meant I'd found the knife! I yelped with joy. I turned my hands so that the rope on the top of my right wrist was against the sharp edge.

It was more awkward than trying to cut the rope straight on, but I didn't want to risk a sudden lurch sending the sharp edge between the insides of my wrists.

The rope suddenly gave way. Freedom! But then, the boat lurched again, and I didn't pull back in time. The knife jabbed into the top of my right wrist. I pulled away, gasping in pain. But I grabbed the knife with my right hand. I knew I needed to use the knife to cut Cherry's and Sally's bindings.

"Josie! What's happening?" Cherry cried, from inside the cabin.

"I . . . I think I'm bleeding . . ." I called back.

I felt a warmness seeping from the top of my wrist, and then I became light-headed. What to do? I needed to stop the bleeding. I needed to free Cherry and Sally. We needed to see if we could find flashlights or a radio on the boat. We needed to see what we were bumping into. We needed to get off that boat . . .

Suddenly, I felt like I didn't want to do any of it at all, like I just wanted to collapse and let the dark speckles that were now dancing before my eyes multiply and grow and overtake me.

"What is wrong with you? Just a few seconds ago, you were thinking about how you have so much to live for!"

That was the voice of Mrs. Oglevee, my old junior high history teacher, who was not on the boat, seeing as how she'd been dead for ten years. But the image of Mrs. Oglevee started showing up in my dreams earlier in the year, when I'd happened to get involved with solving a few murder mysteries, in part thanks to my stain-removal expertise, and in part thanks to my natural nosiness, but always purely by accident—really! I'd be snoozing away, in the peaceful warm fuzzy darkness of sleep—much like the sensation I wanted to give into now—and there she'd be, nattering on about how I *should* be involved with solving a murder (whenever I didn't want to) or how I *shouldn't* be involved with solving a murder (whenever I did want to).

Usually she'd show up Cheshire-cat-like, first her face popping into my subconscious sleep life, like a face from backstage poking through the curtains, and then the rest of her would appear, whether I liked it or not—sometimes in an outlandish getup that she'd never have worn in real life, and sometimes in her regular schoolmarm clothes. Sometimes, she'd make things appear that related somehow to the crime that I was trying to solve.

But this time, it was just her voice.

"Now listen here, young lady! You will not crap out on me now. Get a cloth—there's a pile of rags back in the cabin—and stop that bleeding!"

"You know," I said . . . although I'm not sure if I said it aloud, or just in my head, or a little of both, mumbling, "you would have sent me to the principal in a heartbeat for using the word crap . . ."

"That was then! This is now! Get those rags!"

"What if I don't want to?"

"You're going to just give up? Die out here? Abandon Guy's fate to the decision-making of others?"

That stung. Of course I didn't want to abandon Guy that way. Guy is my older cousin. He has autism, and lives in a wonderful group home, Stillwater Farms, north of Paradise, Ohio. His parents reared me from the time I was seven. They both passed away by the time I was nineteen and left me two things: their laundromat business and Guy's guardianship. In the past eleven years, I'd taken both seriously, cherishing them as the foundation of my life.

But then, there probably wasn't any way I was really going to save us from drowning in frigid Lake Erie, and meanwhile, this warm fuzziness was drawing me away from the chilling, miserable cold and my likely tortuous fate, and it was so, so tempting . . .

"Josie! Young lady, you pay attention, now! You can't give up on Sally and Cherry, either! They need you to help them," Mrs. Oglevee snapped.

It was true. Neither of them deserved to die this way,

either. Sally was the single mother of triplets and worked full time as the owner of the Bar-None and part-time as a carpenter. Cherry had finally found the love of her life.

"It's your fault, you know," I said to Mrs. Oglevee, although the words came out fuzzy and as if they were really one word, like iz-yer-all-ya-no. "Investigating your murder got us into this mess . . ."

"That's right, and if you don't get out of this mess, the world will never know the truth!"

That was Mrs. Oglevee; all sympathy and sensitivity. Hah. Once she was subbing in my home-ec class, and I sewed right through my thumb while trying to make the class project—an apron I would never have worn, anyway—and the needle snapped off. Her reaction was, "Do you know, young lady, how much it costs the school system to replace sewing machine needles?"

She wasn't any kinder now, even though my injury and predicament were far more serious than a sewing machine needle stuck in my thumb. Why *had* I bothered to investigate her murder . . . when all of us in Paradise had believed for the past ten years that she'd died of ill-timed heart failure, right before she was scheduled to leave on a Mediterranean cruise?

Truth be told, because I thought if I laid her story to rest, maybe . . . just maybe . . . she'd stop interrupting my sleep cycles.

Then again, if I gave into the dancing dark warm speckles . . .

"Young lady, don't you dare!" Mrs. Oglevee screamed, and then she slapped me.

A cold, sudden, watery slap . . . that was really lake water sloshing over me.

The water-slap got rid of the darkness in my head—it was still dark, of course, all around us—and the sound of Cherry and Sally screaming my name from inside the cabin finished bringing me around.

I was still clutching the knife in my right hand. Carefully,

carefully—despite the cold, the water, the panic—I cut my ankles free from one another. Then I crawled back into the cabin and clattered into something else . . .

The battery-powered camper's lamp! I fumbled around until I was able to turn it on, and a greenish glow filled the cabin. I saw the box of rags, shoved under the captain's chair. Had Mrs. Oglevee really just told me about those rags . . . or had I noticed them earlier and filed them away in my subconscious?

At that moment, it didn't matter.

I grabbed a rag.

Right. First to staunch the bleeding on my wrist. Then I'd free Cherry and Sally. Somehow we'd make radio contact with someone, before we were launched overboard or sank . . .

And to think this whole mess began—more or less—with a simple coffee stain . . .

2

"Just imagine 'em all naked," Cherry had told me four days earlier, on the evening of December 28. "Then you won't be so nervous!"

That had been Cherry's advice for handling my jitters at giving a speech for the second time in my life. On the eve of that speech, we were at the Bar-None, the jukebox joint on the edge of Paradise, owned by my other good pal—and cousin—Sally. And Cherry had had several too-many beers. She wouldn't tell us why, although Sally and I suspected it had something to do with the unusual absence of Cherry's boyfriend, sheriff's deputy Dean Rankle. But we couldn't pry any details out of her even after three beers and a bowl of honey-roasted peanuts, so the subject had turned to my own woes.

Uppermost: the fact that the next day, I was scheduled—doomed, was more like it—to give the speech at the Mason County Public Library's ribbon-cutting ceremony for the new Pearl Oglevee Regional History Collection.

Sally took away my empty glass and replaced it with a fresh one, filled this time around with just Big Fizz Diet Cola on the rocks, hold the bourbon. One mixed drink an evening was plenty for me, I thought virtuously, frowning at Cherry, who was now humming along to "Your Cheatin' Heart" on the jukebox.

"I've heard tell of some survey that said the fear of giving a speech is greater for lots of people than the fear of death," said Sally, trying to be helpful.

I moaned and put my glass back down on the bar. "Just shoot me now, then," I said. "Better yet, add a shot of bourbon."

Sally added something closer to a trickle of bourbon to my glass. "Now, if I know you, you've done more research than ten other people combined would have, and rehearsed your speech endlessly."

"True. But it turns out that there just isn't that much to find out about Pearl Oglevee."

"Pearl?" Cherry and Sally said at once.

"That's right. Pearl was Mrs. Oglevee's first name."

We'd all had Mrs. Oglevee in junior high social studies. She'd half-heartedly taught government and American history, and only really lit up when she taught local and Ohio history, but through it all she was overly strict, made it clear she thought we were unappreciative dolts (which, to be fair, was sometimes true) who couldn't possibly understand the importance of what she taught. Plus, for some reason I've never quite figured out, she took an especial disliking to me.

Other than that we vaguely knew that she was divorced, had no children, and was very stingy, living in a small house on Poplar Street and wearing out-of-fashion second-hand clothes that went with her unsmiling, plain face and mousy brown hair-in-a-bun.

She was, in other words, the stereotypical schoolmarm kids love to hate. She'd shocked us only twice in her life: ten years before (just two years after retiring), she made sure everyone in Paradise knew she was finally, finally going on the Mediterranean cruise she'd always dreamed of. (She had? That was news to everyone.)

And then, just days before she was scheduled to depart on her dream trip, she'd died, some said of stroke, some said from a heart attack. I didn't know anyone who went to her funeral or burial.

"Besides the fact she was named after a jewel that starts life as an irritating grain of sand, Mrs. Oglevee was born and raised in Port Clinton," I said to Sally. Cherry had wandered off to the dance floor to bump-n-grind with some cowboy wannabe, which surprised me. I thought she'd foresworn her old ways to devote herself to Deputy Dean, who I knew was madly in love with her.

"Port Clinton?" Sally echoed, sounding shocked.

"Are you going to repeat everything I say?" I asked irritably. "It's not exactly shocking to be named Pearl and grow up in Port Clinton, Ohio. In fact, there's nothing shocking about Mrs. Oglevee's life. She and her sister Rose—one year younger—grew up in the well-to-do Armbruster family, who made their wealth long ago in fishing and shipping. She got her bachelor's of education from Bowling Green State University, near Toledo."

I snipped off the end of each sentence as if I were biting off bits of bitter lemon.

"Met and married Millard Oglevee. He was a manager at the Mason Quarry—" that was not far from Paradise, as Sally knew—"and Mrs. Oglevee started teaching at the junior high in 1958. They divorced in 1961. Mrs. Oglevee kept teaching and being bitchy—"

"Now, you're not saying that in your speech, are you?" asked Sally, who seemed to have recovered from whatever was a shocker about Port Clinton.

"Of course not. I'm going to say, 'contributing to the educational development of adolescent Paradisites.' "

Sally shuddered.

"Exactly. Anyway, besides that, the only thing to say about Mrs. Oglevee is that she loved Ohio history. I don't even know why. But she did."

"She did get a little nicer—and more interesting—when

we got to that unit each year. Like she didn't mind teaching so much."

I snorted. "More like she was so lost in her own world— remember the time she dressed up like a Shawnee Indian maiden? Went on and on even after the bell rang? Anyway. She died in 1996—heart attack."

"I heard stroke."

"Dr. Fulmer confirmed heart attack," I said. "I always do my research."

"Hey, Sally, how about another beer?" called a regular from the end of the bar.

"Just a minute, Karl, I'm in the middle of something!" Sally hollered back.

Bar-None is just on the edge of Paradise. The nearest alternative is about twelve miles away, and it was closed earlier in the year by the county health department. All of which meant Karl would wait for his beer with only mild grumbling.

"Go on," Sally said.

She was patronizing me. I knew it. I didn't care. I went on.

"So, her niece—Eileen—"

"She had a niece?!"

"Why does that surprise you?"

"It's just weird to think of Mrs. Oglevee with any family at all."

I considered that. Sally had a point. Mrs. Oglevee had always seemed so . . . alone. And like she liked it that way. It was hard enough, as kids, to imagine even our warmest, nicest teachers with lives outside the classroom. I remember how shocked I'd been the summer I was sixteen and ran into Mrs. Sicillens—my high school biology teacher—at the FoodTown in Masonville. She was there with her *four* kids, trying to help them select *three* Jell-O flavors for a buck— lemon, watermelon, raspberry? Lime, grape, cherry?—and looking most unteacherly in short-shorts, tank top, silver ankle bracelet, and orange flip-flops. After all . . . she was *old*. Twenty-nine!

Which is how old I was, I realized. For two more days.

I moaned again.

"Josie? Mrs. Oglevee's niece?"

"Oh, yeah. Eileen was her sister's only child, and Mrs. Oglevee's closest relative. So she was named executrix of her estate. In the event of Mrs. Oglevee's death, Eileen was to invest the proceeds of Mrs. Oglevee's estate, and when they reached a hundred thousand dollars—"

"Whoa!"

"I know. But Mrs. Oglevee never went out to eat, rarely bought new clothes—and remember when she did, we joked that they must come from the Little Sisters of Charity shop up in Masonville, pretending to recognize family members' clothes that had been donated—"

"I remember," Sally said, looking a little guilty.

"And she never got to go on her cruise."

"Due to her untimely heart attack."

"Right. So, a few months ago, Mrs. Oglevee's investments reached a hundred grand, and off they went to the Mason County Public Library, with the stipulation that most of it would be used to convert a rarely used meeting room into the Pearl Oglevee Regional History Collection room—bookshelves, regional and state history books, novels by Ohioans, and so forth. Winnie tells me there's still room there for meetings, if needed. And the rest is kept in trust at the library for future purchases for the collection."

Winnie Logan is a good friend of mine, and the bookmobile librarian. She comes to Paradise on Tuesdays and Thursdays. I let her use my laundromat's small parking lot to park her bookmobile.

"Sally—another beer? Please?" Karl was sounding desperate.

"Just finish off the honey-roasted peanuts, and I'll get there when I get there!" Sally grumbled.

The Bar-None doesn't exactly have *Cheers* ambience going for it. Although occasionally a *Cheers* rerun appears on the big-screen TV over the bar. But if Ohio State is playing football or basketball and the game is televised, changing the channel to TV Land would result in a riot. Go Bucks!

"Well, that's interesting background," Sally said, encouragingly, finally starting to tap a beer for Karl. I'd been about to crawl over the bar and do it myself. "So, what's the speech?"

I crunched an ice cube between my teeth. "That was the speech."

Sally put Karl's beer mug on the bar and stared at me. "What?"

"What I just said. About Mrs. Oglevee, where she was born, all that—that was the speech. Mrs. Oglevee's entire life, as neat and tidy and simple as a crisply folded stack of clean laundry."

Sally kept staring.

"Sally?" Karl's voice was very soft now.

"That was all the information Eileen—that's the niece—said she had when I interviewed her on the telephone. Well, I do have a few mementos Eileen sent to Winnie, who passed them on to me. Childhood photos—just a few—and a clipping about Mrs. Oglevee winning a singing contest when she was younger, and her wedding photo. Scanned it all for a PowerPoint slide show to go along with my comments."

Sally moved on to the end of the bar, to Karl's relief.

My stomach knotted tighter than pantyhose in a washer. Sally was right. I didn't have enough to say. This speech was going to be awful. But what could I do? I'd talked to Mrs. Beavy, the town's self-appointed historian, to teachers, even to my old principal, other students of Mrs. Oglevee—and we all came up blank. No one had been her friend or even her acquaintance in all her years in Paradise. Her love of Ohio and regional history was well known—and that was it. She'd just been too distant, too prickly to let anyone get too close.

A question weaved across my mind. Why? Had she wanted it that way, to be alone and unloved? It seemed she did . . .

"What's up?" Cherry said, plunking back down on the bar stool next to me.

"I am absolutely, completely going to suck tomorrow morning when I give my speech to dedicate the Pearl Oglevee Regional History Collection."

"Oh." Cherry popped a lip gloss and tiny mirror out of her gold-sequined purse (which matched her top) and reapplied her bright red gloss. I pulled a ChapStick from my jeans pocket and moistened my own pucker, wondering if I should ask what had happened to the lip gloss that had been so bright on her lips just a jukebox dance ago. Then I decided I didn't want to know.

"Well, then," Cherry said, dropping the gloss and mirror back into her purse, "let's move on to cheerier things. So . . . facing the big three-oh in a coupla days, eh?"

I groaned.

"Oh, come on, I turned thirty last year, and I'm doing okay!"

I looked at Cherry. It was true that she wore so much makeup it was hard to tell if she'd aged all that much. Her makeup base filled in all the crevices. And her attitude hadn't aged at all . . . since junior high. That's when Sally and I had met her. She'd been held back a year and so, even though she was a year older than us, she'd been in our graduating class, seventh grade through senior year.

"So, who are you gonna go out with to celebrate turning thirty? The rumpled, witty but cute in his own way, brainboy Caleb Loudermilk?"

Caleb is the new editor at the *Paradise Advertiser-Gazette*. We'd been dating—casually—because I'm still on the mend from my breakup with Owen Collins, my ex-boyfriend who had just moved to Kansas City to be near his son . . . and ex-wife. The move wasn't really the cause of the breakup, but instead it was over the fact he couldn't be truthful with me about major events in his life. From his point of view, I'd been too demanding, too pushy. My girlfriends all assured me he was wrong. Of course, I agreed with them.

Caleb and I had also kept our dating casual because he's a professional colleague—and the guy who first got my column picked up by regional newspapers all across Ohio.

My Stain-Busters column was now in thirty-two newspapers in Ohio, four in Kentucky, and three in Indiana. Plus I'd just been contacted by a Columbus TV station about coming on a newsmagazine show the coming February. And I was working with Chip Beavy to develop a Web site to help promote my column and stain-expertise. (Chip is the grandson of Mrs. Beavy, the local historian. He occasionally fills in at my laundromat and is studying web design at Masonville Community College.)

All of which made me, suddenly, Mrs. Oglevee's most successful student—at least, of those still living in Paradise. A few had gone on to become doctors and lawyers and engineers, but they'd moved away from Paradise. So, I'd been picked to give the dedication speech the next morning about the Pearl Oglevee Regional History Collection.

"Or," Cherry was going on, "maybe you should go out with hunky Randy." Randy Woodford was the handsome, muscular, contractor who was renovating the two apartments over my laundromat into one big apartment. I'd never had much luck renting out the second apartment, and since I owned the building, I'd decided it was time to make my home into what I wanted it to be: bigger, airier, and with plenty of space for bookshelves and books.

Randy was great with power tools, delicious to look at, and a great kisser—which was why I was casually dating him, too. But he couldn't understand why I'd want more space for books, of all things. Or why I wanted to talk about subjects other than Nascar.

"Randy could probably make you feel fifteen again." Cherry waggled her eyebrows meaningfully.

I scowled at her. "Ew. At fifteen, I still hadn't had my first kiss, Cherry."

"Seventeen?" Cherry amended. "Twenty?"

"Cherry, you wanna know what I'm going to do on my thirtieth birthday?"

She nodded eagerly.

"I'm going to make a chocolate Coca-Cola sheet-cake." That was my favorite. Aunt Clara always made it for me on my birthday when I was a kid. "I'm going to sing happy birthday to myself—alone. Blow out my candles—alone. Have a piece of cake—alone. And then start in on my To Be Read pile—again, alone. Sometime between December 30 and January 1, I'm making a list of goals."

"Goals?" Cherry looked genuinely confused.

"You know, achievements people try to reach. That sort of thing." Cherry was thirty-one and genuinely happy living day-to-day, running her beauty salon and dating, dating, dating . . . at least she had been, until Deputy Dean came along, and then she seemed happy sticking just with him, and he was definitely overjoyed to be with her. Except, where was he?

I shook my head, tried to refocus. "I'm going to be thirty. I have responsibilities," I told Cherry, feeling virtuous. The greatest—and most joyous—of which was that I was my cousin Guy Foersthoefel's guardian. "I need to think about where I'm really going with this column, what I want to do . . ."

I stopped. The tangled-pantyhose-knot feeling in my tummy tightened. The truth was, I felt overwhelmed by everything—the column, the speech, the apartment renovation (which was already costing more than I'd planned), my role on the search committee for a new director at Stillwater, since our beloved previous director had taken another position closer to his parents . . .

"She's planning on hiding in her apartment for her birthday," Cherry said, her tone dripping with disgust. "Told you so."

I looked up. Sally was back at our end of the bar.

"Yeah, and I'm doing the same the next night, too, for New Year's Eve!" I said, defiantly.

Cherry held out her hand to Sally. "Pay up."

I glared at them. "You two were making bets on my plans for my birthday and New Year's Eve?"

"Yep," Cherry said. "I bet you'd squirrel yourself away from the world, whereas Sally thought you'd at least show up here as usual . . ."

Sally frowned at Cherry. "Hush up! Josie has a lot on her mind, what with the big speech tomorrow."

"Thanks," I said. "Cherry's harassment had almost made me forget." Well, not really. But I was feeling more than a little prickly.

Sally leaned across the bar, closer to me. "Hey, about that speech . . . why don't you just ask Mrs. Oglevee what to say? Maybe she'd have some insight."

I sighed. Sally and Cherry were the only two people who knew my dirty little secret: that the specter of Mrs. Oglevee sometimes haunts my dreams, especially when I start poking around in things that a lot of folks say are really none of my business . . . although in my defense, I'm usually just trying to help.

But, just like the real-life Mrs. Oglevee had, specter-Mrs.-Oglevee would always nag me and find some reason why what I was doing wasn't quite good enough.

Spirit? Figment of my subconscious? I wasn't sure. I didn't care. I just wished she'd go away so I could go back to the dreamless sleep I used to enjoy.

"It doesn't work like that, Sally," I said. "It's not like I can conjure her up and ask questions."

"Wouldn't that be great, though?" Cherry said. "To have a sort of dream-genie you could ask for advice?"

"She's not real, she's just a dream-invention that my subconscious cooked up for some reason . . ."

"Hmmm. Maybe you should consider counseling. Karl, here, has a brother-in-law who's in that line of work," Sally suggested. "Hey, Karl," she hollered, "what's your brother-in-law's name? The one who's a shrink? Josie here needs to talk to him."

I hopped down from the bar stool and shoved my glass back at Sally. "And you two wonder why I just want to hide for my birthday and New Year's?"

"Hey, that's right, we do . . . did you ever answer that question?" Cherry wondered.

"You're driving her home, right?" I said to Sally.

"Of course," Sally said. "Hey—where're you going? What's wrong?"

"Nothing," I snapped. "I just need a good night's sleep!"

I started to the door, ignoring Karl, who was hollering after me—"Hey, Josie, my brother-in-law the shrink, his name is . . ."

3

Coffee stains are, by their very nature, unique in the world of staindom.

Notice, sometime, how a drop of coffee on, say, a blouse, spreads like any other stain. But as it dries, something different happens with a coffee stain than with other stains. The color travels right to the edge of the stain, so that once dry, the stain's edge is darker than its middle. Scientists have studied this, and they precisely understand it.

Personally, I think maybe it's just in the nature of coffee stains . . . they gotta do what they gotta do, and what they gotta do is send their dark little molecules scurrying to the edge of where they've soaked into the cloth, but no further.

Still, I wonder, why do they do that? Why don't they just keep on traveling? What's in the middle of their stainy souls that makes them scurry away from the center, away from each other, as far as they can go, but no farther? I don't know. It's a mystery: coffee stains . . . right up there with human nature.

And, of course, on the morning of my big Mrs. Oglevee speech, minutes before I was to go on, I was sporting a big coffee stain—right smack in the middle of my blouse.

I had tossed and turned all night long, trying to think up ways to make my speech more interesting, and by the big morning of Josie-Gives-a-Speech-and-Dies-from-Embarrassment, I wished I did have Karl's brother-in-law-the-shrink's name *and* his phone number on speed dial.

Not so I could get his advice on purging the Mrs. Oglevee specter from my dreams—if you don't sleep, ghostly visitors can't disturb your slumber—but so he could talk me out of my absolute terror about giving the speech.

By the time I finally got to the Mason County Library— main branch, in Masonville—I was shaking so hard I could barely carry the ninety-nine-cent latte-to-go I'd picked up at Beans-Gone-Wild Café, which is what the Pump-N-Save calls its variation of Starbucks.

(Truth be told, Beans-Gone-Wild is really two coffee machines and a rack of stale pastries, right next to an even bigger rack of tobacco chew. From my tiny dot on the map, you have to get near Columbus before you see signs for Starbucks. That's right. I'm livin' in a Beans-Gone-Wild outpost in a Starbucks world.)

And by the time I got to the Mason County Library, I was shaking so hard from caffeine and nerves that Winnie Logan immediately escorted me to the media-processing room behind the checkout counter. She hung my coat up on a peg behind the door, while Jenny, another librarian, took my PowerPoint disc and went to set up the slide show.

I sat down in a chair, started to tell Winnie how I was thinking of maybe zesting up my speech with a few recollected renditions of the historical characters Mrs. Oglevee liked to play-act in class now and again, and . . . in a sudden tremor of terror . . . sloshed coffee on my pale yellow blouse, the one I'd bought especially for this event.

Now, I know just how to get out coffee stains.

Rinse and soak in cold water . . . pretreat with a mix of one-third white vinegar and two-thirds water . . . and I told Winnie all about that, but she took off before I got to the vinegar part.

I sat shaking for a few more minutes, and finally Winnie came back. I think of her as an Earth-Mother type; she wears big, cotton peasant skirts of 1960s vintage, lots of jangly silver jewelry, patchouli perfume, and a concerned expression at all times. The kind of person you look at and just know she bakes her own bread, whole wheat. (Which she does.)

She's perfect for the bookmobile. Everyone loves her, and she knows all her patrons by name and book preference. Usually she's great at calming people down, but I had a hyperadvanced case of the nerves.

"Here you go," she said. "A paper towel with cold water—will that help the stain?"

It would lessen it, though not get it out as completely as I'd like, but I just nodded. I, Josie Toadfern, stain-removal expert, would have to give my speech while wearing a coffee-stained blouse. I was sure that Mrs. Pearl Oglevee—wherever she was—was loving that.

"There's a nice-sized audience in the meeting room," Winnie said.

I moaned, dabbing at my blouse with the damp paper towel.

"Now stop moaning!" she said. "You'll be fine. Just inhale slowly—relaxation in! And exhale. Tension out! That's my girl. Okay, Cara Tickham—" that was the library system director—"is ready to introduce you when you come out. Your PowerPoint is all set up. I'll just tell Cara you need a few moments, and then I'll walk you over, okay?"

"Okay," I said weakly, more interested in the sudden appearance of dancing points of light than in Winnie's fading voice . . .

"Josie? Josie! Inhale and look at me! Now exhale."

I looked at Winnie's anxious face.

All right, I told myself. I had to do this. I couldn't embarrass Winnie. Just get through the speech, and then tell Caleb to pull the plug on the column. If making it a success meant doing things like this, then I couldn't do it. I'd just have to cancel the renovations on my apartment, find some other way to make more income to ensure I could take care of Guy . . .

"Josie, this is for you."

Winnie was poking an envelope at me.

"What . . . what is it?"

"It's a note from Eileen Russell."

I stared at Winnie.

"You know," she said with exaggerated patience, "Pearl Oglevee's niece? The executrix of her estate? The woman who gave you the background for your speech, who so generously sent the photos and mementos you scanned for your PowerPoint?"

"Oh, oh, yes, and I have everything here, in my bag, in a big envelope, to send back . . ."

I started pawing through my tote bag.

"That can wait, Josie," Winnie said. "After your speech. Frankly, I'm a little surprised—"

She stopped. My curiosity radar went "ping, ping." "What?" I said.

"Well, it's just that Eileen didn't sound at all interested when I invited her to come to the dedication ceremony." Winnie had been assigned to organize the ceremony, although it was the library director and the president of the Friends of the Library who had asked me to give the speech. "And meeting her, she doesn't seem at all what I imagined from the phone conversations . . ."

Winnie shook her head. "No matter. You also have a surprising number of fans out there, so your presence is good PR for the library—and for the Pearl Oglevee Regional History Collection! Isn't that great? You're already a success, and you haven't even been officially introduced. Now take a few seconds, and I'll be right back. You'll be fine."

And then Winnie left me sitting there, surrounded by books and videos and CDs and DVDs that needed to be shelved, and holding an envelope. I spied a copy of *Little*

Women. I'd loved that book as a kid. Maybe I could just hide in a corner, reread that instead of giving this speech?

I sighed. No, I'd have to be brave—just like Jo March. She wouldn't have had a problem giving a speech . . .

That's just like you, Josie, always wanting to do something other than the task at hand . . .

I shook my head. Great. Now I was hearing Mrs. Oglevee's voice in my head, and I wasn't even asleep.

. . . the task at hand . . .

I looked down at Eileen's envelope in my hand. It smelled of cigarette smoke and was plain white, letter-sized, unlabeled—and sported a coffee stain in the corner.

From my blouse? No. This coffee stain had dried, and left the tell-tale dark-ringed brown splotch. I lifted my eyebrows at the coincidence, and then shrugged.

Some people like to believe coincidences are nudges from higher powers. I like to believe they're . . . just coincidences.

I opened the envelope. For a moment my hand stopped shaking as I read the unsigned note. In fact, my whole body went rigid with shock, even as I read it again:

Josie:

You think you know all about Mrs. Oglevee? You don't. But I'm her daughter, and I do.

And my mother, Pearl Oglevee, was murdered.

4

"Mrs. Oglevee was a long-time dedicated teacher at Paradise Middle School," I was saying. I pressed the button on the remote control and behind me on the portable screen appeared the official photo of Mrs. Oglevee that had been in the school's yearbooks from 1958 to her retirement in 1996.

She was unsmiling, could have been any age from the twenty-nine she was in the photo (My age! For just one more day! a spare part of my brain observed) to her fifties. She wore a pale blouse with a ruffle and had her hair teased into a do that looked like it had all the touchability of a scouring pad.

"The main class she taught was history, with a particular interest in local history . . ."

You're droning, Josie. Are you trying to put the audience members into comas?

There was Mrs. Oglevee's voice in my head again. And I swear I thought I could feel her staring at the back of my head from the big screen.

Plus I was all too aware of the note in my pants pocket. Mrs. Oglevee had a daughter? Mrs. Oglevee was . . . murdered?

One part of my brain kept my mouth moving, reading the speech I'd carefully typed out in an 18-point font, pressing the little remote button to move through the few slides I had whenever I came to a note that said NEXT in bold.

"Mrs. Oglevee—Pearl—had a quiet life in her native Port Clinton, although she was honored as a spelling bee champion at age eight, as shown in this newsclipping . . ."

Another part of my brain—the spare part that also noted that Mrs. Oglevee had been my age when she moved to Paradise—busily analyzed the note still in my pocket.

Was it a prank? A mean trick that someone I knew had organized?

No. Winnie had been adamant that Eileen Russell, Mrs. Oglevee's niece, had directly given her the envelope. Why would she pull such a mean joke on me, right before I delivered this speech about her aunt?

On the other hand, why would she share such shocking claims with me, and in a note? If she had such suspicions, she should really share them with the police.

"Pearl Oglevee remained a highly diligent student through high school. Here's her high school yearbook photo. Her freshman year, she took Latin I, Biology I . . ."

Was that a snore I heard from the middle of the audience? The heat was too high and the lights had been dimmed for my PowerPoint presentation—factors that weren't in my favor. I didn't dare look up from my speech to see if someone in the small room was about to fall off his or her chair.

Never mind that! The calm, spare part of my brain cajoled. What about the note itself? It had the coffee stain—a much smaller droplet than the big splotch smack dab in the middle of my blouse—and it also smelled faintly of smoke. So whoever wrote it was a coffee drinker and smoker, or had written it around someone, or several people, who were.

The message had been penned in firm, dark blue block letters, as if the person wanted to disguise his or her

handwriting. It had taken time to create such careful lettering, which suggested the note had not been dashed off as a
last-minute prank.

Then again, the coffee stain suggested haste. How does
someone get coffee stains on something they're writing?
Maybe just plain clumsiness. But also by hurrying, sloshing,
spilling. Whoever had written it hadn't taken the time to re-
write it on fresh paper.

Somehow, the stylized, careful handwriting and the sloppy
coffee stain didn't fit. Were two people involved?

And were there fingerprints on the note? By now it probably wouldn't matter. Winnie had handled it. I'd handled it.
Then, just before I went out to give my speech, I'd thought-
lessly shoved it in my pants pocket.

"In her senior year, Mrs. Oglevee took Latin IV, Chemistry II . . ."

Maybe someone had given Eileen the note, asked her to
pass it on to Winnie to give to me, as a prank. But again, I
couldn't think of anyone who would want to be so mean
to me. And besides, wouldn't Eileen have questioned why
someone wanted her to give the note to Winnie for me, instead of simply giving it to Winnie or me directly? Plus,
who here would know Eileen? She was from Port Clinton,
and, as far as I knew, had never ventured to Paradise.

On the other hand, it seemed impossible to believe Mrs.
Oglevee had been murdered. She'd died of a heart attack.
Dr. Fulmer had confirmed it. No one had ever questioned it.
I doubted seriously there'd been an autopsy. Although there'd
been former students of Mrs. Oglevee's who had joked that
there should have been—since how could Mrs. Oglevee die
of heart failure when she hadn't had a heart?

To my credit, I'd shushed them when I overheard such
comments in my laundromat.

"Now, we don't have too many spontaneous photos of
Mrs. Oglevee, but here's one from the yearbook that shows
her chaperoning my class on the traditional eighth grade

field trip to King's Island amusement park, over by Cincinnati," I read.

I glanced back for a moment at the photo that appeared on the screen behind me. I'd scanned this one from my yearbook. On the big screen, the faces that had been just dots in the yearbook now loomed.

Sally was in the front row, wearing a big jester's cap she'd won at some ring-toss game, the cap blocking at least three girls' faces. I suddenly recollected how the girls had nagged her to take it off, but she refused, gleefully enjoying the fact she was annoying them, since they had made fun of Sally for being tomboyish and because her daddy had showed up a mite tipsy at the chorus recital the week before.

I was in the back row, my face a pale shade of jade, due to too much cotton candy and riding "the Racer" roller coaster fifteen times in a row, so as to win a bet with Jimmy Joe Johnson. If I won, he'd have to kiss me, which I was hoping would get the attention of John Worthy—now our chief of police and one of my least favorite people—but then I thought he was mighty cute.

Cherry was next to me, hair teased into a glorious swirl that covered the top half of her face, a huge bubble-gum bubble filling the bottom half of her face. I only knew it was her because I remembered being unable to resist popping that bubble seconds after the photo was taken.

It was easy to find Mrs. Oglevee's face amongst all the other teachers; she was the angry-looking one. I'd had the bad luck to be assigned to her bus and on the way to the amusement park, she'd railed that Ohio was the home state of presidents, astronauts, Thomas Edison, the Wright brothers, Paul Laurence Dunbar, and the site of important events such as the Battle of Lake Erie during the War of 1812 . . . and yet Paradise's school population was so moronic that every year the eighth graders voted to go to an amusement park?

Not particularly understanding of her, I'd thought back then. We were just fourteen-year-olds who wanted to celebrate having survived junior high before going on to survive high school, but now as I looked at her face, I realized that she looked sad as well as angry. Was it because every year she tried, really tried, to impress her students with the history of our state, but every year, she felt she'd failed?

Or was there some other reason she was always so angry . . . some reason that had nothing to do with her students?

"Um, Josie . . ."

I startled and saw Winnie on the front row, smiling encouragingly, and worriedly, as she said my name. I had, I realized, gotten off course and stopped talking.

Then I saw Caleb Loudermilk, editor of the *Paradise Advertiser-Gazette*—and the bum who'd insisted on getting my Stain-Busters column into all those newspapers—sitting next to her. When had he slipped in? I didn't know he'd planned on coming.

I frowned at him.

He smiled at me—also encouragingly. Uh oh. Caleb never smiles encouragingly. When everyone else as a little kid was playing Candy Land, he was probably playing a warped version called Sarcasm Land, and he'd never left. If he was trying to look encouraging, I must really be doing terribly.

My hands shook. My stomach knotted even more tightly, and then threatened to undo itself on the spot. I swallowed and tried to ignore the bitter bile taste at the back of my throat. I found my spot in my speech and started up again. "Mrs. Oglevee didn't care much for amusement rides—"

Hey! That at least got a chuckle! Which, for a few seconds, masked what was most definitely a snore.

"—but she did care a lot about history. Some of the people she taught us about were Thomas Edison, the Wright brothers, Paul Laurence Dunbar . . ."

I went on with my speech, while the spare part of my brain kept puzzling over the note in my pocket.

It had to be some weird prank. Maybe a column reader who didn't like my advice? Who forgot to follow my admonition to always check that the stain was completely removed before heat-drying an item, since heat sets stains?

Mrs. Oglevee's entire identity had been that she was a grumpy teacher for many years, only occasionally lighting up when she taught about local history.

That was it. Period.

The fact she'd left behind money and had a niece was a shocking enough revelation.

Why would anyone want to murder her? True, no one particularly liked Mrs. Oglevee. But then again, no one murders someone just because that person is unlikable. No, murder requires extreme motivation and passion, and it was impossible to imagine Mrs. Oglevee inspiring either.

Besides, why would her niece (or daughter) tell me? And why now . . . ten years after the fact?

Should I just throw the note away as a ridiculous prank?

Should I turn it over to the Masonville police?

"So, as we can see, Mrs. Oglevee had a real passion for local history. The books of local, state, and regional history will make a fine addition to the library, and I'm sure we'll all benefit from the Pearl Oglevee Regional History Collection."

I came to a stop. I looked up from my paper and stared at my audience as the lights came back up. Three people had nodded off. The back row had thinned considerably. Everyone else stared at me with expressions that were uncomfortable mixtures of glazed and amazed.

Cara Tickham, the library system director, stood up and faced the audience. "Thank you so much for attending today the dedication of the Pearl Oglevee Regional Collection. And thank you, Josie, for that, um, stirring speech."

Stirring? From the look of the audience, my speech had been about as stirring as dirty laundry left to soak in a bucket.

But someone at the back of the audience stood up and started clapping slowly, in an odd, syncopated way . . . not the usual rhythmic clapping. A few other people joined in. Then Cara started talking about the amount of Mrs. Oglevee's bequest, the renovations planned for the room we were in, and the books already purchased for the collection.

But I wasn't really listening—I was staring at the back of the small crowd. The arrhythmic clapper had gotten my attention because she'd stood up as she'd started clapping, and was now working her way out of the middle of the back row toward the door.

I knew I saw a stain—brown? Coffee?—on the front of the woman's white sweatshirt, which was decorated with glittery gold snowflakes. Did I also see a resemblance to Mrs. Oglevee? A younger version, but the same sharp nose, same critical slant to the eyes? She was so petite that I had easily overlooked her in my nervous scanning of the audience. Now that she was standing, her head and shoulders were just above the tall, broad man who had been sitting in front of her this whole time.

And as she got to the end of the row she stopped and looked at me, fixing me with an amused, knowing stare.

I started to lurch away from behind the podium, to follow the woman, but then I heard Cara's voice.

"Josie, I'm sure we have time for a few questions, don't we?" She asked the question in a manner that answered itself: of course we did!

Still, I thought, questions? Why did she want to open up the floor for questions? I glanced at my watch and gasped. Somehow, the speech I thought would take twenty minutes had only taken ten. I'd rushed through, eager to get it over with.

And I knew I'd been deadly dull. My first speech as a "regional celebrity," and I'd blown it big time. I'd been so distracted by that darned note. Somehow, I knew that Mrs. Oglevee, wherever she was, was laughing so hard she'd probably wet her granny panties.

"I have a question," said the man who had been blocking the coffee-stained woman I suspected was Mrs. Oglevee's niece. Or daughter. Or, anyhow, the person who'd given the note to Winnie for me. "I'm Mike Darby, from the *Mason-ville Daily Press*. Since you're Mrs. Oglevee's greatest success story—" the man paused . . . and actually snickered—"I wondered if you could share a memory of how Mrs. Oglevee influenced you to become a stain-removal columnist."

I glanced at the audience members, who were all staring at me with cautious hope—hope, I realized, that I'd finally, actually tell them something that brought Mrs. Oglevee back to life. That captured her essence as someone who would care so much about regional history that she'd take pains to make sure her estate was used to preserve and promote it.

All I had done, I realized, was find some facts about Mrs. Oglevee's life, a list of classes taken and taught, the dates of milestones (birth, marriage, divorce, death), and . . . that was all. Mrs. Oglevee, I realized, was still a complete mystery to me and everyone else in Paradise.

Maybe she'd wanted it that way. Maybe her anger was a force she used to keep people at a distance, so no one could ever know the real her. But why?

And did the note I was so uncomfortably aware of in my pocket have anything to do with the answer to the "why?" of Mrs. Oglevee's shuttered, cloistered life?

"I-I-" I stuttered to a stop. "Um, Mrs. Oglevee was a stickler for perfection," I tried again. "She expected the best out of each student. I guess you could say I apply that to my efforts as a stain-removal expert. And now as a columnist."

Except, of course, I'd actually gotten that work ethic from Aunt Clara and Uncle Horace, who'd taught it by example and with compassion as well as zeal. Mrs. Oglevee had used the fact that no one ever quite achieves perfection as an excuse to belittle others' failings.

"Well, if you learned so much about perfection from Mrs. Oglevee," I heard a cranky, creaky voice cackle from the middle row, "then maybe you can explain something to me. My sister Missy Hinckle—"

Uh oh, I thought. Missy Hinckle was the Baptist minister's wife in Paradise—and Missy did not like me. I think it had something to do with telling her I didn't have space for her "get saved or burn in hell" tracts at my checkout counter, although I always had plenty of room for the flyers advertising the community thrift sale, held annually in the Methodist Church's fellowship hall. Or for the flyers promoting Paradise Historical Society happenings, or Ranger Girl cookie sales, or . . .

"—she sent me your Stain-Busters column until it started running in the *Masonville Daily Press* a few weeks ago." She glanced back at the reporter, as if it were his fault my column started taking up space. He gave a don't-blame-me-shrug, and Caleb turned to glare at both of them. "And you said in a column that white vinegar is a good deodorizer," she said accusingly.

"It-it-is," I said.

"Now, I'm sure Josie would love to share her tips later, but if we could just keep the questions focused on Pearl Oglevee and her incredible donation—" Cara started.

But Missy's sister—I dubbed her "Prissy" in my head—went on. "You also said that baking soda is a good deodorizer."

"It, um, it is," I said, having a bad feeling that I knew just where this was going.

Sure enough, Prissy continued: "So I poured both in a bucket at once, thinking I'd soak some . . . well . . . uh, never mind that—"

No one likes to talk publicly about their dirty laundry, it seems.

"And you had quite a mess then, didn't you," I said, trying to rescue the situation. "Because vinegar is acidic and baking soda is alkaline, the two react and . . ."

I caught Cara glaring at me, the whole audience staring at me in bemused bewilderment now, Mike Darby (the *Masonville Daily Press* reporter) grinning as he took notes, and Caleb and Winnie looking horrified on my behalf.

". . . and, well, as Mrs. Oglevee would say, there's always more than one way to approach solving a problem, but those approaches don't always mix."

A few audience members chuckled appreciatively. I'd finally shared something real, something from my personal knowledge about Mrs. Oglevee. Of course, I'd entirely made that up. I had no recollection of her saying any such thing. She'd have just said all my problems were of my own making, and I would never get out of them.

"Well, on behalf of the Mason County Library, thank you all for coming today. Please stay and enjoy the cookies and punch!" Cara said, indicating a table spread with goodies at the back of the room.

Everyone stood up at once. About half hurried toward the exit, and the others wandered toward the punch-n-cookies table. Everyone avoided me, except Winnie and Caleb, who came over as I gathered up my notes, fighting back tears and my own urge to run out the door.

Hmmm. Maybe if I did, I could catch up with the woman I suspected had passed the "Mrs. Oglevee was murdered" note to me, ask her a few questions one-on-one. Obviously I was better at that than at answering them in front of a crowd.

"Well, congratulations Josie," Winnie said too heartily. "That went . . ." her voice trailed off.

"Wonderfully, right?" I said. "That's why people are rushing over here to tell me what a great job I did."

"Everyone's nervous about meeting celebrities—" Caleb said.

"I am not a celebrity!" I hissed. "These folks are avoiding me and I don't really blame them. What could they possibly say to me? 'Josie, any tips on blood stains? You see, in desperate boredom, I chewed my arm off during your speech!' And then I could say, 'Why sure! Let's find a vat of hydrogen peroxide . . .'"

"It's your first speech in a long time," Winnie said soothingly. "Maybe if you joined Toastmasters International . . ."

"And it's my last," I said. I glared at Caleb. "If having my column in all these newspapers means I have to do this kind of thing, I quit. I didn't help my new columnist career today . . . I hurt it! And when that reporter, what's his name—"

"Mike Darby. And I've worked with him in the past and he's a jerk. Probably mad that your column going into the *Masonville Daily Press* meant that his weekly drivel got cut."

"It did?" I hadn't thought about that kind of thing happening.

"Don't feel badly—and yes I know you, and you are feeling badly, aren't you?" Caleb said.

I didn't answer.

"Your column has generated more positive feedback in a few weeks than his rants did in a year. I've worked with him before; don't worry about him. Now then, Winnie's suggestion about Toastmasters is actually pretty good—"

Before I could protest, Prissy-sister-of-Missy walked over. "I still say," she interrupted, "that if you're going to dispense advice, you need to forewarn people that they might end up with a foamy mess . . ."

"Ma'am, it is so nice to meet you. I'm Caleb Loudermilk. And you are?" He held out his hand.

Prissy-sister-of-Missy looked as though she might swoon as she shook Caleb's hand and stared up into his baby-blues. I rolled my own gray-greens. Winnie patted my arm and wandered off to talk with Cara—probably to beg to keep her job despite the fact she'd been one of the people who'd recommended me for this speech.

"Evangelina Castrucci."

I did a double take at the name, and then thought nastily that "prissy" really did fit better.

"Ms. Castrucci, as Josie's editor, I have to point out that Josie is an esteemed stainologist."

Stainologist? *Stainologist!* He actually said that with a straight face, except his mustache was twitching at the corners. He thought this was funny? This day had been a disaster: a disturbing message that Mrs. Oglevee had been murdered, my speech a bore, and finally this woman blaming me in front of everyone for her suds bucket turning into a baking-soda/vinegar volcano.

"And as such, she has had the foresight to include at the end of her Stain-Busters column a disclaimer about not all methods working on all fabric types, and about testing methods on a discrete section of the stained item, and warning against mixing some types of cleaning products."

"Well, but, um, she didn't warn about vinegar and baking soda specifically, and my sister Missy says . . ."

"Ms. Toadfern cannot possibly cover every caveat in every column," Caleb said. "That's like saying that every time we print a recipe we should point out that if you eat food right out of the oven or microwave you might burn your mouth. Some common sense is called for in life, you know."

Prissy—a.k.a. Evangelina—gave Caleb a pouty look, although she still had a glare left for me. "Well, I still think you wrote about baking soda and white vinegar in the same column on purpose to set people up. Missy says you have a mean streak!"

I was about to ask why, then, Missy sent my columns to her, when she added triumphantly, "I'm just going to go back to bleaching everything!"

I gaped at that, ready to beg her to please, please not do that. I hate it when people think the answer to problems is to just blast them with the strongest possible solution.

But the woman stomped off before I could share that particular tip.

Caleb grinned at me. "That's the price of fame, Josie—there will always be a flake at events like these who will want to question your authority. You'll just have to get used to it. Now, about Winnie's suggestion, maybe some speech coaching is a better choice if you don't have time for Toastmasters. Or I could give you pointers. As your fame grows as a stainologist—"

There was that word again. I couldn't stand it.

"I quit!" I said.

And turned and walked out the door, hoping to catch up with the woman I reckoned had sent me the note via Winnie about Mrs. Oglevee being murdered.

5

I stood in the Mason County Public Library parking lot, leaning against the back of my minivan, looking around. There were cars, and scant snowflakes lazily drifting down from a gray, overcast sky.

But no mystery-coffee-stained-woman for me to ask, "Were you the one who passed along the note claiming to be Pearl Oglevee's daughter, instead of her niece, and stating that Mrs. Oglevee was murdered?"

After I'd stomped out of the room that would become the home of the Pearl Oglevee Regional History Collection, I'd gone back to the media processing room and grabbed my tote bag, coat, scarf, and gloves. I'd done a quick walk-through of the library, hoping to find the woman, but had no success.

Then I'd come out and walked around the parking lot, and again had no success. I was leaning against my van, considering whether I wanted to go back in and ask Winnie if Eileen was the woman-with-coffee-stain. I was also trying to decide what to do about the note.

Then I saw Caleb crossing the parking lot toward me.

"You okay?" he asked.

"Fine—"

"Good. Now about quitting your column—"

"Caleb, you heard me," I said. "I was an awful speaker. When the column was just for fun, a way to get a few more people into my laundromat, it was one thing . . . but I just don't think I'm ready for the column taking off as it has. It's just too fast. Now, I appreciate what you've done and all, but I really need to focus on running the laundromat, taking care of Guy . . ."

"Josie, look, it was just one speech. And it wasn't that bad—"

"Caleb. Please."

Caleb hesitated. "Okay. It was awful. But you'll get better! Come on, now, I stuck out my neck to convince the powers at the publishing company to get your column in all their regional newspapers. Your column is getting a great response. Why, it's possible that in a year or two, you could be nationally syndicated, on radio, on TV, publishing books—"

"You are delusional," I said firmly.

But Caleb only looked at me with puzzlement. "Why? You don't just dispense stain tips. There's hominess to your writing voice—"

I stared at him.

"I mean," he said, trying again, "the style in which you write. You toss in anecdotes, tell stories about how you tested stains tips. Your column has a mix of warmth that people love and good old-fashioned home remedies that people like in a world that's so high tech and fast and . . . you don't know what I mean, do you? Which is part of your charm."

"Don't you dare patronize me, Caleb, or I'll toss you and this column aside faster than old soaking water. I have a sense of what you mean, yes, but—"

"So why not capitalize on it? Keep the column the same, but add in housekeeping tips, too?"

I'd already thought about that. Stain-removal tips for

laundry could only last so long for a column. And the truth was a lot of what I'd researched for my laundromat customers also applied around the house. For example, did you know denture cleaning tablets are a fast and great way to clean a coffee mug of coffee stains?

I'd learned that one from my Aunt Clara, and many more household tips, besides. She'd been thrifty and inventive, making the best of tips she'd learned or created, to stretch Uncle Horace's and her budget so that they could put aside every spare dime to ensure Guy would always be taken care of. And she'd taught me every tip she knew.

"And besides," Caleb was saying, "today you were nervous because you were talking about Mrs. Oglevee. But when you start talking about all the tips you know, and the chemistry behind them, you really light up."

True. But still, the thought of maybe becoming . . . famous in some way for my knowledge. My . . . style. My . . . my . . . *voice*, as Caleb had said. The thought made my stomach knot up again.

"And if you could grow with this column, how would that be for both of us? More money for you, a promotion for me since I'm the one who discovered you . . ."

I huffed out an annoyed sigh, which turned into a white puff on the cold air. Well, semicold air. Although right below freezing, it wasn't nearly as cold as one would expect for December 28 in Ohio.

"You did not discover me, Caleb. I developed my own stain-removal expertise on my own, long before you ever even heard of Paradise or Toadfern's Laundromat. I had a little monthly column in the *Paradise Advertiser-Gazette* a year before you came onboard. Don't try to hitch on to my talent, claim you discovered me, and use that as a ticket out of Paradise," I said.

Caleb's eyebrows went up. "Still touchy about Owen, huh?"

"That has nothing to do with—" I shook my head. "Never mind. I'm going home."

I started toward my minivan's driver's side.

But Caleb caught my arm in his hand. I glared at him. He grinned. "You know, if you put that kind of passion in your speeches, people might listen instead of nodding off."

"Well, it doesn't matter, because I quit already, remember?"

"Why don't you think it over for a day or two before you make that decision final? You know you'd miss the column."

He was right. I would. And I had to admit that, although the jump in income wasn't huge from being in regional newspapers weekly instead of just one monthly, the little extra was nice. I was putting it all aside, just in case, for Guy. I had a trust fund for him from my aunt and uncle, but what if that didn't last? I could get by on my laundromat income, but expenses for Guy's care were greater than my aunt and uncle had ever anticipated. Maybe I should think about letting Caleb see how far he could push my column.

"I will think about it—on two conditions," I said.

"Oh?"

Caleb packed a lot of insinuation into that "oh." I blushed. Never date a colleague . . . well, he was just a sort of colleague. But still. I tried to look dignified—I was going to be thirty the next day after all—and said, "Condition one—no speech coaches, thank you very much. And number two—don't ever, ever call me a stainologist again. That's just plain hokey."

"Really? I thought it was kind of cute."

"Hokey."

"Okay, fine. I will forevermore only call you . . . well, what do you want me to call you?" He waggled his eyebrows at me.

"How about stain-removal expert. Or columnist. Or just plain . . . Josie!"

"Fine. And I'll give you tips on giving speeches myself."

I started to protest, but he put a gloved finger to my lips.

"I used to be terrified of speaking in public, too, Josie. If I can do it, you can do it."

I grabbed his finger and moved it away from my lips. "Fine," I said.

"Just one condition of my own, though, my dear stain-removal expert."

"What?"

He started to say something, but then he pulled me toward him and kissed me. Right there, in the cold library parking lot, not exactly romantic, and yet . . .

His kiss made more than my lips warm. I felt a warmth buzzing through my whole body, even though his kiss was sweet and simple—no tongues, no groping, just a tender kiss that was like a little question: is this okay? A nice start? Can we do this again?

I answered back with a little kiss of my own: Maybe. I'm not sure. My heart's still sore, but then again . . .

Caleb stepped back, smiled at me. I was tempted to look away, but I made myself hold his steady, dark gaze.

"Will you have lunch with me at Suzy Fu's Chinese Buffet?" he asked.

What could I say after that little kiss? Plus, I was hungry, Suzy Fu's is my favorite restaurant, and it was just down the street. And Caleb offered to drive and pay.

I felt a little better by the time Caleb and I pulled into the Masonville Square strip mall parking lot.

Earlier in the month we'd had a big snowstorm, with about six inches of snow. But most of that had melted. The only reminder of that snow was a mound plowed up against the light pole in the Masonville Square strip mall parking lot.

Caleb parked just a few spaces away from it. "Crowded for a week day," I said, surprised at all the cars in the lot.

He shrugged. "It's a holiday week," he said, "between Christmas and New Year's . . ." He gazed at me meaningfully.

I didn't want to go through, again, why I wanted to spend my birthday—thirty on the thirtieth—and New Year's Eve alone, so instead I grinned at him, said, "Last one to the top of the snow pile is a rotten egg!" and hopped out of his car, slamming the door shut.

A few seconds later, I was standing at the top of the snow pile, giggling, and staring down at Caleb. At five two, I'm usually the shortest person around, so I have to admit it felt good to be towering a good four feet higher than Caleb.

He stared up at me, his arms folded. He looked like a serious businessman in his tweed coat, scarf, and leather gloves. "Come on Josie, you could slip and get hurt. Come on down."

I sighed and crossed my own arms. "That's the exact thing my Aunt Clara always said when I'd run off to scramble up one of these. Then she'd say, 'That dirty snow's been no telling where!'"

Caleb tried not to laugh, but did anyway. "She didn't say that."

"Yep, she did. Anyway, I'm not coming down until you get up here."

Caleb groaned. I held back my giggles as he scrambled up to the top. We stood awkwardly side by side, staring out at the car and truck tops.

"This is your idea of living out a midlife crisis?" he teased. "Defiantly climbing dirty snow piles?"

"This is no midlife crisis," I said. "I'm only turning thirty. This is just me reaffirming my youth . . ." My voice trailed off. Was that Cherry's bright red Mustang, parked at the far end of the lot? Sally's extended-cab Ford truck? Clarice Martin's blue late-model Toyota Corolla?

"I recognize a lot of the cars here. That's Clarice Martin's Corolla," I said, pointing.

"Josie, do you know how many blue Corollas there are in the world?"

"With a bumper sticker that says, DUMB PEOPLE SCARE ME? And a dent with red paint on the right side?"

"You memorize people's cars?" Caleb asked.

"I recognize them from helping carry out laundry. Clarice Martin has a bad back, so I always help her in and out with her baskets," I explained.

"Hmm," he said thoughtfully, and then added suddenly: "Last one down's a rotten egg!"

He started scrambling down, and I followed, protesting that he wasn't being fair—he'd caught me off guard. I was still protesting when we went into Suzy Fu's Chinese Buffet. Suzy Fu herself was there to meet us at the door. "No room in main dining room," she said, before I could even say hello or start to take off my coat, "this way, this way, overflow back here—"

She rushed us toward the banquet room at the back of the restaurant, even as I glanced back and saw that the crowd was about typical for a weekday, even a holiday weekday.

I never got a chance to make my observation heard, though. She opened the door to the banquet room, and I stepped in right beside Caleb—and suddenly I realized why I'd recognized so many cars in the parking lot from my snow pile viewpoint.

The cars' owners—Cherry and Sally and Clarice and Chip and Mrs. Beavy and at least twenty-five others were all there, in the banquet room, hollering, "Surprise! Happy Birthday, Josie!"

Well, my birthday was the next day, truth be told. But I smiled in delight, anyway, and blinked extra hard as my eyes teared up, just a little.

6

"Now, of course we know your birthday is actually tomorrow," Cherry was saying. It turned out that she, my cousin Sally, and Winnie—who arrived shortly after Caleb and me—had been planning this surprise birthday lunch all along, which came complete with a buffet of my personal favorite Chinese dishes—crab Rangoons and Happy Family and hot and sour soup. And even the perfect gift—a gift card for Between the Covers Bookshop, just several storefronts down.

I had gone from surprised to touched to delighted to amazed and back to touched since we'd arrived. And in between, I'd enjoyed my friends and neighbors celebrating my thirtieth, and been relieved that the ones who had also been at my speech didn't bring it up.

Suzy Fu had even allowed Cherry and Sally to bring in several Coca-Cola chocolate sheet-cakes—my favorite—and vanilla ice cream. We were all enjoying dessert then, as Cherry pointed out the obvious—the celebration was a day early.

My warm emotions about-faced to wary. Cherry was speaking in that "Now, Josie" tone of hers, the one she uses to try to convince me to change something about my appearance, which she's constantly picking over.

"But there's a good reason we threw this party *today*," Cherry went on. "Because we have another surprise for you!"

I looked to Sally with a "help me" expression. But she just grinned mischievously. I groaned, recognizing the look she'd had when we were kids while convincing me to help her pull some prank or another.

And I didn't think Caleb, to my right, would be any help. He, after all, had been responsible for getting me there.

Randy Woodford sat to my left. I looked at him. He was staring at Cherry's boobs. I sighed. He wasn't going to be any help. I was doomed.

My next thought: No. I was about to turn thirty! Just because Cherry and Sally weren't aging gracefully didn't mean I couldn't. With great dignity, I could decline whatever they'd cooked up . . .

My thought after that: Oh no. I sounded like a fuddy-duddy already! Not even knowing what they had planned! Assuming I'd hate it! After all, they were my best friends and they'd been great about seeing me through my breakup with Owen, so maybe I should be open-minded about their birthday surprise. Maybe it was shelving for my laundromat. The original shelving, where I kept small boxes of laundry products on sale for customers on an honor system, was getting a bit rickety, and . . .

Uh oh. Was I thinking like a fuddy-duddy again?

"What we have planned for you," Cherry was saying, "is an all-expenses-paid chick trip for a long weekend . . . to the Great Walleye Drop!"

I stared at her. Then I looked back at Sally. They were both grinning widely. And they were not kidding.

"The Great Walleye Drop," Caleb said thoughtfully. "Hmm. I think I heard about this on the *David Letterman Show*. You know Josie, you could make one of your columns a report on your adventures and give tips on removing fish stains and smells. A walleye is a fish, right?"

We all looked at him, several of us saying at once, "Yes!"

"Now, folks, Caleb isn't from Ohio, so he probably isn't familiar with all the great fishing up north in Lake Erie," Winnie said.

"Right. Where I'm from, catfish is the thing—"

"I like catfish," said Randy. "And walleye. I've had 'em both."

"Let's go back to what Caleb said about removing fish stains and smells," said Cherry, her expression suddenly nervous. "This isn't a real fish that's being dropped, is it? Or a bunch of them, to stock the lake . . ."

Sally snorted. "Nobody stocks Lake Erie, Cherry. It's self-stocking. Fish sex."

"Do fish have sex?" Randy asked. "I thought they dropped eggs or something and that's where caviar comes from . . ."

"The lake's probably half frozen this time of year," Sally broke in. "So you couldn't drop a fish in, anyway. It'd bounce on the lake's surface. Or maybe skid. Anyway, I read about it on the Internet, and what happens is on New Year's Eve, a six-hundred-pound fiberglass walleye—known as Wylie . . ."

"Stop!" I said.

"Oh, good idea," Cherry said. "I reckon Josie hasn't seen this on Letterman—you know how she loves the movie channel, especially with all the weepy romance movies—"

"Poor Josie," Caleb said, rolling his eyes. He hadn't approved of Owen and thought I was wasting my time mourning his loss. I kicked him under the table. He winced, most satisfyingly.

"I like weepy movies, too," Randy said. He started to put his arm around me. I shrugged it away, which was not particularly satisfying as he then sniffled in a way that made me feel a little guilty. For such a big strong guy, he had very easily hurt feelings.

"And she'll want to be surprised by all the great activities at the Great Walleye Drop," Cherry went on . . .

"No," I said. "This is . . . very nice of you all . . . but I'm not going. I just can't. I-I have a lot to take care of, and . . ."

Cherry sighed dramatically. "Josie wants to spend her birthday and New Year's Eve alone, can you all believe that?"

"She could spend it with me," Caleb said, giving me a half-smile and a wink. We'd spend the time verbally sparring, which would be fun . . . until I started longing for a real conversation.

"Or with me," Randy said, in a me-too voice. His arm started snaking around my shoulder. I pushed it off, more gently this time. The physical pleasures of his company would be fun . . . until I started longing for real romance.

"No," I said again. "I'm going to spend those days alone, okay? I have a lot of paperwork to look over for Stillwater's search for a new director, and organizing to do before Randy starts on the renovations again after the first of the year"—he smiled at me, pleased to have been mentioned again—"and emails from column readers to catch up on, and . . ."

But no one was listening.

"She always does this, tries to hide away at holidays," Cherry was saying.

"Well, after this past Thanksgiving, I can kind of understand her impulse," said Caleb. My long-lost parents (as opposed to my parents of the heart, Aunt Clara and Uncle Horace, who had actually reared me) had returned to town, very briefly, this past Thanksgiving, and my Uncle Fenwick had been murdered, a crime for which my father was accused. To get them to skedaddle back out of town, I had gotten involved in solving the crime—but that's a whole other story.

"Oh nonsense. Whose family doesn't have issues— especially at holidays?" Sally was saying. My eyes goggled in her direction. Murder is a far sight more serious than "issues," in my book. "She always did this as a kid, too, whenever she was nervous about something . . . usually hiding away with a book, or—"

"Enough!" I hollered—and the whole room, not just my end of the table, went still and silent. Everyone stared at me.

My stomach clenched and for a moment I felt just like I had behind the library's podium.

I smiled nervously. "Oh, uh, I was just, um, saying—th-thank you all for a really wonderful surprise party. It's been great and I'm really grateful and even though Cherry and Sally just told me they were planning on whisking me away for a chick trip weekend . . ."

Before I could say anything else, Cherry broke in with "Of course, Josie here doesn't want to go. She thinks she should just stay home and—"

"I have paperwork to look at for the director search we're doing at Stillwater—"

"That can wait!" called Mary Rossbergen, the assistant director at Stillwater Farms, where Guy resided.

"And we packed that file for you, anyway, because we knew you wouldn't relax without it," Sally said.

"What?" I glared at her and Cherry. "You broke into my apartment? Went through my papers?"

Sally rolled her eyes. "You gave me a spare key over a year ago, remember? Besides, the file was on top of your magazines."

"I've already said I'd watch the laundromat," said Chip Beavy, "although I don't think you'll have too many customers between now and January second."

"You work too hard as it is," added Mrs. Beavy, Chip's grandmother and one of my favorite customers.

"Although maybe the break would help you come back refreshed to your column—and speaking—career," Caleb said.

"And less grumpy about the apartment renovations. This kind of job is pretty big . . ." Randy said.

"No," I said firmly. "I need to be nearby because of Guy."

"No you don't," said Mary. "He isn't expecting your visit in the next few days. And you shouldn't use being his caretaker as an excuse to not live your own life."

The room went silent again. I stared at Mary. Is that what

she really thought of me? Had I been doing that? I'd never seen my devotion to Guy as anything other than something I was happy to do.

The silence was becoming uncomfortable, and then dear Mrs. Beavy spoke up. "The Great Walleye Drop sounds most exciting," she chirruped. "Just where did you girls say it takes place?"

"I don't think we had," said Cherry.

"It's in Port Clinton," Sally rushed in. "Just a few hours drive north, Josie, so if anything would happen with Guy or your laundromat you could get back pretty quickly."

"It would be good for you to get used to being gone a day or two, for when your media presence starts rising—" Caleb said.

"Maybe I could get more work done while you're out of the apartment," Randy added.

"Chip loves to fill in at the laundromat," Mrs. Beavy said.

"I do," Chip agreed.

"And you do need to take care of yourself, which includes a break now and then," Mary said.

But I only half heard any of them. I was staring at Winnie, and she was smiling at me. Port Clinton. That was where Pearl Oglevee was from. Where her niece, who had sent along a few of the photos and clippings, was from.

And who—although I was the only one at the time who knew it—had slipped me a note via Winnie claiming that Mrs. Oglevee had been murdered, and had *not* died of natural causes ten years before like we all thought.

Winnie's grin broadened. I knew what she was thinking. There was no way now I would be able to resist this marvelous coincidence—Cherry and Sally wanted to whisk me away to the very city where Mrs. Oglevee—and her niece—were from. How was I going to resist the opportunity to go and talk to the niece?

Of course, if Winnie had known about the note, she wouldn't have been grinning at me. She'd have been pleading with me to stay put after all, and turn that note over to the police.

But I figured they'd just take it as a prank, which was probably what it was. At least that's what the logical part of me thought. The intuitive part of me wasn't so sure, and was issuing little siren pleas: "Warning! Warning!"

Naturally, the curiosity-gifted part of me won out. Why not go to Port Clinton, and take a few minutes to ask Pearl Oglevee's niece a few questions? Maybe she'd say something that would help me get to know the real Mrs. Oglevee. Truth be told, I'd never really known her, and I was growing more and more curious.

Plus . . . the Great Walleye Drop did sound like fun. Or at least interesting.

And I could tell from the expressions on Cherry's and Sally's faces that this meant a lot to them.

So I said . . . "Oh, okay, I'll go."

7

Pearl Oglevee was pretty when she was eighteen, I thought. I was looking through the envelope of items I was going to return to Eileen, up in Port Clinton, studying Mrs. Oglevee's high school graduation photo. There was already something a little sad about her look that edged her sweetheart-of-the-Midwest prettiness toward beautiful. Her dark eyes were intense, as if she were searching for something. Her brunette hair was styled in an early 1950s puffy flip. Her full lips were sexy, pouting, and promising all at once.

I put the photo in the envelope, the envelope in my backpack. The envelope now also held the unsigned note that Eileen had passed along to me. Winnie had confirmed that the harsh-looking, coffee-stained and tobacco-scented woman had introduced herself as Eileen before giving her the note. Winnie had looked curious about, but didn't ask, what the note said, and gave me Eileen's address at the end of my surprise lunch.

Then I'd checked for myself, and sure enough in the covered bed of Sally's pickup truck was my suitcase plus a tote that contained my Stillwater search-for-a-director file, and books. Sally had a suitcase, a cooler, a bag of snacks, and two boxes of wine (one red, one white). All that took up a small section of the bed; Cherry's suitcases took up the rest.

When I confirmed that, yes, we were just going to be gone until January 2—not a month, as Cherry's many suitcases implied—I climbed into the back seat of Sally's extended cab—cleared of booster seats for her triplets, who were spending the next few nights with her ex's parents—and immediately felt drowsy. Post-Chinese buffet syndrome.

While Cherry went on in the front seat with a long story about how difficult it was to perm Ida Blanshaw's coarse hair, I reviewed the contents of the envelope to fight drowsiness, until trying to read in the backseat made me a mite queasy, and then I stared at a mystery stain on the back of Sally's seat. Sally'd done a great job mucking out the back of her truck, but as the single mom of triplet five-year-old boys, she could only do so much. I wondered if I was gazing at Kool-aid, blood, or some mix. But mystery stains can only intrigue even me for so long, so I started staring out the window.

Now, Mrs. Oglevee had taught us that during the Ice Age, glaciers bore down on what some twenty-five-thousand-plus years later would be known as Ohio, and gouged out the deep well that would fill in and become Lake Erie, and flattened northern and western Ohio. If you looked at the state, she said, and drew a diagonal line from the southwest to the northeast, anything in the north half was pretty much smooshed (I don't think she used that exact term), and the rest was left hilly. In the southeast, we have the Appalachian Mountains. Okay, the nubbed down part of the mountain range. Still. Ohio's not made up of entirely flat terrain, as folks who live elsewhere seem to think.

But we were heading north to Port Clinton, right on Lake Erie's coast, and soon we were out of our familiar rolling hill terrain and on State Route 4, driving on a two-lane state highway that stretched through miles and miles of cornfield—all frozen stubs now, of course, dusted with snow. The sky was filled with barrel-shaped, gray, angry clouds that seemed to press down to the earth. Occasionally, there was a small town—even smaller than Paradise—or a farmhouse or a grain silo or a billboard proclaiming salvation while threatening its alternative, a sorry place that would be far warmer than what we were driving through.

One such billboard proclaimed Jesus was coming soon and showed a big clock, with the hour hand at twelve and the minute hand at eleven. The billboard was unclear as to whether its clock was depicting a.m. or p.m.

I checked my watch. It was two o'clock p.m. I'd either missed my chance or still had ten hours to reconsider my radical viewpoint that God loves us all, whatever we may feel about Him. Or Her.

I closed my eyes against the landscape and such weighty considerations, telling myself I'd rest just for a second, and then try to catch up on whatever Cherry was saying.

The truck was hot. Sally's truck heater had only two settings—hot as the alternative to salvation proclaimed on the countryside billboards, or freezing cold, which if you ask me, would be an even more torturous form of hell, even if that's not traditional theology, either.

As my eyes drifted shut in the warmth, and I felt the rhythmic bouncing of the truck (even though we were on flat, straight pavement, because Sally needs new shocks but can't afford them just yet, what with the soaring cost of gas to heat her trailer home in the Happy Trails Motor Home park), I started to lose the battle against falling asleep, and Cherry's droning about Ida morphed into the memory of Mrs. Oglevee's voice lecturing about glaciers ironing out Ohio . . .

"What do you mean, 'glaciers ironing out Ohio?'" Mrs. Oglevee shrieked at me.

I moaned. There she was, the Mrs. Oglevee of my junior high and high school days, looming over me in my dreams. She looked just like she did back then, too: heavy set, steel-gray hair in tight bobby-pinned bun, dark rimmed glasses making her dark eyes look narrow, matronly cotton dress with an unfortunate blue cabbage-rose print that made her ample chest look even bigger, and, of course, no makeup.

Only in this iteration, the clothing was accessorized with a cheap tin-and-rhinestone tiara and an ostrich-feather boa. Her sensible brown, flat lace-up shoes had been replaced with clear high-heeled glass slippers. Lucky me, my dream-vision was so clear, that I could see through the slipper toe-tips that her toenails were manicured hot pink, a detail that made me moan unhappily again.

Mrs. Oglevee looked as though she'd been visited by some wickedly mischievous fairy godmother whose wand gave out halfway through the makeover.

"I would never have referred to glaciers as 'ironing,' Josie Toadfern," Mrs. Oglevee lectured. "Glaciers are obviously quite cold. Therefore, they can't iron, because irons are hot. It's an incongruous image! But then, of course you'd come up with some ironing image, because your whole career focuses around doing the wash."

She said this last part with a sneer. Mrs. Oglevee, in my subconscious life, never approved of the fact that I am a laundromat owner and self-taught stain-removal expert. She always manages to imply that this career choice is beneath me.

I'm not sure why. When she was my teacher in real life, she'd laughed at me on career day when I announced to the class I wanted to go to college to study chemistry, and said I'd be lucky to get a minimum-wage job. So I'd have thought she'd be pleased with my career path—but no.

"Why are you bothering me?" I asked. "And why are you dressed like that?"

Mrs. Oglevee snorted. "This was the dedication day at the library for my new local history section." She preened a little, adjusting her tiara. "It's only fitting that I should dress up."

She tossed one end of her ostrich-feather boa over her shoulder, sending a flutter of feathers flying, all of which aimed themselves at me. She chortled as I ducked. So far, she and her other worldly antics in my dreams hadn't done me any harm, but I wasn't particularly keen on taking chances.

Mrs. Oglevee had first shown up in my dreams when I started investigating the murder of a media star who was visiting our town. Since then, Mrs. Oglevee's shown up in my dreams whenever I've been under stress, such as getting involved in other investigations. Or during the final days of my breakup with Owen, when she kept popping in my dreams to holler at me, "What did you see in him, anyway? He was nice enough, but you had to sense there was no real future there . . ."

She hadn't shown up in my dreams for a whole week, not even when I was stressed over preparing for that morning's speech about her. And I hadn't missed her at all.

"In real life, you'd have never shown up with shoes like that or a tiara or a boa," I said. "You'd have been in some knit gray suit and brown flat shoes and pearls."

"Oh, really?" Mrs. Oglevee glared at me. "You think you know me so well? It sure didn't come across in that speech of yours this morning—"

"That's not fair," I protested. "I was nervous—"

"If you'd taken Speech in high school as I recommended, you wouldn't have that problem—"

"—and it's not like I had a whole lot of fascinating material to work with. You try filling a whole half hour with the story of your life!" I paused. I wasn't entirely sure that that made sense.

But I reckoned Mrs. Oglevee knew what I meant, given that she suddenly looked hurt. I felt a little guilty, but I went on. I'd never gotten the best of Mrs. Oglevee before.

"I mean, there wasn't a lot to go on. You were married, and quietly divorced. No kids. You taught at the junior high, that's all. And made everyone miserable with your grumpy attitude. And you should be thankful I didn't put *that* in the speech!"

Mrs. Oglevee's tiara and glass slippers started diffusing into mist. The boa's feathers started molting, as if the boa, along with Mrs. Oglevee, was suddenly disheartened. But I went on, emboldened.

After all, Mrs. Oglevee had picked on me often, meanly and without cause when I was a kid, and had recently started doing so in my dreams, too. And I was tired of it. I was about to be thirty! It was time to speak up for myself, right? Besides, it's not like Mrs. Oglevee could give me detention anymore . . . right?

"I mean, there's nothing even remarkable about your youth. No rebellions. No jaunts with the Peace Corps. No travels. Just growing up in Port Clinton, college at Bowling Green, and then teaching in Paradise. You could have gone anywhere! Done anything! But you didn't!"

By now her tiara and shoes were completely gone, and I had to admit, Mrs. Oglevee looked pretty vulnerable in bare feet, even though her pedicure had remained intact. The only thing left of her boa was a thick strand of yarn.

But there was still some spark left in her. "Like you," she said quietly. "You could have gone anywhere, done anything, but you were always content with what you had."

I shook my head. "Don't try to turn this around on me. And don't try to convince me that you were only mean to me for my own good. You were just mean. And bitter. And I don't get it. I stay put because I'm responsible for Guy— and glad for that. And I have plenty of friends who are like family to me. But you . . . like I said, you were just mean and bitter and alone—until the day you died of that heart attack."

Mrs. Oglevee was staring down at the ground now, slump-shouldered. I tried to convince myself that it was okay to vent at an apparition that somehow, bizarrely, I'd made up. So it couldn't matter that I was finally shouting the things at her I'd wanted to shout all along, could it?

But I still felt bad. Damn it. One of these days, I'm going to figure out how to be a mean girl for at least five minutes without feeling bad. Cherry seemed to have it mastered. Maybe she could give me lessons.

Mrs. Oglevee looked at me. "You think you know me . . . my identity . . . so well?" she asked. "Every life has a secret."

"Really?" I fumed, still trying to hold on to my outrage. "Well, yours must be quite a doozy—because your niece Eileen left me a note that she's really your daughter and that you didn't just die of a simple heart attack. You were murdered!"

Now, at that point, here's what I expected to happen: Mrs. Oglevee to snap back into her usual angry, critical mode, rant about what an idiot her niece had always been, and proclaim that she'd died of a heart attack, just like the conventional, traditional woman she was—nothing as unseemly or scandalous as murder for her. Then, I expected her to say her death-by-heart-attack proved her rotten luck, and how unfair life was, given that she'd been just a week away from the cruise of her dreams, which had been the only thing that had kept her going until she could finally retire from teaching ungrateful brats . . .

But here's what actually happened . . . well, as much as something can actually happen in a dream.

Mrs. Oglevee said in a near whisper: "I don't know."

"You . . . don't know? How you died?"

Mrs. Oglevee looked thoughtful. "I was packing, getting ready to go on my cruise."

I nodded. That fit with what I knew so far about the days before her death.

"I was a little dizzy; I kind of remember that. Everything else is foggy, from days before. My last real sharp memory of life was being at Sandy's Restaurant."

Mrs. Oglevee frowned and pursed her lips, pulling the soft slackness of her expression back into its more customary pinch. "I remember I was just paying my tab for breakfast when Mr. Johnston said, 'Well, looky here, Miss World Traveler.' That didn't sit well with me. I told him I didn't have to be nice and polite anymore, now that I was retired, and put up with parents who think their brats are just the most wonderful creations God ever made—"

I sighed, which Mrs. Oglevee didn't notice, she was so intent on her rant about how awful Mr. Johnston and his son, Alex, had always been. My surge of sympathy for Mrs. Oglevee—and my guilt over my earlier comments—started to subside. Oh, yeah, that's right; that's why no one liked her. Any chance to be hateful, she took it. As much as I preferred the original explanation of her death—heart attack—I was starting to see that lots of people could have harbored murderous feelings toward her. Like anyone who'd ever known her . . .

"Josie Toadfern, are you listening to me?"

"Yes, ma'am!" I automatically replied. Some habits are hard to break. Annoying.

Her tone and look softened again when she saw she had regained my attention. "After that encounter with Mr. Johnston, things are a little hazy. Packing . . . dreaming of the trip . . . scrambling eggs for a quick supper. And being upset about something, and a tightening feeling in my chest and light-headedness . . ." Okay, I told myself, that fit with a heart attack. ". . . and then after that, nothing, until . . . this."

She waved her arms around to indicate "this." I reckoned she meant the afterlife. I've never made up my mind where she'd gone and I don't particularly want to know. Every answer I'd come up with raised troubling theological questions, so I just stopped wondering about it.

"And I've always wondered . . . just how I did get here?"

And I was wondering, where *did* she go when she wasn't wandering into the middle of my dreams, mucking up my REM sleep? But I wasn't about to ask. Just in case Mrs. Oglevee might see fit to answer.

Instead, I thought about what Mrs. Oglevee had just said. I don't spend a lot of time thinking about the afterlife, but I guess if I had to give an opinion, I'd say, yeah, I reckoned there was one . . . and that in *that* life, all mysteries would be resolved, all questions answered.

I for one would want to know the whys of why some people, like my cousin Guy, are dealt conditions such as autism. Is there some higher purpose? Is it just genetic lotto? And if it's that—then there's another "why." I suppose even in eternity, there could be an eternity of questions to be answered.

And of course I would just assume that I would know the details of how I died. Like, say, I was hit by a car and died some time after that. Even if I was in a coma between being hit and my death, I'd reckon I'd be able to kind of review a film of my life to know what all had happened—who'd visited me in the hospital, and so on.

But then again, I'd also heard some folks believe in ghosts. I don't, or at least I never had until Mrs. Oglevee showed up in my sleepy-time subconscious, and I still like to think she's some figment of my dreaming imagination. Anyway, those who do believe there are ghosts say that spirits are restless if they have unresolved issues left over from their lives, preventing them from moving on to whatever the next life might be. Issues such as untimely death. Or murder.

And certainly, Mrs. Oglevee seemed to be struggling with the unresolved issue of not knowing just how she died . . .

"Josie!"

I refocused on Mrs. Oglevee. Her gaze had turned sharp, probing—like it had been when she suspected (usually correctly) that I'd been passing notes with Sally.

"I need to ask you something, young lady!"

Her voice was sharp, too, barking out every word like a command. But suddenly, I realized that at least in this case, in my dream, the sharpness was a cover for nervousness. And I wondered—had it been in real life, too?

I held her gaze, something I had *not* been able to do in real life.

Mrs. Oglevee cleared her throat. "Josie, would you . . . find out for me? If I died the way you say everyone says I did—a heart attack. Or if I was murdered?"

I staggered back. "What? No—no way—I've had enough of mucking about in investigations I have no business in . . ."

"I don't believe that for a minute!" Suddenly Mrs. Oglevee looked angry. "Nosey Josie, *not* investigate something like this? I've watched you, even tried to talk you out of some of your cases, and I know if it were anyone else, you wouldn't hesitate! You're just trying to get back at me . . ."

"And so what if I am," I challenged her. "What's in it for me?" Even as I asked, I knew my curiosity was piqued. That I'd pick at the question—was there truth to that note?—like an old scab. I'd tell myself I wouldn't, I'd try to resist . . . and yet . . .

"I'll tell you what's in it for you. If you find out for me, tell me the truth, what you learn, then I will give you a choice. Either you can have me pop in now and again, and give you much needed advice—"

I snorted at that.

"Or you can ask me to go away and I . . ." Mrs. Oglevee's voice dropped. "I will."

"But—why can't you just find out yourself?" I asked. "I mean, if you're in the afterlife, and not just a figment of my imagination—"

Mrs. Oglevee gasped and looked hurt.

"—then why can't you go swooping into other people's lives, like, like . . ." I paused, as the realization dawned on me . . . "like the person—or people—you must suspect, because you wouldn't want me to check this out, would you, if you didn't think there was some possibility . . . oh my Lord! You suspect you *were* murdered, don't you?!"

Mrs. Oglevee shook her head. "It doesn't work like that. I can't really explain it, but I can't control where I go all the time, and I can't look up records, or interview people, or get into their heads at will," she said, ignoring my last question,

I noticed. She flashed me a harsh look. "And believe me, I don't know why I show up in *your* head, of all places."

Oh thanks, I thought. Now that's softening me up for this little request: Josie, please jeopardize your life for your mean old former junior high history teacher and investigate her death. That's a good girl!

"So why should I believe that if I do this for you, I can tell you to go away and you'll do it—or even be *able* to do it?"

Mrs. Oglevee's harsh look faded, thoughtfulness again taking its place. "I don't know. I just think that is how . . . how it would work . . . once this was resolved . . ."

Mrs. Oglevee looked at me. "So. What is it going to be, Josie? Will you find out the truth behind my death? If it was murder or heart attack?"

I hesitated just a second before saying, "Yes. I will . . ."

Mrs. Oglevee looked relieved. "Thank you," she said. And she started to fade, Chesire-cat-like, from the feet up. And recede at the same time. I hated it when she did that.

"Wait!" I hollered. "Give me some hint, some clue . . ."

"Josie . . . Josie, come on wake up!"

I moaned. I knew that voice. It was Cherry, trying to wake me up. But I couldn't wake up, not yet. If I was going to do this thing, I needed more than just a note and a dream vision of Mrs. Oglevee . . .

"Josie, sheesh, girl, wake up!"

Something poked me in the shoulder.

I moaned. "I need a clue, a clue . . ."

But Mrs. Oglevee was gone. There was nothing but whiteness, a growing sense of being about to wake up—

And suddenly Mrs. Oglevee's voice—just her voice—again: "Oh, for pity's sake's Josie Toadfern! Can't you remember *anything* I've taught you? Now, tell me, what did Commodore Oliver Hazard Perry *say* after the battle of Lake Erie was over? Word for word, Josie!"

8

"Perry . . . wha . . . what'd he say . . . wait, wait . . ."

Something dug hard into my shoulder, and I winced.

"Josie, wake up! We're in Bucyrus!"

I slowly opened my eyes. Cherry's face was looming over mine. She stood outside the truck, leaning in over me through the open door, grabbing my shoulder and trying to shake me awake. Her perfume—some patchouli something—and the scent of strong breath mints was overwhelming as she repeated, "We're in Bucyrus!"

I jerked my shoulder from her grasp.

"I'm awake, I'm awake," I mumbled. "Just give me a sec."

"Sorry, Josie," said Sally from the front seat. "I said to let you rest and we'd wake you up once we're in Port Clinton—"

"But we're takin' a pit stop here in Bucyrus," said Cherry, firmly. "We have a photo op we can't miss, and I need coffee!"

I yawned so hard my eyes shut for a second. When I opened them and got my bearings, I saw we were in the parking lot of the Butt Hut, a squat building, the orange and hot pink lettering in its huge window proclaiming: ALL BRANDS! $24.99 A CARTON!

"Sally," I said, admonishing. "You told me you'd been off the smokes for more than a year!"

Sally had been a chain smoker, until she got pregnant with her triplet sons. She quit to take care of her babies' health, and didn't take up smoking again after they were born, although she'd threatened to throughout her pregnancy. After her ex-husband left her for a honey in his motorcycle club, she had a brief two-week relapse into chain smoking, but then one of the triplets (Larry, I think) got a serious ear infection that nearly burst his eardrum, and she blamed herself and quit smoking for good, at least in the teeny trailer home they live in. Although I think she occasionally has one at the end of a long day at the Bar-None, a hazard of ownership.

"I have," Sally said, a mite defensively. "This is Cherry's idea."

"What?" I was confused. "Cherry's taken up smoking?"

She looked horrified. "Of course not! Do you know what smoking does to your skin and nails?"

To say nothing of your lungs and heart and general health, I thought . . . but Cherry's a skin-deep kinda gal. So, in fact, I said nothing.

"She wants the picture," Sally said, "because of the name of the place."

Cherry grinned triumphantly. "That's right. So what if it's a cigarette discount outlet? If we stand in front of the advertising and frame the picture just right, so the words Butt Hut show above us, it could be a, well, you know."

She wriggled her eyebrows. I thought about the implications of what Butt Hut could mean besides cigarettes, came to the right conclusion quickly enough, and groaned.

"Cherry, what are you up to?"

"I just want a picture. To, you know, give Dean." She giggled. But the giggle was kind of forced. And something flashed in her eyes. Uh oh, I thought. Something was up. Something I didn't know about. Something I figured I'd find out about later . . . and regret learning.

"Sally?" I said, plaintively.

"Let's just get this over with," Sally said, sighing. "We argued for five minutes about this before you woke up."

So, a few minutes later, there we were. Posed in front of the Butt Hut, with our backs to some poor forty-something guy who had pulled in after us and was starting across the parking lot to the building when he found himself besieged by Cherry, who charmed him into agreeing to take a picture of us with her camera.

We bent over, and peered around at the camera. Three big behinds, all in a row; the words Butt Hut above our heads, and us grinning back at the camera. Click!

"Take another one, just in case!" Cherry hollered.

In case what? One of us blinked?

But the guy obliged and a few seconds later, Sally and I stood leaning against her truck, our breaths fogging the cold air, snow starting to come down, and watched with a mix of awe and annoyance as Cherry flirted with the guy who'd taken our photo.

"Is she flirting with him?" I asked.

"Yep," Sally said.

"Are they—they're exchanging numbers!"

"Looks that way."

"Sally, what's going on?"

Sally shook her head. "I don't know." I studied her as she stared at the cars passing by, and decided I believed her. Something was up with Cherry, but we weren't going to get it out of her just yet.

A few minutes later, Cherry trotted back over to us, and Butt Hut man returned to his car. We took off, bypassing a McDonald's and Burger King in favor of privately owned Jerry's Drive-Thru, reminiscent of Sandy's Restaurant in our hometown, except Sandy's was a converted double-wide trailer, whereas Jerry's was a 1950s relic. The car-side walkie-talkies had long been pulled out, but there was a drive-up window on the side as well as a walk-up window on the front. We opted to go in, having faith that the building, which seemed to be leaning forward on the front overhang supports as if they were canes, would not choose that day to heave a great sigh and collapse from the tension of all that fast-food competition just down the road.

Which, in fact, we'd only bypassed because Cherry said that Dean had relatives in Port Clinton, and on the trip up for summer fishing, a big family treat had been to stop in at Jerry's for what he claimed were the best burgers ever.

We'd gone in, ordered our burgers, sat at a table near a family of a mom and two young girls, and commenced to eating. The burgers were, in fact, wonderful.

"Don't tell Sandy," I said, "but these rival hers."

"Almost as good as the best burgers of my childhood," Sally said.

"What were those?"

"Got 'em with Daddy when we'd go fishing, at the Bait Shack on the way over to Licking Creek Lake," she said, referring to the man-made lake near Paradise.

"The Bait Shack has burgers?" Cherry asked.

"Did then," Sally said, licking the grease off her fingers. "We'd get burgers for us and worms for the fish."

Cherry wrinkled her nose. "Ew. You got burgers made at the same place that sold . . . worms?"

Sally got that mischievous look on her face. "Yep," she said. "Daddy always told me not to look too close at the burgers. But I figured the worms made the burgers moister . . ."

Cherry looked horrified, and I burst out laughing, nearly spewing cola-with-a-shot-of-vanilla-syrup across the table.

Cherry tried to look nonplussed as she plucked a French fry from our communal pile, holding it delicately between the tips of her long, fake nails as she salted it down. She does that—salts each fry individually.

"Time for change of subject," I said, when I regained self-control.

"Okay. So, who is this Perry, and why haven't you told us about him before?" Cherry asked, glancing up from her fry to give me a look.

"What?" I said, dipping my trio of fries into catsup. Mmmm. These were as good as the burgers. Deep fried to crispiness, not mushy. I hate mushy fries.

"You were mumbling about Perry when we pulled into the Butt Hut." Cherry whispered the last two words and giggled. Sally rolled her eyes and snagged Cherry's fry from between her hot-pink-with-lilac-swirl fingernails.

"Hey," Cherry said, trying to snag it back, but too late. Sally'd already popped the fry into her mouth and was smiling at Cherry with impish glee.

I sipped my cola, staring off into space, hoping the fry distraction would throw Cherry off the Perry line of questioning. It didn't.

She plucked up another fry, gave Sally a warning look, started meticulously salting the fry, and then looked at me. "Perry," she demanded.

I sighed. I'd told Sally and Cherry about my Mrs. Oglevee dream visitations—or whatever they were—in a moment of weakness. Naturally, they found the idea of Mrs. Oglevee nagging me in my sleep to be quite a hoot. I reckon they'd think differently if she popped up some night in their REMs.

Sally frowned at me. "What are you thinking? You've already got two boyfriends. Who is this Perry?"

"I do not have two boyfriends—" I started.

"Caleb," said Sally.

"Randy," said Cherry, and waggled her eyebrows at me.

"And now this Perry character?" Sally said.

"Caleb is a colleague and friend and someone I just enjoy going out with occasionally," I said, through gritted teeth.

"Long-winded way of saying boyfriend," Sally said.

"And Randy," I went on, ignoring her, "is renovating my

apartment and is just someone I enjoy going out with occasionally . . ."

"Well, he'd be a hunka-hunka burnin' love if you'd just let him," Cherry said. Oh Lord. We weren't even to the Great Walleye Drop, which, Sally had told us earlier, included an Elvis act, and she was already quoting the King. Before I'd drifted off on the drive up, she'd told us about how she'd looked up the Great Walleye Drop on the Web, and sure enough, there was an Elvis impersonator—Lenny T.— scheduled to entertain the crowd in the hours before Wylie-the-Walleye was lowered from his hoist to ring in the New Year. "And given how he looks, I don't know why you'd hesitate to stoke that fire . . ."

"And Perry . . ." I started, and both Sally and Cherry leaned forward eagerly, wanting to hear more about my new, secret lover. I was sorely tempted, I confess, to just make up something. I had done that once, in eighth grade, made up a boyfriend who I claimed lived in Kentucky on a rich horse farm, and managed to get everyone to believe me for about three days. The soap opera love yarn that I spun got so intense that I had to break up with my imaginary boyfriend.

". . . is as in Commodore Oliver Hazard Perry," I said.

Cherry went totally blank.

Sally scowled. "What? You're dreaming about some old crusty long-dead military historical figure?"

"Who?" Cherry said.

Now Sally scowled at her. "Oh, for pity's sake, Cherry, how could you forget what Mrs. Oglevee drummed into our heads? I swear she was in love with that old long-dead guy."

Cherry blinked at her.

I had a few more French fries and a sip of cola. Truth be told, I could remember Mrs. Oglevee seeming taken with the story of Commodore Oliver Hazard Perry—which was apparently more than Cherry remembered—but I couldn't remember the details.

Sally focused on me. "So, why were you muttering about him?"

"Well . . . you know I had to give a speech about Mrs. Oglevee this morning," I said. "And, so, well, after I drifted off . . ."

"You dreamed about her, again?" Cherry said. Sally elbowed her.

"Yes," I said, a little defensively. "And she said something about remember what Perry said, some famous quote."

" 'We have met the enemy and they are ours,' " Sally said.

Cherry and I looked at her.

"That's the quote," Sally said. "That's what he wrote down on the back of an old envelope when he and his men on the U.S.S. *Niagara* defeated the British squadron in the Battle of Lake Erie."

Cherry frowned—then quickly lifted her eyebrows high to smooth out the space between her brows. She's starting to develop a frown line, she says—no one else can detect it—and she's on a mission to never frown again, or at least undo the effect with what she calls Extreme Eyebrow Lifting. (She talked about, but hadn't followed up on, looking into getting the concept trademarked.) She did a few reps, and then said, "How do you remember that stuff?"

" 'Cause it's interesting," Sally said. "Now, what else did Mrs. Oglevee say in this manifestation?"

I shrugged. "Kinda vague," I said. I wasn't ready yet to share about the note or about Mrs. Oglevee saying in my dream that she didn't know how she died.

"So, what do you all remember about Mrs. Oglevee?" I asked.

"Josie, if we remembered anything other than the basics, we'd have told you last night," Sally said. "Besides, you found out a lot more than either of us knew."

"She did?" Cherry said, looking confused. She apparently didn't remember much about the night before.

Sally filled her in on what I'd shared with her, the recitation of facts that had formed the basis of my speech.

"But, see, those are just facts," I said, when Sally finished. "What made her tick? What motivated her? The facts don't tell us that. Can't any of us remember anything that gets to her . . . her essence?"

Cherry and Sally ate a few more fries, considering my question.

Finally, Cherry said, "Well, she was mean, remember? And always so uptight. No wonder she didn't have any friends."

"Well, sure, that's how we saw her as kids," Sally said, "but Josie's point is that it's kind of weird that she didn't have any real relationships at all. Her whole identity was being a teacher, and something of a self-made expert on local history, but she never seemed to enjoy any of it. I mean, who goes their whole life with so few connections and so little joy?"

"Maybe someone who is depressed?" Cherry asked. "Nowadays there are medicines to help people with depression—"

"Well, there were back in the seventies and eighties, too—" Sally said.

"But maybe Mrs. Oglevee didn't know about them. Or just couldn't get herself to go get help—maybe she felt stuck," I said. I felt a little trill of excitement. I'd never thought of Mrs. Oglevee as anything other than simply unpleasant because she was . . . unpleasant. Not a surprising view for a teen. And I hadn't updated my view since.

But maybe there really was a reason for her attitude . . . a reason that might have something to do with her being murdered. Assuming she was, and the note wasn't just a prank.

"Maybe she didn't want people to get close to her, because she felt guilty about something, and that's why she didn't have any real activities outside of work, or relationships with anyone," Cherry said.

"Or maybe she was trying to hide something from her past, and that's why," Sally said.

"Oooh—how about this: she was trying to protect something or someone or some piece of information, and that's why she kept everyone at a distance and was so secretive,"

I said. It turned out that there were any number of reasons why someone might have chosen the life Mrs. Oglevee had! I was starting to feel it . . . the excitement of the puzzle, of trying to figure this out . . .

"Or maybe she really was just a bitchy grump."

"Or grumpy bitch," Sally said.

"Now watch your language . . . this is a family restaurant . . . not your bar!"

"Just calling it like it is," Sally said, "and besides, I've heard you use language in the Bar-None that could set the CDs to playing backwards in the jukebox . . ."

I sighed, suddenly feeling deflated, tuning out their squabbles. I took a long sip of my soda. For a second there, I thought we were on to something, reasons that Mrs. Oglevee was so, well, grumpy and bitchy. Reasons she might have been murdered. But then, Sally and Cherry had to bring it back to the most obvious reason: Mrs. Oglevee just wasn't nice. Maybe I'd been looking for something more to Mrs. Oglevee's identity than that because I wanted to believe it was there and because I didn't want to think she'd tormented me in junior high just for sport. But what if she had . . . and her niece was cut of the same cloth, slipping me that note just to rile me before my speech, just as a practical joke?

Maybe Mrs. Oglevee had told her niece about all the times I'd skipped her class, pulled pranks on her to get back at her for her meanness, and this was her niece's way of getting back at me on her aunt's behalf. It was a real possibility, I thought. I'd be sure to ask her about it when we got to Port Clinton. No use bringing up the possibility of murder with Cherry and Sally. I'd check this out with Eileen, Mrs. Oglevee's niece, get that over with that very night, and then have a nice time with Sally and Cherry, let Mrs. Oglevee know in my next dream she hadn't been murdered, dismiss her from my mind forevermore, simple as that.

Oh my Lord. Was that a whiff of wistfulness I detected, curling forth from the back of my brain, at the thought of

Mrs. Oglevee disappearing forever from my subconsciousness?

The question was interrupted by a sudden giggling fit . . . from Sally. I looked up. Cherry was staring at her in wonderment, her expression reflecting my thoughts: hey, wait! Cherry's the mad giggler! Not Sally!

"S-s-sorry," she managed. "Must be our posing in front of the Butt Hut that made me think of it . . . but there is something that kind of fits trying to figure out Mrs. Oglevee. Josie, do you remember when—"

She started sputtering with laughter again.

The woman and her two young daughters at the next table were staring at Sally. The youngest, who I reckoned to be about three, started puckering up, like any second she'd start wailing.

"Sally, you're starting to scare young children," I said, elbowing her. "Just say whatever it is."

Of course, I ended up almost immediately regretting my admonition, 'cause what Sally said next was: "Okay, okay. Recollect the time Paradise Middle School got a brand-new photocopier, and Mrs. Layton, the secretary, was all proud of it?"

I pressed my eyes shut, remembering suddenly, and wishing I didn't. I'd gone years happily suppressing the memory. But I couldn't any longer, because Sally went on, barely able to get the words out, she was giggling so hard.

"And Josie and I, we snuck into the school office after hours, and photocopied our butts! I was sitting on top of the photocopy machine when Mrs. Oglevee walked in. Josie had already done her photocopy and had zipped up her jeans, and there I was, my jeans and panties around my ankles, the photocopy machine whirring away, spitting out copy after copy of my behind . . ."

Sally's sputtering rendition of our unfortunate tale was interrupted by a piercing wail. I opened my eyes. Sure enough, the three-year-old blond girl at the table next to us was now hysterically screeching. Her tantrum seemed to have nothing to do with what Sally was saying—the girl's bigger sister had dumped her milkshake onto little sister's fries, and was happily eating them. But, mama, who was now trying to clean the older child's hands and calm the younger daughter, was glaring at Sally as if somehow her use of the word "butt" in a public place had caused the whole scenario.

By the time the harried woman at the next table had calmed and cleaned her little ones, gotten them into their coats, and shooed them away from their table, Sally had finally calmed down, too, although she still erupted with an occasional giggle.

Cherry stared at me. "Did you really photocopy your butt?"

"Why're you looking at me? Sally did it, too. And it was her idea in the first place!"

"Yeah, but it's not surprising Sally would do that. But you were always just Nosey Josie, curious about what everyone else was up to. You never actually *did* stuff yourself . . ."

I scowled at her. "That's not true. And you know how I hated that nickname—"

"But it fits. And, kinda like the shoe, if the nickname fits, wear it—"

"Look, little Miss Cliché," I said. Okay, that was a little harsh. But I didn't like being tagged with that nickname, even if it fit. "I didn't get that nickname until years later—"

"But it was true even in junior high," Cherry said.

"Well, it was true that you were stuck up in junior high, the ultimate cheerleader cliché." Oh, shut up, Josie, I told myself; Cherry's eyes were welling and her lips pouting just like the three-year-old's had moments before. But somehow I couldn't stop. She was my friend, true, but somehow she always brought out the defensive cat in me. "Big hair, big boobs, big butt, strutting around like—"

"Hey, hey, hey," Sally broke in, suddenly serious. "C'mon gals, we're not even to Port Clinton, and you two are getting into a catfight?" She glared at Cherry first. "Apologize to Josie. This is her thirtieth birthday trip, remember?"

"Sorry, Josie," Cherry muttered, barely getting it out through her glittery, glossed lips. How did she manage to keep the coat of lip gloss intact, I wondered, while eating fries?

Sally turned her glare on me. "Josie—your turn."

I sighed. "I'm sorry. I just hated that nickname. And I always was jealous of how glamorous you looked, even then."

Cherry's eyes welled up, but she managed not to let tears spill over. "Aw, really?"

Nothing like being the envy of her friends to calm down Cherry. I smiled. "Really," I said.

Sally rolled her eyes. "Yeah, yeah, Cherry was the hot cheerleader, Josie the nosey bookworm, and I was the dumb jock that scared all the boys because I could out run 'em all—and hit a baseball farther than they could. Now that we've detoured down memory lane about what our identities were back then, let's get back to Mrs. Oglevee.

"So . . . she caught us in the act of photocopying our butts. Remember, Josie?"

"Yeah, unfortunately. Because while your daddy thought it was funny, Aunt Clara and Uncle Horace were not amused. They were horrified. The two days' suspension we each got wasn't enough, as I recall. 'Cause I was also grounded for a week and spent the whole time cleaning the cellar."

"Yeah, but what else do you remember?" Sally asked.

Where was she going with this? "Um, I remember we were going to write stuff on the photocopies to get back at some boys who had been mean to us. I think . . ." I paused, trying to recollect. "Oh, yeah. I was writing 'To Johnny, you showed me yours, here's mine,' right across the picture, and I was going to put it on John Worthy's locker, to get back at him for calling me flatchested in front of everyone. The idea was to embarrass him anonymously. And weren't you planning to—"

"I was going to write, 'Kiss mine, dumb . . .' and then leave a blank line next to 'dumb,' and leave it on Toby Hugh's locker, to get back at him for telling me I might as well be a boy since I outran him in the hundred yard dash. But then Mrs. Oglevee came in." Another giggle bubbled forth, but she forced her expression back into sobriety. "And what makes me laugh is the completely horrified expression she had on her face."

"As I recall now," I said, "right after you grabbed a handful of paper to cover your private parts, you started laughing."

"Yeah. Because that look—it was like she had never seen anything so awful in her life. She had this look like there was this horrible taste in her mouth, like she'd just stumbled upon the commission of a terrible crime. It was so over the top," Sally said. "I mean, yeah, we shouldn't'a been doing that for all kinds of reasons, but really, in the grand scheme, a coupla kids photocopying their butts as a prank isn't that awful."

"Well, it is kinda gross," Cherry said. "If I'd have been Mrs. Layton I'd have gone over that machine with a whole bottle of Windex. Besides, doesn't it fit Mrs. Oglevee that she'd be horrified by finding the two of you doing that? I mean, she was so upset when she found out I was trying to make fake fingernails with glue in the pencil tray inside my desk. You'd have thought I was permanently defacing property."

"Yeah," Sally said. "It fits. But what doesn't fit is that for just a second, that terribly angry expression dropped from her face. Like a mask dropping. And she looked so sad. I don't think you noticed it, Josie."

I shuddered, at the image of the mask slipping, and then tried to shrug away the creepy chill that suddenly danced between my shoulder blades. "No," I said. "I didn't. I was too busy trying to crumple up the evidence and figure out how I was going to explain this to Aunt Clara."

"Well, she did look sad. Very, very sad. And then, suddenly she was so angry, screaming at us—remember?"

"Yeah, I remember now. She was screaming about how we were loose, nasty, promiscuous girls, how we were going to grow up to be strippers or hookers, and proceeded to shriek some unlovely variations of the word hooker at us . . ."

Cherry's eyes were wide. "Wow. I didn't even know she knew about such things."

"Exactly," Sally said. "Mrs. Belham, the principal, thankfully was walking down the hall and overheard Mrs. Oglevee's rant, and came in. She had to calm Mrs. Oglevee down."

"That's right," I said, remembering. "By then we were crying."

"I was more terrified by this sudden, weird explosion from Mrs. Oglevee than anything else. And remember, Mrs. Belham seemed to be more upset by that than by our antics."

"We still ended up with two days' suspension," I said. "And I still had to clean that cellar."

"Yeah. But Mrs. Oglevee was gone for a whole week," Sally said. "I don't know if that was because she'd called us names, or because for some reason she needed the break. I mean, she shouldn't have been that traumatized by finding us like that."

"Okay, so what does this have to do with the original question about Mrs. Oglevee?" Cherry said. She frowned, then immediately lifted her eyebrows. "Wait— what *was* the original question?"

"It was—what did any of us remember about Mrs. Oglevee, except that she'd been uptight all the time," I said. "And since she had such a quiet life, was there a reason for that . . . or was that just her way?"

"Oh," Cherry said. "So what does this story have to do with that?"

I looked at Sally. "Because," I said, understanding finally. "Sally remembers seeing Mrs. Oglevee crack—she saw a glimpse of great sadness in Mrs. Oglevee, and then she saw Mrs. Oglevee either try to cover it up by ranting at us . . ."

"Or, did the rant really have anything to do with us? I think what was so scary was not what she yelled at us . . . but that while she was yelling it was like she wasn't even there. She was somewhere . . . else," Sally said.

We all thought about that for a long moment, about how maybe that glimpse behind Mrs. Oglevee's mask told us something about Mrs. Oglevee. Or maybe not. Maybe we were just fishing, hoping to catch some truth or other that made sense of Mrs. Oglevee. It was too soon, though, for us to know if Sally's memory told us anything.

In any case, it was getting dark outside, and we still had about an hour's drive. So we cleared our table, put on our coats, and headed out.

At a booth near the front door, I saw the man who'd taken our picture in front of the Butt Hut. For just a second, I thought he'd noticed us, but then he stared out the window, away from me.

I couldn't say why his presence bothered me, but it did. That creepy chill started up again between my shoulder blades, icing up my neck, but I shrugged it off again. After all, Bucyrus was a lot bigger than Paradise, but it was still small enough that it wasn't at all surprising that the man had ended up in the same restaurant as us.

9

The rest of the way into Port Clinton, we sang along with the country station. When we got tired of that, we sang along to a station playing 1980s tunes, all of us crooning with especial gusto to Joan Jett's rocking lament, "I hate myself for lovin' you . . ." Which I could understand for Sally and me, but I wondered what was up with Cherry.

But after that we started cracking stupid jokes that we'd cracked a hundred times before.

Here's one that Cherry can never remember, and so she breaks up laughing every time she hears it: What kind of socks do pirates wear?

Aaaaargyle.

I know, I know. Scottish pirates in colorful diamond-patterned socks? But on and on we went, making up variations, each as nonsensical as the original.

What's a pirate's favorite pet? Aaaarmadillo.

His favorite novel? *A Farewell to Aaaarms.*

(Sally and Cherry had to think about that last one. I'm the bookworm of our trio, and in any case, Hemingway would never make their To Be Read piles—if they had them.)

See, once you're out of the metro areas (the big three

being Cincinnati, Columbus, and Cleveland), there's a whole lot of Ohio that's nothing but cornfields and silos and farm-houses and tiny towns and two-lane state routes ribboning in and out and amongst all of the aforementioned. That's where we were, in an area just like where we were from, except it was colder and a lot flatter. Our region has rolling hills and some tobacco farms to break up the monotony of corn.

So we entertained ourselves with the radio and our silly jokes. It would turn out to be the best part of our chick trip.

Eventually we were on a four-lane, divided state route, seeing signs for Cedar Point, the big amusement park not far from Port Clinton and right on the edge of Lake Erie. I've heard tell that from the top of the Ferris wheel, you can see Lake Erie, but I don't know this for sure, having never been to Cedar Point. I felt a little twinge of longing. I was a day shy of thirty and I'd never been to the state's big amuse-ment park!

Then I shook my head to clear it, went back to bad "Arrrr" jokes and then the next thing I knew, we were back on an ordinary two-lane state route, passing through a west Port Clinton neighborhood of clapboard-sided two-story houses with tiny lots, huge trees, and overburdened front porches.

Once we got to the center of town, we easily found our motel, the Perry Inn, which was across the street from the docks and around the corner from the town square, where the Great Walleye Drop itself would take place in two evenings.

The Perry Inn was made up of two buildings. The main building was a beautiful old house that had a two-story ad-dition on the back. The second, just across the parking lot, catty-cornered to the old house, was a regular-looking two-story motel building. I studied the motel setup and thought about how odd it was that Cherry had insisted on us resting in Sally's truck while she took care of getting us checked in. It wasn't like Cherry to be so thoughtful.

But rather than pulling a mean-girl moment and com-menting on that the minute Cherry left Sally's truck, I said,

"Wow. The Rhinegolds sure would think this is something."

The Rhinegolds own the Red Horse Motel, just on the outskirts of Paradise, a one-story structure, with a filled-in pool in the back that Greta Rhinegold plants with flowers in the spring and advertises as a "courtyard."

"Yeah," Sally said. "You know, I've always admired their marriage. Wonder how they do it?"

"I don't know. Maybe it has to do with choosing well?"

Sally laughed. "Is that more a comment on our exes' bad taste—or ours?"

"Ours," I said, definitely. "We're perfect."

Sally laughed again, and Cherry came out of the front of the building. "And yet," Sally said, "look at Cherry—not perfect. Self-absorbed. Primps all the time . . ."

So much for avoiding a mean-girl moment.

"Hey! She thought up this treat for my thirtieth birthday!"

"True," Sally said, "But you know what I'm saying."

"Yeah."

"And she ends up with a great guy like Deputy Dean!"

"Yeah," I said again, sighing a little. Not over Deputy Dean. He was a nice guy and all, but not my type. Still, what did I want from my life, at nearly thirty? That billboard before Bucyrus claimed Jesus was coming any second. The Good Book says it's foolish to make such predictions, so on that account I could dismiss the billboard's message. On the other hand, the billboard had stirred in me a sense of time slipping by.

I loved Guy and my hometown and my business . . . but what else did I really want?

I shook my head. No. This chick trip was just supposed to be for fun—not contemplation.

"I think by spring, our boyfriend-of-the-month-gal Cherry is going to be fussing over her wedding dress."

"Really?"

"C'mon, now, haven't you been payin' attention to Cherry

and Dean when they come into the Bar-None? They're moon-eyed together. In a serious sort of way, not just pawing each other."

Truth be told, I'd been so focused on my own breakup with Owen—and the pleasant if not completely satisfying distractions of Caleb and Randy, plus my apartment renovations, and my expanded Stain-Busters column—that I hadn't really noticed that Cherry and Dean's relationship had taken a serious turn.

"Now, you know she'll ask us to stand up with her at the wedding," Sally went on, "at least she'd better, after all these years we've had to put up with her heartaches—thank the good Lord she's finally with a man with sense who also makes her happy—but she'd better not try to get me into anything with ruffles. Lace I could maybe manage, but I just can't abide by ruffles—"

She stopped as Cherry got to the passenger door. We composed expressions of innocence. Cherry opened the door, and peered in at us suspiciously. "What?" she said.

"Nothing," I said.

"Room number?" Sally asked perkily.

"One-twelve," Cherry said, still casting suspicious looks.

Sally pulled into the parking space in front of Room 112, which was on the first floor at the end of the extension to the old house.

I glanced around. The parking lot was empty, save for Sally's truck. "We're the only ones here."

"Just wait," Cherry said. "Place'll start filling up tomorrow, and be packed by noon day after tomorrow."

We got out of Sally's truck. Cherry had the key, but she also had the most luggage, so within minutes Sally and I were at the front door, patiently waiting for Cherry, who was trying to lug two large suitcases, an overnight bag (which probably held her makeup and hair stuff), a large purse, and a shopping bag.

"Hate to see what she'll pack for her honeymoon with Dean, if this is what she brings for three nights," Sally muttered.

Cherry was casting us "help me," looks, which we were happily ignoring.

"If they go to a Swiss chalet in Gatlinburg, like Cherry's always said she wanted for her honeymoon, they'll need a U-Haul," I said, softly.

"Hell, she'll have a suitcase just for bikinis for the heart-shaped Jacuzzi," Sally said, and snorted a brief laugh.

I giggled, feeling a little guilty. After all, Cherry had arranged this chick trip just for us, in honor of my thirtieth birthday. "Maybe we should help her," I said, as we watched Cherry drop the overnight bag onto her own foot, then yelp a curse and lament the likely fate of her Opi nail polish.

"Nah," said Sally. "Hey, Cherry, toss us the keys. It's freezing out here! We'll unlock—"

"You can't toss a key card," Cherry said. "When's the last time you went to a motel that wasn't the Red Horse?" The Rhinegolds' motel still had old-fashioned keys.

Sally didn't answer—just turned a little pink, I noticed—and went over and snagged the key card from Cherry. "Hope you got three of these!"

"The other two are in my pocket, which I could get to if I wasn't struggling with—"

Sally unlocked the door and we went into the room, ignoring Cherry's whining. Then we stopped, staring at the bed. Of which there was one. King-sized.

"What the—" Sally said, and went over and dropped her duffel bag on it. The bed rippled and the bag tumbled off the side.

"Holy sh—"

"That," I interrupted. "Is. A. King-sized. Water bed."

"Cherry!" Sally and I hollered in unison, and turned around, intent on going back outside to confront her in the parking lot.

But Cherry was standing in the doorway, her supersized purse over one shoulder, the overnight bag over the other, a suitcase and shopping bag in one hand, and another suitcase in the other. The expression on her face—that she was carrying the weight of the world—had nothing to do, I realized, with all of the stuff she was holding.

She stared at us for a second, and then suddenly burst out sobbing. Wailing, really.

Which was when I knew Cherry was truly upset.

She doesn't make her mascara run over just anything.

10

A half-hour later, we had everything more or less sorted out. First, I had to get Sally to stop hollering that she wasn't sleeping in a king sized waterbed with two other women even if they were her best friends and how Cherry could just sleep in the tub for all she cared. Then I had to get Cherry to stop blubbering and wash her face. A raccoon-eyed Cherry is a disturbing sight.

After that, while Sally glared at her, and I tried to stay calm and objective, Cherry shared her tale of woe.

"Dean booked us this room—I didn't know he'd asked special for the king-sized water bed . . . I just assumed it had two double beds . . ." Cherry said as primly as she could, given that she was hiccupping. Sally rolled her eyes. I swatted her arm.

"Anyhow, Dean wanted us to come up for the Great Wall-eye Drop for a special New Year's Eve," Cherry went on. "He had lots of fond memories of fishing up here with his grandpa, who took tourists out to fish for walleye."

I nodded encouragingly. That part made sense. After all, we'd seen several signs on the way into town proclaiming Port Clinton as the Walleye Capital of the World. This, I reckoned, made it also the Walleye Capital of the Known Universe, as good a point of pride as any.

"The thing is, Dean let it slip that he was planning to . . . to . . . propose to me this weekend!" Cherry's voice rose on a wail as if this was a horrifically evil plot.

Sally elbowed me and gave me a told-you-so look.

"Well, I reckon I surprised Dean—and me, too, really— by telling him I'm just not ready for a lifetime commitment. He was hurt, I could see that, but that's no excuse for what he said next. Said I'd sure been acting ready from almost the minute he'd met me. Said maybe there was another man he didn't know about—'cause I definitely had *that kind* of reputation."

She looked at us, as if we might argue that she didn't have *that kind* of reputation. But, of course, she did, and up until now, she'd taken a gleeful joy in that fact. It was just part of who she was: Cherry, good-time party girl and heart-breaker.

Cherry shrugged at our silence. "Well, anyway, I got mad and told Dean I not only wasn't going with him to the Great Walleye Drop, but I never wanted to see him again, and then I thought, well, he'd already paid for the room, and it was in both our names, so why not come up here anyway with my two best friends in the whole world?"

She tried to charm us with a big smile. We didn't smile back.

"You expect us to believe you just wanted to come up for a getaway with us so you could forget your woes?" asked Sally.

"Uh—yeah."

"Uh huh," Sally grunted. "What kinda rumors did you get started about our little trip?"

Cherry cut her eyes away, "Well, maybe I did mention to Janine Johnson when she was in my beauty shop a few days ago that we were coming up here and I planned to see if I couldn't lure a fine catch during our wild walleyed weekend."

"Janine Johnson? As in wife of Tommy, one of Dean's coworkers?" I asked. Janine also came regularly to my laundromat. No wonder she'd given me a funny look a few days before.

"Yeah," Cherry said, so quietly we could barely hear her.

"And in the town where Dean has so many childhood memories?" Sally said. "Now, that's low."

"And those Butt Hut pictures," I said, realization dawning.

"I thought I'd send 'em to Dean," Cherry said.

"Trying to prove his point and make us look bad at the same time?" Sally asked angrily.

"I—I just wanted to get back at him. I—I didn't know he'd especially booked a room with a king-sized water bed! That's so . . . so . . . thoughtful . . . see, I told him about this fantasy I have of—"

Sally poked her fingers in her ears and started singing, "la, la, la!" I held up my hand and hollered, "Too much information!" before Cherry could hiccup out any more details.

"I don't understand," I said. "I thought you and Dean, well, I thought maybe you two were the real deal."

Cherry looked at me. "I thought so, too, but I'm just not ready . . . I mean I've always been this happy-go-lucky party girl. Settle down? Get married? I—I don't know. That would be such a big change for me."

It wasn't that she didn't love Dean, I realized. She just was terrified because committing to that love would mean exchanging her old identity, one she was comfortable with, for a whole new one.

Which made me feel sympathy for her, until she said, "'Course, I don't want to be an old maid forever like Josie—"

"What? I'm a year younger than you! How come you get to be party girl and I get to be old maid?"

"Oh, Josie, you know you're not party girl, and you've never talked about wanting to get married."

"She's got a point," Sally said. "I've always assumed you

were so busy with taking care of Guy and working that you never wanted to marry or have a family of your own."

"But, but . . ." I spluttered.

They weren't listening to me. "And what if I do get married," Cherry went on, "and things don't work out, and we've already had kids? I don't want to be like you, Sally, and be known as that poor divorced woman stuck with all those kids . . ."

"Hey!" Sally said.

I looked at Sally. "Hah!"

"I just don't know what to do!" Cherry wailed.

We told her exactly what she—and we—were going to do. We'd stay, but Sally was calling down to the Bar-None to tell her ex-mom-in-law (who filled in at the bar when Sally wasn't there) to tell Dean that we were most definitely not up here hoping to hook fellas. As Sally said, Cherry might not mind a racy reputation, but Sally had her boys to think about and I had my columnist future to consider.

My job was to see if we could get a room with double beds. I shrugged on my coat and trotted to the lobby in the original old house, looking around while I waited for someone to come from the back office to the front desk.

It was a sight different from the Red Horse. There was a cozy fireplace, with a fire going, and comfy-looking overstuffed sofas and chairs, with comforters and pillows tossed artfully here and there, everything in shades of green and burgundy and tan. In an antique china hutch was a display of scented jar candles, homemade and for sale. I took a whiff of the one labeled CINNAMON BUNS. Mmmm. Maybe I'd splurge and spend five bucks for the candle before we left—a memento of the trip and a to-me-from-me birthday gift.

The clerk—a tired-looking, middle-aged woman—came to the front desk, listened to my request, then told me she was sorry, we could move tonight to another room if we liked, but then we'd lose the room we had for the next two nights, because the motel was booked after tomorrow through January 1.

So I requested two cots and learned we could only get one—fire hazard laws being what they were about overstuffing rooms. She also told me, in a warning voice, that the Great Walleye Drop was a wild time.

With visions of people dressed up in fish-scale necklaces, fish-head hats, and fish suits dancing in my head, I said the one cot would be fine, thinking Cherry could sleep on it, and Sally and I would share the king-sized bed. Unless, of course, it being a water bed, we kept rolling to the middle.

In which case Sally and I would sort out who got the water bed and who got the cot, and Cherry could sleep on the floor. Or in the tub. Or standing up against the wall. Whatever. That "old maid" comment really rankled.

I settled down for a few minutes on the lobby's couch, and gazed at the cozy fire, trying to collect my thoughts. I needed a few minutes before I walked back into Room 112's scene, which I figured was more of Cherry blubbering and Sally hollering that Cherry was a fool for letting Dean go, that there might be more fish in the sea—or walleyes in Lake Erie, as the case might be—but she wasn't going to find a nicer, kinder catch than Dean. Plus he had an adorable tush.

The door opening behind me startled me out of my reverie.

I got up to leave, and saw standing at the lobby desk the man we'd seen at the Butt Hut—and later, at Jerry's Drive-Thru. He glanced at me and for a second our eyes locked. A look passed across his face—like he was annoyed I'd seen him—but then he recovered, and smiled and nodded without saying anything, ignoring me, as if we'd never seen each other before.

I tried to push aside my unease—which, for Nosey Josie, isn't easy. Still, I'd never been all that comfortable with that nickname, so I thought maybe now that I was turning thirty, I should try to be a little less nosey.

So I told myself that it wasn't surprising he'd forgotten me—after all, he'd been focusing with much embarrassment on three women's butts, not our faces. Told myself it wasn't surprising he was here, either—after all, apparently this Great Walleye Drop was pretty popular in this region of Ohio. Told myself to stop worrying so much and to get back to Room 112.

'Course, it's not that easy to get away from your own identity. Later on I'd think now that I was turning thirty, I should just embrace being Nosey Josie!

By the time I got back to the room, Sally and Cherry had, thank the good Lord, calmed down considerably. Cherry was still sniffling a little, although she'd reapplied her makeup. They'd decided to go out, maybe check out the downtown, see if they could find a place to get a drink and play a game of pool or two, try and put the fight behind us.

I myself was still smarting from the fact that Cherry hadn't really planned this whole chick trip to celebrate my birthday—just used my birthday as an excuse to come up here anyway to get back at Deputy Dean. So I said I was tired and would hang out in the motel and wait for the cot.

After they left, I told myself I'd enjoy the time alone. I picked up my book tote and sat on the edge of the water bed, and immediately rolled back. I wriggled around to sit back up, feeling a surge of sympathy with upended turtles everywhere.

I finally made it from the bed to a chair and looked through the contents of my book tote. I smiled when I saw the contents. Sally must have packed for me. She'd stuffed in the top titles from my To Be Read pile—*What's the Worst That Could Happen?* by Donald Westlake and *Heat* by Joyce Carol Oates. Cherry would have bought out the Pick-N-Save's fashion magazine rack, hoping to convert me into a fashion-holic like her.

I started to pick up a book, but suddenly felt restless—not like me when I have a book in my hands. I wandered into the bathroom, planning to check my look in the mirror, suddenly worried that maybe Cherry had a point. I'd be thirty the next day. Most of my wardrobe was jeans, sweaters, T-shirts. My hairdo was a short chin-length crop that I just washed, combed, and let air-dry, just enough effort to get my straight hair to fall into place, except for the Forelock from Hell, as I call the strand at the center of my forehead, which seems to have a life of its own.

My makeup was a smudge of mascara, a coat of lip gloss, and a dash of tan eyeshadow. I only add a slash of blush for dressup occasions like major holidays and weddings and funerals. My fragrance is a splash of Jean Naté.

As I gazed in the mirror, it hit me that the only thing that had changed about my look since high school was that I no longer tried to tame the Forelock from Hell with hair gel and headbands. Forelock always managed to wriggle free. That . . . and . . . were those a few wispy lines at the corners of my eyes? I suddenly felt sympathy for Cherry and her Eyebrow Lifts.

And was that . . . a gray hair?

I plucked the hair, examined it under the light. Maybe it was just a silverier shade of medium brown . . . a taupe, perhaps . . .

I shook my head at myself, and dropped the hair into the toilet. That's when I saw them—the towels on the floor. Smeared with Cherry's makeup and mascara.

To remove: soak in cold water and a degreasing dishwashing detergent, such as Dawn. Then launder as usual . . .

I groaned, even as my mind went immediately to this stain tip. I had been in the laundromat/stain-removal business so long, that it had become one with my identity. A fact of which I was usually proud. But suddenly, I just felt stodgy.

For all my adult life, I'd been three things: Guy's caretaker, laundress, and chick with a pathetically laughable love life.

The first part of my identity was rock solid. The laundress part had always seemed like a good gig, a way to continue my beloved Aunt Clara's and Uncle Horace's heritage while taking care of myself and Guy, although these days, the income wasn't going as far as I'd like, which was why I'd been willing to expand my column. I had no idea where that would lead, which left me a little shaky because I also didn't know where I wanted it to lead.

And as for the last part of my identity . . . I shook my head at myself, partly to get rid of the memory of Caleb's warm kiss . . . Not going there, I told myself. Do something productive!

I went back to my book tote. Sally had also packed my file folder with the sheets about the candidates for the new director at Stillwater Farms.

Why not look at those?

I settled down in one of the two chairs with the folder and dug a Big Fizz Diet Cola out of the cooler, and sipped as I looked through. My review was interrupted almost immediately by the delivery of the cot, which fit beside the bed, after the young man—he looked like the son of the clerk—moved the guest chairs.

Then I settled down again with the files. I was familiar with most of the candidates we'd narrowed down to: Terry Whitaker, Serena Page, and Mark Peters. But at our last committee meeting I'd gotten the résumé of a new, late-comer candidate. Mary Rossbergen, Stillwater Farm's assistant director, had insisted that we all take a look at this candidate's dossier. I'd tucked the manila folder to the back of the expanding folder that contained all my info.

I pulled it out. Levi Applegate. Impressive credentials, I had to admit, more so than the other candidates. He also had a sister with autism, who had died from an unrelated cause (breast cancer) recently.

I felt a knot turn in the pit of my stomach. I couldn't imagine losing Guy, so I felt sorry for this Levi. But I wasn't sure how I felt about the fact he'd had an autistic sister. On the one hand, it explained his devotion to adults with autism and his motivation to work with them. On the other, would he be objective enough?

Then I frowned as I scanned a photocopy of an article he'd written recently, supporting the idea of breaking routines systematically rather than always following them, as a way to test for areas in which an adult with autism might be successful in expanding his or her abilities.

I knew how comfortable Guy was with his routines, and how distressed he became when they were varied at all. Even though I respected Mary's opinion—despite the fact that she pushed me too hard, I thought, to take breaks from my own routines in visiting Guy—I didn't really know that I could support this Levi. What if he tried to make Guy comfortable with the color red—a color that always sent Guy into a panic? What if he tried to take away Guy's pet project, cultivating pumpkins in the greenhouse?

I flipped through Levi's background check. Single, never married. From New Mexico.

I wondered what he looked like, feeling a sort of strange draw to the guy. I frowned. The old maid comment must have really hit hard.

It bothered me that, if he took the job, he'd have to move from so far away. Not that I have a thing against New Mexico. From the Travel Channel, it looks like a fascinating state.

But Owen had moved here from Seattle and chafed at fitting in in the Midwest. The other candidates were all from the Midwest or had lived in the Midwest in the past.

My frown deepened. Was I really going to let a personal issue with a romance-gone-bad get in my way of making clear-eyed decisions about Stillwater's future director?

I told myself not to frown, did another Cherry Eyebrow Lift, and then shook my head at myself. This was pointless. I wasn't going to be able to think clearly, waggling my eyebrows at this dossier. Levi Applegate would have to wait for later.

I packed up the file and tucked it back in my book tote, then sat back down. I pulled out a book and read for about ten minutes . . . and then heard, through the thin walls of the motel, the voices of a man and a woman entering the room next to us.

And just seconds after that, their words turned to moans. Loud moans. Groaning moans. Whoops and hollers and "Oh, Jesuses!" I didn't think this was in response to the JE-SUS IS COMING—ARE YOU READY? billboard we'd seen earlier in the day, although the couple seemed more than ready. Primed, even.

The whole thing made me groan . . . in despair, not sympathy. I turned on the TV, cranked the volume to dull next door's Hallelujah Chorus of Hot Motel Sex into vague making-out Musak.

I flicked through channel after channel until I hit a *Saturday Night Live* rerun. So, the show debuted around the year I was born. I still liked catching the older shows, more than the recent ones.

In a few seconds, I was watching a skit with John Belushi and Gilda Radner and I sighed as it started. I always sighed when I saw an image of Gilda. Poor thing. Dying so young of ovarian cancer.

Woman (Gilda) enters a laundromat, looking for a washer. Man (John) bumps into her, also looking for a washer. Only one washer available, so they share it. He drops in socks; she, pantyhose. He, shirt; she, blouse. He, pants; she, skirt. He, sleeveless T-shirt; she . . . shyly . . . starts to drop in her bra and he offers her a rose . . . from his laundry basket. That's enough to convince her to drop in her bra.

Next, he deposits underwear into the washer. She has panties, but is again reluctant . . . until he produces wine and glasses from his laundry basket.

Finally, he puts in the money to start the washer, she closes the lid, he pulls out and lights two cigarettes, and she accepts one, and then they sit in front of the washer and smooch . . .

Commercial break.

I realized I was crying. Other than the cigarette part (see . . . things were different in the past) it was just so, so . . . romantic. Would a man with a laundry basket containing red wine and roses and laundry he'd like to tumble around with my laundry ever show up in the laundromat of my life?

Oh, for pity's sake, I thought, snapping off the TV and rolling my eyes at my silly, maudlin self. Owen was gone for good, and I needed to move on. Besides, Aunt Clara had always told me: honey, just pursue your own life and the right man will come along sooner or later . . . and if he doesn't, that's better than going out and hooking up with the wrong one just for the sake of having a man.

Good advice.

But now it was too quiet. Even in the next room.

I decided to take Aunt Clara's advice and pursue life. Or at least not sit alone in a motel room on my thirtieth-birthday-eve.

I got up, put on my coat, scarf, knit hat, gloves. Made sure I had the room card key and the manila envelope of photos and articles from Eileen, and her note about Mrs. Oglevee being murdered, in my backpack purse, and stepped outside.

No one was in the parking lot—just the same car that had been there when we arrived, and a truck parked in front of the motel room next to ours.

I started to walk toward the lobby when the door of the motel room next to ours popped open. A tiny, frowzy, red-haired woman, dressed only in a chiffon dressing gown, popped out. She was wearing flip-flops and had a lizard tattoo on her very pale left ankle. She was tired-looking. Huh. The *Saturday Night Live* laundromat skit couldn't have taken more than five minutes.

I saw movement behind her and caught a view of Butt Hut man. I lifted my eyebrows at him, and he scurried out of sight, clearly unhappy that I'd seen him.

The tiny, too-young redhead lit up a cigarette—never mind the NO SMOKING sign on the outside of the motel room door.

"You know, you had that TV on awful loud," she said, no hint of irony in her voice. She wasn't shivering, either. This was one tough woman. "These walls are mighty thin!"

I stared at a spot on her dressing gown that wasn't there. Then I looked back up at her. "You know, I'm a stain-removal expert. And that's a mighty nice dressing gown. I could tell you how to get that stain of—"

She gasped, pulled back into the motel room, and slammed the door shut.

And I admit it. I smiled to myself as I headed toward the entrance to the lobby, certain the clerk could give me directions to Eileen's, since Winnie had given me the address.

It was time to ask some questions.

11

I was right. Rhoda—the desk clerk—knew exactly who Eileen Russell was. And the fact I was from out of town but knew someone in town didn't faze Rhoda a bit. She just said, "So, you know her, eh?" I noticed that people on the north shore of Ohio tended to add the "eh" as if we were in Canada or the Upper Peninsula of Michigan, a fact that I would never point out.

After all, this was still Bucks Country. Meaning Ohio State University Buckeyes, Buckeyes being the university's nickname as well as the state tree, and Bucks being short for Buckeye. Northern Ohio and southern Ohio are different places in many respects except one—all of Ohio is Bucks Country. And lots of people fly the red "O" flag right alongside their U.S. of A. Stars and Stripes, and with as much pride.

Not only that, but the team every Bucks fan loves to hate is the University of Michigan (the Wolverines). So pointing out that some Northern Ohioans have a bit of the Upper Peninsula clip to their voices would be about as wise as pointing out that the state tree's leaf . . . a symbol on many an official state document . . . looks an awful lot like the foliage of, well, marijuana plants.

Anyway, I told Rhoda that I was a friend of a friend of Eileen's—which was sort of true—and that I had her address, which I rattled off from memory. That made Rhoda lift her eyebrows just a bit, but then she gave me directions and told me Eileen lived in walking distance from the motel.

She didn't ask why I wanted to visit Eileen, but I had a feeling that everyone she knew would know before the night was out that I was visiting Eileen. I wasn't sure yet why Eileen was a person of such interest in Port Clinton, but I figured I'd soon find out. In any case, the fact that Rhoda looked like she just couldn't wait to pick up the phone and call her buddies was proof to me that, although Port Clinton's a sight bigger than Paradise, a small town is a small town anywhere.

I thanked her for the directions and then told her about the couple in the motel room next to ours. Not about their Hallelujah Chorus of Hot Motel Sex, but about the smoking. She frowned and said the room was registered to one guest, male, and asked what the woman looked like. I told her, including the lizard tattoo, but leaving out the imaginary stain I'd goaded the woman with.

Rhoda got a knowing look, and I figured her friends might have to wait before hearing about my visit to Eileen's house.

To get to Eileen's house, I just needed to go out the front door of the Perry Motel, turn right, and walk along Perry Street, which faced the shore of Lake Erie. Then, I'd find it, the fourth one down of the "big, grand houses," said Rhoda.

I didn't go there directly, though. After all, Eileen wasn't expecting me. Why not do a little exploring?

At the corner across the street, I noticed the banner hanging from the lamp post: "Exp*erie*nce Our Lake Erie Heritage." Always appreciative of a good pun, I smiled, and thought about what a nice town this seemed to be—never mind the Butt Hut man and his honey next to our room.

Then I crossed the street to the Port Clinton Municipal

Pier and had it all to myself, passing bars and the Port Clinton Fishing Company and fishing boat charters, all bedecked with CLOSED FOR THE SEASON signs. *Miss Lindy-Loo*, *Irish Mist*, and *Scooby*—cheerfully named fishing boats—were all up on cinder blocks for the season. There wasn't even so much as a cat or dog roaming the alleys between the buildings. The area had been completely abandoned for the winter.

As I walked, I thought I smelled the tang of fish—although it was so cold, I wasn't sure if it was left over from seasons past or if I just imagined the odor. I definitely heard the distant caw of seagulls, invisible as they circled above in the dark. Seagulls in Ohio. Might sound strange to folks from other states, but I'd read somewhere that seagulls had become a nuisance in northern Ohio, flying inland from the northern coast as far as fifty miles.

At the waterfront, the breeze, which I'd barely noticed at the top of the pier, suddenly snapped with bitter gusto. In the water was a pole with a green light on top to guide in fishing boats, I reckoned, although no one was going fishing again until March or April. Ice chunks clanged against the pole.

I hurried back up the pier, then crossed into the city park, and followed a paved path along the water's edge. After just a few steps, I stumbled in a sudden gust of wind. I quickly regained my balance, but my heart was thumping. I wouldn't want to plunge into the icy water. Anyone falling in might have five minutes—maybe ten, tops—before the cold water would claim them.

But I kept walking—mindful of my balance—to the path's end by a municipal parking lot, empty save for one white car. I stared across the lake, to where the water and sky met and smudged into one. How far was I looking, I wondered?

Not very, I reckoned. But eventually, from there, one could reach the ocean.

Then I thought about the islands of Lake Erie—Kelley

and Big Bass and South Bass. Maybe, I thought, I could return to Port Clinton in the summer, when the place was alive
and bustling. Go fishing. Visit an island . . .

Then I shook my head at myself. My home, my life, was
in Paradise, Ohio. I'd always been at peace with that fact.
And I needed to stay at peace with it—for Guy's sake, and
mine as well. Paradise was part of who I was, part of my
identity. But still, there was a little part of me that wondered
about exploring the great wide world beyond my little
spot . . .

I pulled my attention from the strobing white light, the
rhythmic sloshing of water pulling itself toward shore, the
gonging of ice against metal, the caws of the invisible
seagulls, and started back up the walk.

Then, suddenly, I stopped.

Was that . . . the odor of tobacco?

I stared across the municipal parking lot, saw nothing except the white car, which I knew didn't belong to Butt Hut
man, because I'd seen his vehicle in front of his motel room.

Was I just imagining that odor, like I'd perhaps imagined
the odor of old fish?

Sure, I told myself. Pure imagination. Still, I hurried
toward Eileen Russell's house.

The houses along Main Street were gorgeous—Victorian-
era mansions, with front-yard floodlights that showed off
their gingerbread-confection architecture. I gawked at the
fancy turrets and frilly details and the sheer size of the
houses, as well as their elaborate Christmas decorations.

Eileen's house, well lit by front-yard spotlights, was an
ornate yellow and white three-story with a wraparound
front porch, and a turret on its northwest corner. The holiday decorations included a floodlit manger scene near the
house, and closer to the sidewalk, deer made of wire and
white lights, nodding their heads to the ground. And from
the top of the turret, a precariously balanced—and again,

flood lit—Santa Claus cheerily dipping a fishing pole—
complete with a fish (walleye, I reckoned)—up and down.

I stared for a moment, surprised at the wealth the house
and its trimmings suggested, and at the whimsy of the decorations that cheerfully made a mishmash of several Christmas themes. Maybe I was judging too fast. Eileen's harsh,
angular face—the way I imagined a younger Mrs. Oglevee
would have looked—popped into my head . . . and I couldn't
quite get what I assumed about her from her manner, expression, and dress to match up with that house, that display. I'd
have guessed a more modern house for her, and few if any
decorations.

I went up to the front door, pressed the doorbell, which
triggered a cheery chiming of "Jingle Bells."

Just as the chiming got to "one-horse open sleigh" and I
was starting to hum along, the door opened. A short woman,
shorter even than my five feet two inches, stood in the doorway. She had short white fluffy hair, a cheerful, round, ruddy
face, and was on the pudgy side, comfortably dressed in a
green velour warm-up suit, with a necklace made of a bell
on a strand of red yarn, and jingle-bell earrings, and she
wore red elf-style house slippers, which also had bells on the
pointy tips of the toes.

I resisted the temptation to say, "Mrs. Claus, I presume?"
and instead said, "Hi. I was told Eileen Russell lived here,
and I was hoping to chat with her—"

"I'm Eileen," the woman said happily.

I stared at her. "But . . . but you can't be . . . I met Eileen,
well, just saw her really, for a few moments, and . . ."

The woman's round face puckered into a tight little frown,
as if an invisible drawstring had just pulled her lips, forehead, and eyes closer to her nose. She started to shut the
door.

"Wait!" I said. "Sorry—let me start again. My name is
Josie Toadfern and I wanted to talk to Eileen to return the
photos and clippings of Pearl Oglevee she loaned for the

ribbon-cutting ceremony for the local history collection in her name at the Mason County Library . . ."

I stopped. Eileen—or whoever this woman was—stared at me for a long moment, considering what to do, rocking back and forth on her feet, jingling from head to toe.

Finally, she stopped, and sighed. "I think," she said, "you'd better come in."

12

I hesitated before going in. Maybe it was just because I'd felt spooked at the waterfront when I imagined I'd caught a whiff of tobacco. But, after all, this woman wasn't who I thought Eileen was, and no one knew I was here.

Of course, my overdeveloped sense of curiosity won out. Eileen was Mrs. Oglevee's niece, after all. And I had no leads about why someone would pretend to be Eileen . . . and pass me this note about Mrs. Oglevee being murdered . . . and no way to find out who the harsh woman pretending to be Eileen really was . . . unless the real Eileen could give me some help.

So I went in, reassuring myself with the knowledge that I had my cell phone and a handy can of pepper spray in my mini backpack. Not that those things would necessarily help me out if, say, she decided to whop me over the head and leave my bludgeoned body in the turret where the fishing Santa stood guard. Although I couldn't imagine why she'd want to. She'd seemed pleasant enough, hadn't known I was coming, and had been agreeable with Winnie. She wasn't the one pretending to be Eileen.

So I followed her into the parlor, after she graciously took my coat and hung it on an old-fashioned coat tree in the foyer. I sat down in a comfy, overstuffed chair by the fireplace, and glanced at the gas log.

"I'll get us some hot chocolate—or do you prefer tea? I have chai, spiced . . ."

"Hot chocolate is fine," I said. I took her absence as an opportunity to look around the front room—and was startled by what I saw.

The room—with its big pane window, off-white walls, traditional furniture, and flickering gas fireplace—was very conventional.

But the accent pieces . . .

It turned out the fishing Santa had only been a hint of what awaited inside the house—at least in that room. I counted thirty different fish—stuffed and mounted—on the walls. The coffee table and end tables were covered with fish and fishermens' knick-knacks. The bookshelf held a few books—and a lot of fishing trophies. Even the sofa's cross-stitched pillows portrayed images of fish.

The only non-fishy décor were the pictures and pine needle roping on the mantel. I stood and looked at the pictures—Eileen and what I guessed was her husband and two sons and a daughter from various stages in their family life. About half were traditional portraits—graduations and weddings. The other half were of the family members proudly holding up fish they'd just caught. I reckoned some of the fish in the photos were also the fish on the walls—a concept I found a little creepy. But the people in the photos all looked happy and healthy and cheerful, images of lives well lived.

"Here's our hot chocolate," Eileen said, as cheerfully as if she hadn't had a moment of concern back at the front door.

"Your family?" I asked, taking one of the two mugs—Christmas ones, of course, decorated with images of Christmas trees—and settling down again into the cozy chair.

"Yes," Eileen said, sitting down on the loveseat across from me. She sipped from her mug, and gave an mmmm of pleasure. "Ghirardelli," she said.

I'd heard of Ghirardelli, of course, although I'm a Hershey's girl. I took a sip. Mmmm. Just as good as Hershey's.

Eileen looked at her mantle. "Harvey—he's my husband—passed away a year ago." A look of sadness pulsed across her face. "Our sons—Charlie and Ryan—are grown. Charlie and Ryan have families and live elsewhere now—Charlotte and Atlanta." She chuckled. "Escaping their cold Ohio roots."

"Do they both still . . . fish?"

Eileen laughed. "Oh, yes. People are often taken aback by my fish collection. Harvey always said I overdid it. But I loved fishing with my daddy as a girl, and sport fishing was always a big part of our family life, too."

She sighed, looked a little sad. "I don't go as often now that Harvey's passed on. I was never good with the boat, so I sold it after he died, and just go on charters now and again." But then she brightened. "But I am still involved with volunteering to put on the Great Walleye Drop every year! I was on the original committee, ten years ago, for the first drop."

Eileen stood, got a picture off the mantle, and handed it to me. I looked at it. She was standing next to what looked like a one-ton fish.

"That's an awfully big fish," I said.

She laughed. "That's Wylie, the fiberglass walleye that gets lowered for the drop each year."

Ah. Of course. Lake Erie fish don't get as big as Moby-Dick. I knew that.

In the photo, Eileen was holding something near Wylie's mouth. I pointed to it. "What are you holding?"

"Oh, you can barely see it. It's a good-luck lure. That was my idea. I collected favorite lures from the various captains in the area and we attached them to Wylie. Each year, after Wylie's lowered, we add one more lure, from the fishing captain of the year. It's just a good-luck ritual, but I'm proud I came up with the idea."

"It's a good one," I said. "Rituals have power if they make people believe in their own abilities."

Eileen looked pleased as I handed the photo back to her. "That's right!" she said, putting the picture back on the mantle, and then sitting back down.

She took a sip of hot chocolate and waited for me to make the next conversational move.

"So you live here alone?" I asked.

"Everyone comes home at Christmas and for a summer visit—although as the grandkids get older and more into their own activities, I'm guessing that will fall off," she said. She had the same clipped accent as Rhoda, the motel clerk. "Charlie and Ryan and their families have already returned home. Next spring, I'm thinking of putting this house on the market—maybe getting one of the new condos just down the road that overlook Lake Erie, and another in Arizona," Eileen went on. "I'd originally thought about Florida for a winter condo, of course, but with the hurricanes, I'm not so sure."

As Eileen went on about the relative merits of winter abodes, I set my mug of hot chocolate on the coaster on the end table, and opened up my backpack purse. First, I pulled out the manila envelope of clippings and photos that Eileen had sent Winnie several weeks ago.

Eileen wrapped up her winter-home commentary. "These are the clippings and photos you sent Winnie Logan," I said, holding the envelope out to her.

She nodded and took it, and put the envelope on the coffee table without bothering to open it and see if I'd returned everything. "Thanks for returning them. But I have a feeling you didn't come all this way just to do that."

I grinned. "I'm here with some friends for the Great Walleye Drop."

"Oh, good," Eileen said eagerly. "Maybe I'll see you there."

"You're going?" I stopped, smiled, glanced around the room. "Of course you are. It's just, so far we've heard it's a wild evening, and—" I stopped.

"And I don't seem like the wild type?"

"Well, no."

"I'm not. I've lived a pretty traditional life, and I like it that way. The only extraordinary thing about me, I guess, would be my passion for sport fishing. Usually, that appeals more to men." Eileen shrugged and laughed. "My husband always said that I was the exception that proved the rule."

Then Eileen gave me a funny look. "You do know that this is the twenty-ninth, and the Great Walleye Drop is on New Year's Eve?"

"Yes, I know. But tomorrow happens to be my birthday, too—I'll be thirty on the thirtieth." I gulped. What a mature sounding age. "So this is a combined birthday and New Year's trip my friends set up. It's just a coincidence that Mrs. Oglevee grew up here, and that the photos and clippings came from you, and—"

Eileen interrupted my commentary with a snort. "It's my experience there are no coincidences."

I startled at her words and suddenly uptight tone. For a moment, there, she sounded just like her Aunt Pearl. But then she smiled. "The photos and clippings were among the few things I received from Aunt Pearl's estate, and I'd be just as glad to let them become part of the collection at the library. I guess I should have told Winnie that."

"You were the beneficiary of Mrs. Oglevee—your aunt's—estate?"

Eileen laughed. "Not exactly. I was the executrix. I didn't get anything from the work and time I spent fulfilling that role except the comfort of knowing that it would please my mother."

At my questioning look, Eileen sighed, and went on. "My mother and Aunt Pearl were sisters. Very close, as children and teens, with the usual ups and downs, according to my mother, may she rest in peace," Eileen said. "She died ten years ago, but I still miss her. A lot of these things were collectibles she bought my daddy. The other rooms have other things she collected—dolls and tea cups and ceramic lighthouses. I just couldn't bring myself to throw anything of hers away."

Interesting, I thought, that Pearl and her sister had died at about the same time.

"You said Mrs. Oglevee—Pearl—and your mother were close?"

Eileen nodded. "They even ran off to New York City for a while, to pursue acting and singing careers. They eventually returned, of course—not together. My mother returned first to this house—"

My eyebrows went up. Eileen smiled. "Oh, yes. This was my parents . . . and my grandparents' house. Aunt Pearl never had any children, and I was an only child. It passed on to me. Fortunately, my husband earned enough that we could keep it in good repair. Anyway, according to my mother, Aunt Pearl came home long enough to have a talk with Grandfather Armbruster—Pearl's and my mom's dad—pack up a few things, and then go to Bowling Green State University, where she earned her teaching degree. She got married to a man named Millard Oglevee, but no one from her family went—it was just a quick civil ceremony. They moved to Paradise, Ohio, where Aunt Pearl started teaching at Paradise Middle School."

And continued to torture adolescents for the next gazillion years, I thought.

"Uncle Millard worked as a security guard at the penitentiary down there." Eileen paused, and then gave a little laugh. "It feels odd to call someone 'uncle' that I never met."

"Why didn't you meet him?"

"I was born several years after Aunt Pearl moved down to Paradise," Eileen said. "We only visited her a few times, my mom and I. The first time was after Aunt Pearl and her husband divorced. Another time was after my grandmother— my mom and Aunt Pearl's mother—died. By then, my grandparents were living in a nursing home. Not long after, my grandfather died, but we didn't visit Aunt Pearl then."

"She didn't come to her parents' funerals?"

Eileen shook her head. "No."

"Why not?"

A shuttered look came over Eileen's face, as if she knew she had suddenly keeled into choppy, dangerous waters. "I don't know. I—I was just a young girl when we visited Aunt Pearl those two times."

"What do you remember about the visits?"

She shrugged. "Not much. Just that it was a long drive to Paradise. That Aunt Pearl seemed uncomfortable around me, which I thought was odd, since she was a school teacher. That's about it. Well, thank you so much for dropping by. But, really, feel free to take the items back to the library collection—"

She was trying to hint me out the door now, and I was having none of it. I wriggled back further into my seat. Eileen looked dismayed, as if she suddenly regretted letting me in.

"I think you should know my nickname back in Paradise, Ohio, is Nosey Josie," I said. Eileen gave a little start, as if she might laugh at that despite herself, but she caught herself in time. "I don't like the nickname much, but I guess I've earned it because I ask a lot of questions. So . . . I can ask them of you. Or in the next day or so, I can find other folks—friends, neighbors—who might have known your aunt and grandparents, and ask them. They won't be hard to track down. The clerk at the Perry Inn knew who you were, and told me how to get here."

She stared at me, horrified. I waited for a few beats of silence and said, "You know, one thing I've learned about people is that they don't like having their own dirty laundry aired, but they sure love to talk about other people's dirty laundry."

13

Eileen picked up her mug, her hand shaking. She took a sip, but then quickly set the mug back down as if the hot chocolate had soured.

"Why do you want to know so much about my aunt?"

"Like I said, I'm a former student of hers, and—"

"I have a hard time believing Aunt Pearl inspired so much devotion in a student from fifteen years ago that you're here just to return some old clippings and a few faded photos."

I wondered what Eileen would say if I told her that, for just a second, her expression was just like Mrs. Oglevee's whenever someone had trouble naming all of the Great Lakes.

Instead I asked: "Why would you assume that? If you only visited your aunt twice?"

"You're serious about talking to people around town about my aunt, my family?"

"I am."

Eileen gave me an appraising look, as if trying to decide if I was just that low. I must have looked as though I was, because finally, she sighed, and said, "All right. Here's the lowdown. The few times my mom talked about Aunt Pearl,

I got the impression Aunt Pearl was almost two different people—there was the perky, peppy Pearl my mom grew up with. And then the Pearl who came back from wherever she disappeared to for two years. That Pearl was uptight at best, bitter and hurting at worst."

I nodded. That certainly described the Mrs. Oglevee we'd all known in Paradise.

"She was not pleasant," Eileen went on, "the two times my mother and I visited. I stayed in the living room, looking through her books, and they went into the kitchen and yelled at each other."

"About what?" I took another sip of the hot chocolate.

"I'm not sure. I think it had something to do with Mama wanting Aunt Pearl to come home, make peace with their parents. My grandparents never talked about her. If I hadn't gone with Mom to visit Aunt Pearl, I'd have just assumed that she, like me, was an only child. There were no pictures, no memorabilia, nothing about Aunt Pearl ever on display. So I'm not sure what the story was, why Aunt Pearl cut herself off from her family."

And yet, stayed in Ohio, just four hours away. How odd. If she wanted to cut herself off from her family, why wouldn't she have gone far away . . . like, say, all the way across the country, to Seattle or San Francisco or somewhere exotic like that?

"Port Clinton is a sight bigger than Paradise," I said, "but it's still a pretty small town. I reckon if your family has been here for three generations—"

"Seven," said Eileen.

"—for a long, long time," I went on, "that there'd be plenty of people gossiping about your aunt and whatever caused her to go off like that at age seventeen."

Again, that shuttered look, as Eileen answered, "Not really. Not to me, anyway. After I grew up, occasionally someone would ask if I ever heard from my Aunt Pearl, and I would just say, no, because I never did."

"But you were executor of her estate?"

"To my surprise. I was her closest living relative when she died. I guess she found out, somehow, that my mother died, although I didn't call or write her about it."

I frowned. That seemed awfully cold. "Why not?"

"I was pretty distraught over my mother's death. And we hadn't talked about Aunt Pearl in at least ten years before my mother's death. Before that, Aunt Pearl was more or less a taboo subject. All I knew was that occasionally my mother got letters from her. After she read them, she'd be upset for days, and keep them locked in a safety-deposit box. She was a packrat—just like I am—and she couldn't bring herself to throw them away, but she didn't want them around the house, for some reason."

Eileen gave a little laugh, and I didn't believe for an instant she didn't know the reason. But I'd get to that in a minute. For the time being, I just listened.

"As it turned out, Aunt Pearl died about a month after my mother. I got the letter from her attorney, naming me as her executrix if my mother preceded her in death, and I almost declined, but then I thought that if those letters had mattered so much to my mother, that probably she'd want me to be her sister's executrix. It didn't seem to be an overwhelming task, so I took it on."

"Aunt Pearl's attorney, a Mr. Morgan Holloway, said that my aunt's wishes were for me to have a few personal mementos—you've seen those," she said, gesturing to the envelope. "And that everything else was to be sold, and held in an interest-bearing checking account, until it reached a certain amount, at which time the whole amount was to be donated to the Mason County Library for the purposes you already know about. I, of course, would get nothing for my efforts."

I studied her. A lot not being shared, here. "Why would you do that? Seems a lot of trouble for an aunt who was the family's black sheep, one you'd only met twice. Why not just hire the attorney to be the executor?"

"Like I said, it seemed the right thing to do," she said, her voice clipped.

I considered what I'd heard so far, that I did believe: Pearl Oglevee had been the black sheep of the family, left home at seventeen, returned two years later for a brief visit, went to Bowling Green, earned a degree in education, married, moved to Paradise, became a teacher, divorced two years later, saw her sister and niece twice—once after her divorce, once after her mother's death—was not notified of her sister's death by her niece, died, left niece in charge of her estate, who followed her wishes.

Then there was what I'd heard so far that I didn't believe any more than I believed a walleye might voluntarily hop out of the icy Lake Erie and into a frying pan: that Eileen had simply executed the will out of the goodness of her heart or that she didn't have a clue about the cause of the rift between Mrs. Oglevee and her family of origin.

I reckoned the only way I'd get the real story on those two points would be if I played the ace still in my backpack—the note about Mrs. Oglevee's death really being murder.

But first, I had another point I wanted to clear up.

"At the door, I was startled that it was you who answered. I made a comment that you didn't look like the person who I thought had dropped off these few photos and clippings with Winnie. You also just said that you'd mailed the items. And that the last time you were in Paradise, you were a young girl."

Eileen pressed her eyes shut. "I think you'd better leave," she said. "I've told you all I know."

All you want me to know, I thought.

I pulled the note from Eileen-imposter out of my backpack and held it toward Eileen.

"You might want to read this," I said.

Eileen didn't look at all surprised as she read the note, and I found that telling. She thrust the note back at me, and then stared into the rhythmically flickering gas fire.

"She said she was you," I said. "She came to Mrs. Oglevee's regional book collection ceremony, and gave Winnie this note to give to me. She left before I could talk to her."

Eileen didn't say anything.

"She looked a lot like Mrs. Oglevee."

Eileen suddenly shifted her gaze from the fire to me. "Coincidence. As I said, Aunt Pearl didn't have any children."

I arched an eyebrow at her. "I thought you said you didn't believe there were coincidences."

She sighed. "Aunt Pearl was, from what I surmise, a bitter, angry woman most of her adult life. Maxine VanWort, the woman who brought you this note and pretended to be me, was also. Maybe that outlook shapes people's faces similarly. In any case, Maxine is definitely not Aunt Pearl's daughter."

"Maxine VanWort." I repeated the name, wanting to make sure I remembered it. "Well, who is she, then?"

Eileen hesitated, chewed on her lower lip for a moment. Finally, she said, "She is the granddaughter of Beatrice and Richard VanWort. Richard and my grandfather—Mom's and Aunt Pearl's dad, founded the Perry Commercial Fishing Company together—the oldest in the area. The partnership was a good one. Dinner parties at this house." Eileen gestured, as if taking in the whole of the house. "Dinner parties at the VanWort's, who lived next door. My family's involvement in the company ended when my grandfather died. Tanner VanWort bought out my family's half, and took over the company. He and his wife Amelia had two children, Tanner Jr. and Maxine. I guess, like Aunt Pearl, Maxine is the black sheep of her family. Always stirring up trouble at inconvenient times—like now.

"Tanner Jr. became an attorney—he still practices for his friends, and is, in fact my attorney—and was quite successful at it, but he took over the business several years ago after Tanner Sr.'s death. He bought out Maxine's half, so with investments, she's always been comfortable. Now he's ready to sell off the business. Regulations about how many pounds of fish companies like his can take in are making it harder to make a profit. Plus, Amelia told me Tanner is just burned out on the business."

"You're friends with Amelia and Tanner?"

"I have been for years. It's just Maxine that I'd rather not have anything to do with. Anyway, Tanner is running for Congress next year, and from what I hear, he has a good chance of being elected. The incumbent is leaving office, and Tanner has a good reputation and a good family name to draw upon. His father was once state senator."

"I'm confused. What does this have to do with your Aunt Pearl—with Mrs. Oglevee?"

"Maxine loves double-crested cormorants!" Eileen exclaimed, looking more upset than I'd thought she was capable of.

I, on the other hand, was just confused, which Eileen didn't notice, because she just went on with her rant: "I mean, it's fine that she loves birding—she got that from her father, which I can understand, since I got my love of fishing from my father, but why does she have to focus on cormorants?

"She sends letters to the weekly newspaper all the time! During the height of last tourist season—which is what this town depends on—she even dressed up as a cormorant with a big chest wound and wandered around at the pier, scaring kids and tourists and passing out fliers with all this crap about how the cormorant almost went extinct from DDT and other pollution in the 1960s, and how thanks to them DDT is now an illegal pesticide—you'd think we'd all be neon green if it weren't for the cormorants—and how now that the cormorants are under siege again, the things will be threatened with extinction again! She was so nuts, she ended up in jail for disturbing the peace—and now she's writing letters about how she is going to retire from her job—she's an accountant—and organize her and all of her cormorant-loving buddies to save the damned birds."

Eileen's voice was thick with outrage at Maxine's plans,

which were apparently as disgusting as bird droppings at a tea party.

She stared at me for a long moment, waiting for me to join in her outrage, I reckon.

I finally cleared my throat, and said, "Um, well, now I'm still confused about what Pearl Oglevee has to do with any of this, but in addition I'm also confused about . . . what is a double-crested cormorant?"

Eileen sighed. "You're not from here, or you'd know—" I winced, not liking being on the receiving end of that comment. But how many times had I made a similar comment at my laundromat during our tourist season, summer at nearby manmade Licking Creek Lake, as in, well, since you're not from here, you might not know that you can get a fishing license at Ed's Body Shop and Supplies . . .

"—that a double-crested cormorant is a bird species that nearly died out, but it's come back with a vengeance in recent years, and it's decimating local vegetation, especially on some of the lake's islands, and ruining sport fishing for walleye and yellow perch and other species. Local authorities are looking into what can be done to 'manage the population,' as they say. Those of us who understand that this area depends in large part on sport fishing for its survival say let hunters shoot the damned birds or oil the eggs."

I swallowed. I wasn't even sure I wanted to know what that meant. But she told me, with a small smile. "Simple. Just put oil on the eggs in the nests, and the birds suffocate before they get a chance to hatch."

I must have looked horrified.

Eileen shrugged. "The folks in Ontario don't seem to mind that the government controls their cormorant population with these practices."

"But Maxine does. I get it. I still don't get what this has to do with Pearl Oglevee and why Maxine would come all the way to Paradise today to slip me a note that says Pearl was murdered ten years ago, and that Maxine is her daughter."

Or how, for that matter, Eileen knew that Maxine was the one who'd brought me the note.

"Tanner sees the whole cormorant issue the way I do—the way a lot of people around here do. Cormorants have become a pest that has to be dealt with somehow. Kind of like deer populations elsewhere. When he's congressman, Tanner'll push for more aggressive control of the cormorant population to protect sportfishing. He's already made that clear, and his campaign is just getting started. He'll also work to bring in more industry, so we're not so dependent on tourism. And of course, whenever she doesn't like something Tanner Jr. is doing, Maxine also claims that he is really the child of Tanner Sr. . . . and Aunt Pearl."

"What? But on her note, she claimed she's Mrs. Oglevee's daughter!" I was seriously confused. "Does she think Mrs. Oglevee is both Tanner's and her mother?"

14

Eileen shrugged, as if this was of no consequence. "Who knows why she wrote that. Maybe to get your attention. In any case, I knew she had to be the one who brought you that note, because of the claims she's made about my aunt and her brother. Who else would have brought that note?"

I considered that for a moment. "I tried to follow her out, but she disappeared before I could catch up."

Eileen snorted. "Probably went out to smoke. She could have been the inspiration for the cliché, smokes like a chimney. Does that to her health, pollutes the air around her, and then has the nerve to whine about how evil humans are for wanting to stop the cormorant nuisance?"

"She sounds like a character." Maxine sounded like Pearl Oglevee's daughter in spirit—if not in fact.

"That's one way of looking at it. Crazy is another."

"Sounds like you've known her for quite a while."

"I have. I'm fifty-two. Maxine is fifty-one." That surprised me. Maxine looked so much older than Eileen, but then, I reckoned smoking for a lifetime did that to a person. Even an environmental rights activist. "Her brother, Tanner Jr., is fifty-four, and a very nice man. I dated him for a while."

I worked the numbers in my head. Mrs. Oglevee had died at age sixty-seven, when Tanner Jr. would have been forty-four. This would have made her twenty-three when she had him. Not at all impossible—mathematically, at least.

But how—and why—would Mrs. Oglevee have given her son to the VanWorts? Why would Maxine have claimed, to me, to be Mrs. Oglevee's daughter, when all these years she'd been spreading gossip that Tanner Jr. was really Mrs. Oglevee's son?

I asked Eileen those questions.

She just shrugged. "Like I said, Maxine is the black sheep of the family and always felt slighted by her father. We're close enough in age that we went to school together, and of course we found ourselves at parties at each other's houses. Maxine always told me about how she felt, although I tried to make it clear I didn't want to hear it."

I wondered if Eileen was the sort who never wanted to hear about anything that wasn't rosy. She'd lived a life more blessed than most, so maybe just the thought of someone like Maxine having emotional issues made her so uncomfortable that she decided to blame the victim, as the saying goes.

Or maybe I was being unfair in my judgment of Eileen because she seemed gleeful about killing baby birds by suffocating them within their egg shells. And maybe Maxine was truly nuts.

Hard to say. Maxine had certainly looked like a difficult woman. And her note to me—and its timing—sent off warning bells.

But still, I felt a tug of sympathy toward Maxine, and a little disdain toward Eileen. Maybe a lot of people would say I had my emotional reactions flip-flopped. But then, being an underdog so often myself, I usually pull for the underdog, which in this telling, at least, was Maxine.

"Pamela—Maxine and Tanner Jr.'s mother—died just a few years after Maxine was born. It's been said she overdosed on sleeping pills—"

My eyebrows went up at the bland way Eileen shared that bit of ancient gossip.

"—that she had an unusually long case of the blues after Maxine was born. These days, I guess we'd call it postpartum depression. The official word, though, was that she died of ovarian cancer and that it took her quickly.

"Maybe just knowing about the suicide made Maxine feel unloved. The only way she could seem to relate to her dad was going birding with him. They had terrible fights, otherwise, or just wouldn't talk. I have to admit, as much as I liked Tanner Sr., and like Tanner Jr. and his family, all of the VanWorts have hot tempers.

"Anyway, whenever Maxine and her father fought, she would tell everyone that she was unloved—that Tanner Jr. was the only child her father loved. But in my opinion, Maxine was, sadly, never very lovable. She never married or had kids or even very many friends, other than a few who are as nuts about cormorants as she is."

"No boyfriends?"

"None that I know of. Like I said, the one person she was at least sometimes close to was her dad, especially when they went birding. I have to admit, he's the source for her love of cormorants. He was passionate about the bird, too, which made more sense when the bird was truly about to go extinct. Now it's gone the other way."

"Humankind does have a way of mucking about and throwing nature out of balance," I said.

Eileen ignored that comment. "But other than that, Maxine has pretty much been a loner, for as long as I've known her. Runs a successful accounting business, though, as a solo practitioner, of course. Can't imagine her with employees or partners. She's even taken care of the books all this time for Perry Fishing Company, which I think is very generous of Tanner, considering he bought out her half. For the past eight years or so, she's told this outrageous story Aunt Pearl and her father having had an affair which produced Tanner Jr."

For the past eight years. I turned that number over in my mind. Mrs. Oglevee had died two years before that.

"How did Mr. VanWort—Tanner Sr.—die?" I asked.

"He had melanoma," Eileen said. "He only lived six months after the diagnosis. Anyway, Maxine would never have gotten away with that outrageous story about my aunt and her dad while her dad was still alive. No one's taken her seriously over the past eight years. Pamela Van-Wort was most definitely pregnant two different times. I remember my mother, who was good friends with her, telling me how difficult those pregnancies were. Poor Mrs. VanWort had to go on bed rest for the last three or four months of both pregnancies, back home with her parents in Florida."

"But, why would Maxine make a claim like that? I mean, people would have known whether or not her mother was pregnant."

Eileen shrugged. "I don't know. Maybe just to embarrass her family? Maybe without her dad around to go birding with, she decided she really resented him for all the times in between that she felt neglected?"

"But why do that after he died?"

"Like I said, I don't know. Most people think of Maxine as a crackpot. Her latest nutty defense of the cormorant when most people hate the birds only makes her seem like more of a crackpot."

Maybe Maxine was one walleye shy of a full catch, after all. At least her actions—on the surface, and based on what I knew so far—suggested that. But then, maybe if I could go deeper than just the surface . . .

"Anyway," Eileen was saying, "the talk about Tanner Jr. really being the love child of his father and my aunt hasn't been brought up for years. What I don't understand is why Maxine is now claiming *she's* my aunt's child—and that Aunt Pearl was murdered. The only reason she'd make such a claim would be if she thought it would help her with her precious save-the-cormorants cause. But she hasn't brought up the claim locally. Apparently, you've never met her before."

I shook my head. "I haven't. I can't say I really met her this morning. She delivered the note, getting Winnie to hand it to me by pretending to be you, and I just caught a glimpse of her, and then she disappeared. I'm hoping you can tell me why she'd do something like that."

She gave me a long look. "Maybe she just thought you'd come up and start asking questions—which is what you're doing, after all—and that if an outsider starting asking questions about a claim like that, people would think twice about voting for her brother, and somehow that would help her with her cormorant cause.

"Not that such a plan is going to work. Tanner has the incumbent's and his party's endorsement. I don't think there's anything that could keep him from winning. He'll run in next May's primary unopposed, and the opposing party's candidate—who, by the way, has already lost votes by saying the cormorants should remain fully protected—will just go through the motions, as in all the elections past."

Pretty smug, I thought. "I still find it hard to believe, though, that Maxine just made up this story about Mrs. Oglevee—your Aunt Pearl—out of thin air. There had to be something for her to go on."

Eileen stared at me stubbornly.

I tried my earlier tactic again. "I really just came up here with my girlfriends for the Great Walleye Drop and reckoned while here I'd return your aunt's mementos to you. But the Great Walleye Drop is not until day after tomorrow. This is a quiet-seeming city. Not much to do here in winter. Except, maybe, go around, ask a few questions of folks . . ."

"Okay, Okay," Eileen said. "I can see you and Maxine have a few characteristics in common."

I grinned. "Gadfly? Nosey?"

"Something like that. I'm not sure why she contacted you, except no one here would have listened to her, and you must have been pretty close to Aunt Pearl to be willing to give a speech about her."

I didn't say anything. Gadfly, yes; nosey, yes. Liar, no. But not correcting isn't the same as lying—at least, that's what I told myself.

"When I completed my duties as executrix of her estate," Eileen said, "I received the items you've already seen from Mr. Morgan Holloway. And a few other items I didn't think would be exactly appropriate for your library's dedication of the Pearl Oglevee Regional History Collection." She said the name of the collection as if it were laughable, and then stood up and went over to an antique rolltop desk, and opened a side drawer. She pulled out an envelope, handed it to me.

I looked at the envelope: large, white, glossy, embossed in the upper left corner with a fancy font that said, LINDEN-HURST, HOLLOWAY & SCHANTZ. The firm's address was in Cincinnati.

Inside was a brief letter, addressed to Eileen, and another envelope, this one just a plain manila one.

I read the letter quickly: "Dear Mrs. Russell: Pearl Oglevee requested that I hold this for you until such time as you completed the request that your aunt's estate be invested, and turned over to the Mason County Public Library. Please let me know if I can be of further assistance."

I opened the manila envelope and pulled out another letter, this one handwritten on ordinary goldenrod paper from an old-fashioned pad. Something was paper-clipped to it.

I recognized Mrs. Oglevee's handwriting. Usually, of course, it was looping up the side of my own paper, in red, with comments like: "Needs work!" and "Put on your thinking cap next time!"

This time it was in black ink, remaining dutifully on the lines of the goldenrod paper. The note simply said: "Thank you for administering my estate. Thought you might want to know the whole story of why I left Port Clinton—but not Ohio. I'm guessing you haven't read the letters I've been sending your mother. If you're reading this, she's passed on before me. I'm sure you've kept the letters I sent her, but you probably haven't read them. My last request is that you do so. Here's a little something to pique your interest."

I pulled the letter from the paperclip and saw the yellowed article from the *Toledo Blade*.

It was from forty-five years before, and a photo showed a shamefaced Tanner VanWort being arrested in front of an exotic dance establishment . . . the Femmes of Iniquity Lounge. From a quick scan of the article, I learned that he had been a part owner of the place—and that he'd been arrested for running an illegal gambling scheme there. The following autumn, he'd lost his bid for re-election in the state senate.

Also arrested was Sol Levine, co-owner of Femmes . . . and his girlfriend and employee, Pearl Armbruster.

I stared at Eileen . . . "You mean . . . Mrs. Oglevee . . . was an . . . an exotic dancer?"

Eileen smiled grimly. "Looks that way."

"Her note refers to letters to your mother. You read them?"

Eileen looked away. She shrugged. "No. I threw them away after my mother died. How was I to know I'd get *this* letter ten years later from Aunt Pearl, asking me to read *those* letters?"

I didn't believe her. I know not everyone is as curious as I am . . . but not read those letters?

And even if she'd simply wished to respect her mother's privacy, I just couldn't believe she'd thrown those letters away. She herself said she was like her mother—and never threw anything away—and that those letters had been painful to her mother, but had also meant a lot to her. Plus, it was obvious she'd been close to her mother. I just couldn't believe she'd really thrown those letters away.

"This is ancient history," Eileen said. "Tanner Sr.'s mistake with gambling and the Femmes of Iniquity Lounge have long since been forgotten—or at least, forgiven. He never held public office after that, but he helped get the lounge closed. So this will have no impact on Tanner Jr."

"But Mrs. Oglevee—" I still had trouble thinking of her as this woman's "Aunt Pearl," "wanted you to know about this ancient history, and for some reason she wanted you to know only after the trust was made to the Mason County Library. Aren't you curious about why?"

Eileen stared at me a long moment. "Aunt Pearl was an embarrassment to my family, just as Maxine is an embarrassment to hers. I don't want to get in the middle of learning the details about my Aunt Pearl's murky past. I don't see what it has to do with the present."

"You're afraid," I said.

She looked away for a moment, then back at me. "I'm comfortable, Josie. I have been my whole life. I want to keep it that way—stay here a few more years, sell this house, then maybe move closer to my children."

"I can't believe you're not even a little curious," I said.

"You're a stain-removal expert, a laundromat owner?"

"Yes."

"Then you should know some dirty laundry shouldn't get aired. It should just get tossed away."

I felt a little light-headed. Mrs. Oglevee? An exotic dancer? At the Femmes of Iniquity Lounge? Mrs. Oglevee? Sending that old article . . . and clearly wanting her niece to know about the past, after all those years.

But niece Eileen was clearly not planning to do that, ever. She'd taken care of her aunt's basic request and planned to ignore the one that would take her out of her comfort zone.

"I still want to talk to Maxine," I said. "She went to a lot of trouble to contact me—and then just disappeared from the dedication. Do you know how to get in touch with her?"

"She lives around here somewhere," Eileen said. "I'm not sure where. I—I haven't talked to her in years."

Again, she looked away quickly, and again I didn't believe her. She was a terrible liar.

"If you really want to know how to get in touch with her,

just go next door and ask Tanner. He still lives in his family home, too. Since you don't seem to mind knocking on strangers' doors late at night, I guess you could walk there now."

"It's getting late." I glanced at the clock in the middle of her mantle. It was nearly ten o'clock.

"Or, you could try to talk to him—or more likely, one of his people—at the Great Walleye Drop. He's the emcee this year. My recommendation. I think it will help his campaign."

From her voice, I could tell she was proud of that fact.

I stood up and tried to hand the article and letter back to her. She waved them away. "Keep those. And the other articles you brought back. I'm sorry you went to such trouble, but I really don't need—or want—any mementos of Aunt Pearl. I'm happy just thinking of her as my eccentric, long-gone aunt."

15

I didn't walk to Tanner VanWort Jr.'s house. It was late, I was tired, and—despite Eileen's teasing comment about my boldness—I just couldn't see walking up to another large house, knocking on the door and saying, excuse me, Congressman-candidate-person, could you tell me how to find your black-sheep and possibly insane sister? Who seems to think my junior high history teacher was your real mama . . . or maybe her real mama . . . and that she was murdered . . . a teacher who was the aunt of your neighbor and was apparently an exotic dancer in a club your daddy once part-owned, at least until he was caught in a gambling scheme, and . . .

No, that seemed like a far too complicated introduction. I needed to think about what Eileen had told me—and how much I thought was true. I knew I wanted to talk to Maxine—to at least find out why she gave me that awful note before my speech about Mrs. Oglevee. But that could wait for the next day. My birthday.

Happy birthday to me, happy birthday to me, I hummed in my head, as I walked back to the motel, pulling my coat tightly around me. The lake wind snapped sharply at my ankles—even with the houses and trees buffering me from Lake Erie and any view of it. I could still hear a few seagulls, and my thoughts were like them—circling and cawing for attention all at once.

Mrs. Oglevee had been an exotic dancer. Okay, that was just too freaky—and nasty—to contemplate. Mrs. Oglevee? The uptight teacher of my youth who now haunted my dreams—turning them into nightmares?

And why would Maxine pretend to be Eileen, give me a note that she was really Mrs. Oglevee's daughter—when up until then, she'd apparently been claiming, ever since Mrs. Oglevee's death, that her older brother was Mrs. Oglevee's son? And why would she just disappear after leaving me that note?

There were so many questions. Answering them would be like trying to get the whirling seagulls to stop chattering and start making sense, I thought despondently.

But I quickened my pace, anyway. Maybe if I got back to the motel room—Sally and Cherry would no doubt still be out partying at a bar, especially if Cherry was depressed over her fight with Deputy Dean—I could look over my notes, organize a plan to try to figure out what was going on . . .

My thoughts were interrupted by a snap near me. Was someone following me? I looked around as I picked up my pace and didn't see anyone, but then again, it was dark— even with the house lights and Christmas decorations—and someone could be creeping behind shrubs, trees, or even the cars parked on the street.

I sped up even more. Focus, I told myself. Just one fast but careful step on the sidewalk in front of another. I couldn't run because of the ice. How many more such steps to the motel . . . Fifty? A hundred? Two hundred?

I got about three steps farther when suddenly something whacked me hard in back of the head. I crumpled . . . the blackness of the night suddenly softening as an internal blackness welled up. Little pinpoint stars began sparkling all around me as another whack landed in the small of my back.

I heard a scream—was that mine? It sounded like my voice—and then I felt a leather-gloved hand clap over my face, muffling my scream and my breathing. I started flailing, kicking, elbowing, and felt rough, strong hands on me, dragging me . . .

And then suddenly headlights appeared, blinding me for a second. A vehicle door opened, and an angry voice screeched: "Just what the hell do you think you're doing? That's my *cousin!*"

That's right . . . Sally and Cherry rescued me.

The grasp of my attacker's hands let up for just a second when Sally hollered. That gave me enough wiggle room—and adrenaline—to start kicking and struggling again. I heard a male voice grunt as I stomped backward down on a foot.

By then, Sally and Cherry were both out of the truck, Sally with a tire iron held high and Cherry screeching at the top of her lungs and twirling her purse—no mini backpacks for her—like a sling she was about to set sailing, which she did, just as my attacker unhanded me.

A hail of breath-mint tins, lipsticks, and other stuff came down on us, causing my attacker to pause, and giving me a chance to break free. Then my attacker started yanking on my backpack purse, trying to get it from me.

But by then, Sally was giving chase with the tire iron, and my attacker released me and ran off. Sally, of course, was all for going after him, but Cherry was busily regathering the contents of her purse, and I was moaning, so instead—after Sally hollered at Cherry to "leave the damned breath mints!" and after they helped me into Sally's truck, where I sat in the front seat and shook—we called the police.

It took a few hours before we got back to the motel room. First, we had to explain what we could to the police, who were very nice, but didn't offer much in the way of reassurance that they'd find my attacker. A mugging, they called it. Told me I was lucky my friends had come looking for me.

Of course, they thought it was a mugging because I didn't tell them about my visit with Eileen. I started to tell them a couple of times about the note from Maxine, the letter Mrs. Oglevee had sent Eileen, but it all just sounded so cuckoo. So, I just said I was out taking a walk.

After we finished with the police report, Sally and Cherry insisted on taking me to the urgent care clinic the police officer had told us about. I was reluctant—my health insurance is catastrophic-only—and I didn't like to think about what such a visit was going to cost. At the clinic, the doctor confirmed what I'd insisted on with Cherry and Sally—that I didn't have a concussion. He said that I should ice the welt on my head, and gave me some Tylenol extra strength to help with the pain I'd surely feel in my back in the morning.

Then we went back to the Perry Inn. I got first dibs at the bathroom, changed into my pajama pants and Tweety-bird nightshirt, and crawled onto the water bed. My head felt okay, but my back throbbed as I bobbed up and down, partly because Cherry kept tossing and turning, trying to get comfortable on her side.

Sally took the rollaway cot, and I envied her, but I was too tired to ask to trade. Besides, I reckoned—after her comments earlier—that she'd put up a fuss, and I just couldn't deal with that right then.

It was only as I drifted off to sleep that I realized I never asked Cherry and Sally how they knew where to look for me. I had a feeling that would come up later.

"Aren't you just a pitiful sight," Mrs. Oglevee declared. She was always like that—posing critical statements as rhetorical questions. "Bruised up. Banged up. Having to get rescued by the likes of Cherry and Sally."

Mrs. Oglevee was sitting primly on a wooden, straight-back

chair, which was somehow floating on a lake. At least I assumed she was on a lake. I couldn't actually see water, but the chair kept bobbing up and down.

Mrs. Oglevee wasn't wearing a feather boa this time. She was primly dressed in a grayish-lavender coatdress, her hair in a strict bun, not a wisp out of place. Not a lick of makeup, or a spot of jewelry, except a plain black-banded watch.

She pressed her lips together. "Oh, I know what you're thinking, young lady—"

"That you promised to leave me alone if I found out the circumstances of your death?"

"Have you?" she asked a mite eagerly.

"No," I said, "I've been busy getting bruised and banged up. Now as to what I was thinking . . . well, what am I supposed to think about you having been an exotic dancer? And for someone named Sol Levine? What a hypocrite—"

Mrs. Oglevee gave a snorting laugh, so hard her chair rocked and the waves picked up, bobbing her up and down. "Oh, of course that's what you're thinking. You have no imagination to think anything else. I had one youthful indiscretion, and that's what you're going to focus on?"

"A youthful indiscretion," I said, "is, say, photocopying your butt on the school's new photocopier." She winced at that allusion. "Working at an exotic dance club called Femmes of Iniquity is not just an indiscretion. It's a lifestyle choice that you apparently regretted later—"

"Of course I did! But that's not the point. The point is, did you ever remember what Commodore Oliver Hazard Perry said upon his victory in 1812 against the British—"

"What? What does that have to do—"

"You don't know!"

"Yes, I do," I said. " 'We have seen the enemy and they are ours.' But what does a victory quote have to do with—"

"You only know because Sally told you," Mrs. Oglevee said in disgust.

I started to ask how she knew that, but then shook my head at myself. She knew that, of course, because she just "lived" in my imagination, and my subconscious knew that Sally had provided the quote earlier.

A sudden gust of wind capsized her chair. For just a second only her legs—and the legs of the chair—stuck up in midair. I gasped, horrified, wanting to lunge for her, grab her back out of the water, because drowning—even for someone as crabby as Mrs. Oglevee—seemed a horrifying way to go . . .

Suddenly, the chair righted itself. Bone dry and glaring at me, Mrs. Oglevee bobbed up and down again on the waves. "If you had any sense, you'd be pursuing that angle!"

"What angle? A quote from an old dead war guy?"

Mrs. Oglevee snorted, but didn't answer, perhaps distracted by the fact that from out of nowhere a ski rope landed in her lap. She grabbed it, and suddenly zoomed out of the picture, and I was left with nothing but a gray-lavender fog and a sense of bobbing up and down.

The next morning, I woke up, moaning, on the floor. I must have rolled off the bed sometime after my Mrs. Oglevee dream.

"You okay? I made coffee in the little coffeemaker that was in the bathroom. Brought it out here."

I sat up. I was definitely stiff, but, blessedly, my head didn't hurt. I rubbed my eyes, looked around. Sally was in one of the guest chairs, staring at the TV. From the sound of it, she had on a local TV news program.

A female was talking about the building excitement for the Great Walleye Drop, and then about some business news in nearby Sandusky. That was odd. Sally was not the type to follow TV news. She said with her life, she didn't have time to follow the news and counted on me to relay anything major. It was an approach to the world at large that I didn't understand. Then again, I'm not a single mom of triplets.

I stood up, helped myself to a cup of coffee from the dresser, sat in the other chair.

"What time is it?" I asked.

" 'Bout eight-thirty a.m."

That's when I realized I hadn't seen Cherry, although evidence of her was everywhere, in discarded food wrappers, tissues, makeup bottles and jars all over the dresser. Her clothes were draped here and there, too.

"Where's Cherry?" I asked. How had I slept through the TV noise—and how long had she had it on like that?

"What?"

I grabbed the remote from Sally and turned down the TV, saying as I clicked away, "what's with you? It's not like you to have the news on like this—especially when you could see I was trying to sleep, and—"

Then I stopped. I heard Cherry's voice—in the bathroom. And a man's voice. Deputy Dean. They were arguing.

"I'm amazed you slept through it," Sally said, through clenched teeth. "He got here an hour ago. The only thing worse than when they're fighting is when they start to make up. And when those two start to make up, what you get to hear is . . ."

I turned the volume back up. I'd heard enough the night before of the Hallelujah Chorus of Hot Motel Sex, which, when you're not a participant, is not exactly music to the ears or spirit. Which is what drove me out, in part, to seek out Eileen. Lord, I thought. If the Butt-Hut couple next door got started, we'd descend into the Dueling Banjos of Hot Motel Sex. Yuck.

A commercial for a product promising whiter, brighter teeth, kissably fresh breath, and oodles of sex appeal popped on the TV. I stared at it, trying to follow the logic of girl ignores boy/boy uses toothpaste/boy gets girl.

Then I decided this was ridiculous. If Cherry wanted to be here with Dean, fine. Sally and I would just pack up and go back to Paradise where it was safe. I'd have the quiet birthday and New Year's Eve I'd wanted after all.

But what about finding Maxine? Making that list of questions? Digging to find out what really happened to Mrs. Oglevee? Figuring out who had really whacked me upside the head? Because I didn't believe my attack was really a mugging.

I shook my head to clear it, and moaned once because that hurt, then moaned again upon realizing the bottle of extra-strength Tylenol I'd gotten at urgent care was in the bathroom with Dean and Cherry.

For once, I told myself, I'd do the sensible thing . . . leave this place, forget nosing into other people's dirty laundry, even if it meant having my dreams haunted by Mrs. Oglevee forevermore . . .

And then the commercial broke off abruptly, with the newscaster saying:

"This just in! We've just learned that Eileen Russell, well-known Port Clinton volunteer and widow of prominent businessman Harvey Russell, was found murdered in her home, early this morning. According to her cleaning lady, Mrs. Russell had been beaten and suffered a head wound. Her family's walleye collectibles had been destroyed, as if someone was looking for something in them. However, police have declined to confirm these details . . ."

I stood up, suddenly, sloshing coffee everywhere.

And apparently I was hollering, Oh my Lord!, over and over—at least that's what Cherry and Sally and Dean told me later. All I really remember is that suddenly Sally was trying to calm me down, and Cherry and Dean came tumbling out of the bathroom together, and Dean—his glasses askew and his pants falling down around his hips and his face covered in Cherry's Pouty Plum lipstick—said, "What's going on out here?"

16

"I was at her house last night," I said, when Cherry, Sally, and Dean finally calmed me down.

I sat in one guest chair, legs curled up to chest, a blanket pulled over me. Sally brought me two of the extra-strength Tylenols, and then sat in the other guest chair. I rinsed down the pills with the rest of my coffee—a weak brew that made me long for a real cup, but I didn't tell Sally that. She looked really worried about me.

Dean and Cherry sat on the edge of the water bed, holding hands, their expressions a weird mix of make-up-sex glow and frustration that they hadn't quite entirely finished making up.

"Her house . . . the woman who was just on the news? Murdered?" Sally asked, stating each word carefully. She was worried, I could tell, that the previous night's "mugging" had gonged my brain pan just a little too hard.

Cherry gasped. "You were at that woman's house when she was murdered?"

"No, no," I said, "before that—"

Dean gave me a stern look. "If you witnessed a murder, you have to go to the Port Clinton police with the information."

"We did talk to the Port Clinton police last night—after Josie was mugged," Sally said.

"You were mugged?" Dean asked. He gave Cherry a why-didn't-you-mention-this look. She gave him a who-had-time smile and shrug, and his expression melted back into adoration. That boy, I thought, was hooked for good. And Sally was worried about *me*?

"She was only half-mugged. We got there just in time to prevent a full-scale mugging—" Sally started.

"And I've been wondering . . . how did you know where to find me?" I said.

"Never mind that for now—just—"

"No," I said firmly, "you first. Then I tell about the woman who was just on the news. Then—stop that!"

Cherry and Dean had been massaging each other's palms. They had the good graces to look guilty and primly put their hands back in their own laps.

"All right," said Sally, "we went in town last night first to the Dublin Inn—this bar, no, excuse me, this pub that was trying to be Irish-like . . ."

"Sally said it was too high-falutin' and fake, although I thought it was kind of cute . . ."

"You thought the guys were cute," Sally snorted.

"Baby-kins?" Dean said, hurt.

Despite the facts that my whole body ached, that I wished for real coffee, and that a woman I'd interviewed the night before had been murdered not long after I'd left her house— probably right after my "half-mugging"—I almost started to laugh. But I didn't. Dean truly looked hurt.

"Now, sugar pie, you'd said some mean things about me, and I thought we had broken up . . ."

"Don't worry," Sally said to Dean. "I got her out of there and over to the Cut Bait."

"As in, 'fish, or . . . ' " I allowed myself a small laugh after all, which made me feel better, but I still wished for stronger coffee.

"Yeah," Sally said. "The Cut Bait is a little place with a strobe-lit dance floor, on the second story of one of the buildings overlooking the square."

"The guys there weren't nearly as good-looking," Cherry assured Dean.

"Anyway, we stayed there a while—"

"And met Wylie!" Cherry said excitedly.

"Wylie?" Dean asked, looking upset again.

"A fish. Well, a walleye. Well, a walleye character. Wylie the Walleye, the Great Walleye Drop mascot—"

"I thought Wylie was a coyote? From Looney Tunes cartoons," Dean said.

"That's Wile E.," Sally said, spelling it out. Her sons love old cartoons. "The fish is Wylie. W. Y. L. I. E."

"Didn't you use to visit your grandparents up here?" I asked Dean.

"That was before the Great Walleye Drop tradition began," Dean said.

"Anyway," Sally said, "Wylie is really Henry Steinbrunner, who runs a fishing charter in season, and who is just filling in for the usual guy who does the Wylie gig—I reckon Wylie makes local appearances all through the year—but that guy has the flu, and so Henry's filling in just to make some extra dough. It seems to really bug him though, dressing up in the walleye suit. He kept saying he never thought as a fisherman he'd have to do such a thing. I think it's partly because he has to dance along with Gary Kruetcher, who dresses up as Elvis—"

"The Las Vegas Elvis," Cherry clarified, looking a bit disappointed. After all, everyone knows Blue Hawaii Elvis or Memphis Elvis is much more appealing. But for some reason there are more middle-aged paunchy guys with thick sideburns who want to play Elvis dress-up than slender, muscular guys. Go figure.

"Gary does the Elvis gig year round, though," Cherry was saying. "For parties and such all across northern Ohio. He even has a business card. He gave us one. I have it in my purse, somewhere." She started to push herself up off the water bed.

"We don't need to see the card, Cherry," Sally said. Cherry poofed her lips into a little pout, but settled back down on the water bed and took Dean's hand again. "Anyway, both Gary and Henry are important parts of the Great Walleye Drop festivities," Sally went on, "which they say are wild."

I frowned, then immediately started massaging my forehead where a spasm clenched my brow. "And Wylie and Elvis helped you find me somehow?"

"No, no," Cherry said. "It's just, Elvis was spotted by some wild fans—well, really a trio of women—and had to duck out of Cut Bait, and Wylie was so depressed that he started messing up our mood—"

"—it's getting tougher each year to make a living running his fishing charter," Sally said. "Plus, he's starting to realize he's too old to make it in the career of his childhood dreams."

I just had to ask. I took a sip of coffee first, then said, "Which was?"

"Professional bowling," Sally said.

"Anyway, Wylie—um, Gary—was just too depressing to be around, so we had to get out of there."

Dean looked relieved. Cherry's been known to try to cheer up cheerless Wylies with her affection in the past.

"So we came back here, saw you were gone, and got worried," Sally said.

"It's not like you to take off on your own like that," Cherry said.

I suddenly felt about as interesting as the damp, makeup-stained towels festering on the bathroom floor.

"So we asked Rhoda—that was the desk clerk last night—if she'd seen you leave, and she said yes, she knew where you were going . . . to Eileen Russell's house," Sally said.

Cherry's eyes widened. "Hey! Wasn't that the name of the woman the TV lady just announced was murdered last night? About the time we found Josie having the tarnation beat out of her?"

Sally gave her a look. "Now finally boarding the clue bus, it's Cherry Feinster!"

Cherry frowned at Sally and tried to get off the edge of the water bed, but plopped back down. "Why you little—"

"No bickering!" Dean snapped, and pulled Cherry back down on the bed at her next attempt to get up. "Josie, I think you'd better tell us what's going on."

And so I did, at least as much as I knew about what was going on.

About how Eileen was really Pearl Oglevee's niece. How she'd been executrix of Mrs. Oglevee's estate, for reasons I hadn't yet figured out, considering Eileen hadn't liked or been close to her Aunt Pearl. How Eileen's family had been close in years past to the VanWort family. How Pearl Oglevee had been an exotic dancer as a young woman at the Femmes of Iniquity Lounge. That triggered some gasps of disbelief . . . followed by Cherry having a fit of giggles.

After Cherry's giggles dissolved into mere hiccups, I went on to explain that Tanner VanWort Sr. had been caught in a gambling ring at Femmes and that he'd never fully recovered, politically, but not long after that he and his wife had Tanner Jr., and then two years later, Maxine. I showed them the old newspaper article that Eileen told me to keep.

Then I said that Pearl went on to live the boring life we all knew about, until of course she died of a heart attack, about the same time that Tanner VanWort did, also.

Shortly after that, I said, Maxine made the claim that Tanner Jr. was really the love child of Pearl and Tanner Sr., until she revised the claim just yesterday by posing as Eileen and giving me a note that stated Pearl was murdered . . . and *her* mother.

Oh, and I made sure to work in the double-crested cormorants, too. The egg-oiling concept sparked gasps of dismay.

"What I don't understand," said Dean, "is what any of this has to do with Eileen Russell being killed last night.

The news report was very specific that she was killed in a break-in."

"What about Josie's mugging?" Sally said. " 'Bout the same time as Eileen's killing?"

"Coincidence," Dean said.

"I don't think it was a coincidence," I said, wincing a little, knowing I was echoing poor Eileen. "I think that someone knew Eileen had been in touch with Winnie about Mrs. Oglevee. And that same someone knew Maxine went to Paradise yesterday to tell me that Mrs. Oglevee was murdered. Then I show up at Eileen's . . . what if someone thought I had information from Maxine about Mrs. Oglevee's death, and was passing it back to Eileen?"

Dean stared at me like I was nuts. "What? Why would you believe anything this Maxine says? Like Eileen said, she's probably just a crackpot. What else would make you think Mrs. Oglevee was murdered?"

I didn't say anything. I looked at Sally, then at Cherry. Bless them, they remained mum. I felt goofy enough knowing that they knew about my Mrs. Oglevee dreams. If they told Dean that I'd had a dream in which Mrs. Oglevee asked me to investigate whether or not she was murdered . . . well, Dean would think I was an even bigger crackpot than Maxine.

"I just think it's, well, pretty weird that Eileen got murdered right after I visited her and we'd had this long talk about Mrs. Oglevee's past and her relationship with Maxine's family," I said.

"Did you tell the Port Clinton police about this conversation?" Dean asked, his voice tightening into officer-of-the-law mode.

"Well, no," I said. "After all, I didn't know about Eileen's murder until this morning. My attackers did grab at my backpack, which is where I put the article from Eileen, but then, muggers just after money would grab at my backpack purse, anyway. But it seemed an odd place for a mugging—"

"Yeah. Wouldn't muggers usually be watching for people

leaving bars or something, honey-bunkins?" Cherry asked Dean.

He ignored Cherry. Maybe in cop mode he didn't like being called honey-bunkins. Not that I could think of *any* mode in which being called honey-bunkins would seem appealing.

"—and it felt to me like my attacker was waiting for me," I went on.

"What do you mean, it felt like the attacker was waiting for you?" Dean asked.

"Just . . . a gut feeling." I said.

"Hmm. Josie, I think you should tell the Port Clinton police what you've just told us, and if it ends up pertaining to Eileen's murder, then you'll have been a helpful citizen."

"You think I'm a goof, don't you?" I said, suddenly annoyed. "That my gut feeling about being jumped having something to do with the fact I'd been at Eileen's—and my feeling that Eileen's murder has something to do with Maxine and Mrs. Oglevee—just means I'm a crackpot . . . kind of like Maxine."

"Oh, Dean doesn't think that," Cherry said. "Do you sweetie-doodle?"

"Of course he does," said Sally. "Look at his facial expression."

Cherry edged away from Dean and crossed her arms. "Dean?"

Uh oh. He was in trouble if Cherry was calling him just by his name.

"I just think Josie should simply share her thoughts—"

"—with the Port Clinton police, so they can have the same reaction you're having? That my theory about Eileen's murder being connected with Maxine contacting me yesterday is just as nuts as Maxine's assertion that Mrs. Oglevee was murdered? So everyone can pat me on the head and say, that's nice Josie, you did your civic duty, now go away and be quiet like a nice girl?"

I jumped up, not caring that I was sloshing coffee about. "Well, I'm almost thirty!" I paused, thought for a second, and then said, "Hell, I *am* thirty! And I don't need to be patronized! What I need to do is find Maxine, talk to her, and if I learn anything I think the police will take seriously, *then* I'll talk to them."

"Oh my gosh, that's right, it's Josie's birthday today," Cherry said, suddenly remembering her excuse for bringing Sally and me up here with her.

"Um, happy birthday, Josie," said Sally.

"You can't go off and investigate on your own," Dean said, wobbling for a second on the bed, before lurching to his feet.

"Of course, we had cake and the surprise party and gifts yesterday, but we brought a few gifts for today, too," Cherry said, reaching for Dean's hand. He swatted her hand away.

"I'm not investigating. I'm simply going to have a conversation with Maxine VanWort. She wasn't mentioned on the news story about Eileen's death—which of course was just a tragic outcome of breaking and entering—so no one will mind if I find her and chat with her about the note she gave me, and the note Mrs. Oglevee sent to Eileen saying to talk with Maxine if she wanted to know more about the past. I'm just curious about the notes, that's all, just being good old Nosey Josie—"

"Josie, settle down. Why are you so angry?" Sally asked.

"Because . . . because . . ." I wasn't sure. And that made me even angrier. "Because I just shared what I know about Mrs. Oglevee and Maxine and Eileen, and I think it might have some bearing on Eileen's death, and this guy"—I gestured roughly at Dean—"is patronizing me and I don't like it!"

Of course, a little voice whispered at the back of my mind, Dean doesn't know why you want to look into Mrs. Oglevee's past. Not, the little voice added, that that would help him take you more seriously . . .

"Josie, you need to talk to the Port Clinton police. You were the last person, apparently, to see Eileen alive," Dean said.

I shuddered. He was right . . .

"And then you need to leave this whole thing alone."

I crossed my arms. "I'm finding Maxine, and I'm talking to her," I said.

"We haven't sung 'Happy Birthday' to Josie this morning," Cherry said. "Maybe that would calm her down."

"What?" Sally looked at Cherry like she was nuts.

"C'mon, sing with me Sally . . ."

"This," Dean said, totally ignoring the fact that Cherry and Sally were now warbling a scratchy-throated duet of "Happy Birthday" to me, possibly individually in key, but definitely not in key with each other, "this is not—" Dean gestured wildly to take in the room and everyone and everything in it, before starting up again: "this is not the set and cast of *CSI: Port Clinton!*"

". . . happy birthday, dear Josie . . ." Cherry and Sally held their discordant notes for a long, long moment.

"I am not pretending I live in my own little TV show," I shouted at Dean. "I am simply going to talk to Maxine!"

"Fine, but at least talk to the police first!" Dean hollered back.

"Happy birthday, to you!" Sally and Cherry wavered to a close.

And then, suddenly, we were all quiet.

Tears pricked my eyes.

Happy thirtieth birthday to me. Hoo-buddy.

The silence was interrupted by a knock at the door.

"We're not ready for housekeeping!" Sally hollered.

"It's not housekeeping. It's me. And I'm freezin' my keister off out here!"

I moaned. The voice was muffled, but I knew who was on the other side of the motel door. Only one person I knew who'd use the word "keister" and sound like he thought he was clever for doing so.

Caleb Loudermilk.

17

"I don't get it," Cherry said. "There's not a single walleye dish on this menu!" She poked the laminated paper menu with a long, magenta fingernail.

We (Cherry, Sally, Dean, Caleb, and I) had bundled up in coats, gloves, hats, and scarves and walked over to the Port-O'-Call Diner. Sally had led the way, followed by Cherry and Dean—hand in hand, then Caleb and I—not hand in hand.

I'd filled Caleb in on the previous night's events, the morning's news, and my theory that if Maxine's claim that Mrs. Oglevee had been murdered had any truth, then that might relate to Eileen's murder and my attack the night before.

And, bless him, he simply listened without judging or commenting. It was almost enough to make me want to tell him about my Mrs. Oglevee dreams—especially the one in which Mrs. Oglevee asked me to find out just how she died. But then we got to the Port-O'-Call Diner and I lost my nerve.

Now we were all snugly tucked into a booth—Cherry and Dean on one side, and me between Sally and Caleb on the other—and pining for mugs of coffee, while Cherry ranted about the walleye-less menu.

"I mean, this is supposed to be the walleye capital of the world! Where are the walleye dishes?"

"It's just after eight o'clock in the damned morning," said Sally. "You think walleye omelets are a hot breakfast item—anywhere?"

My stomach flip-flopped at the very notion.

"Yeah, but this menu is for lunch and dinner, too—and there's not a walleye dish to be found. But look, there are clam strips and a shrimp basket . . . and you can't tell me those seafood critters are fished out of Lake Erie," she said. Then she stopped, looking perplexed. "Or . . . are they?"

Caleb started to laugh. I elbowed him.

"Oh," she said softly. "Never mind."

The waitress, an older woman whose back was bent from the ravages of arthritis, served us mugs of coffee, which we all took black except Cherry, who dosed hers with cream and three packets of Sweet n Low. I felt bad for the waitress—her name was Hester, she said—and had to fight the impulse to jump up and help her. But her determined look told me that would offend her.

Hester recommended the buttermilk pancakes but said the biscuits with sausage gravy were good, too. It being my birthday, I splurged on the "hearty size" of two biscuits and a bowl of gravy, instead of my usual one and a cup. Everyone else got buttermilk pancakes, except Dean, who ordered the ham pancakes, which have chopped bits of ham in them. Made me glad there were no walleye dishes on the menu. Walleye pancakes. Shudder.

After Hester left with our orders, I looked at Caleb and said, "So. You're here. You haven't said why."

He shrugged, and stared into his coffee mug. "Word got around that Dean, here, was mighty upset about his falling out with Cherry—"

"People are talking about that?" Cherry said, wincing as Sally kicked her under the table and said: "Well, isn't that how you wanted it? Spreading those rumors—never mind my reputation and Josie's—and then taking photos with the Butt-Hut man!"

Dean looked unhappy again. "The Butt-Hut man?"

We explained. Caleb nearly spewed coffee while trying not to laugh. Cherry said, "Now, honey-bunkins, we've already made up, and really, I wasn't going to do anything with the Butt-Hut man. He smokes." She wrinkled up her nose at the thought.

"Yeah, but you got his phone number, and you didn't seem too unhappy that he's in the motel room next to ours—" Sally winced as this time Cherry kicked her under the table.

"Was next to your room," Caleb said. "He got kicked out for smoking in a nonsmoking room, so I managed to get the room."

"What?" several of us said at once.

"I drove up because, well, I thought maybe Josie—" he stuttered to a stop and turned red, no longer looking as though he wanted to laugh.

"Aw! Caleb's sweet on Josie!" Cherry said.

"No kidding," Sally said.

"Go on, Caleb. Just tell us how you got the room," I said, not really wanting a group hashing-over of our relationship, such as it was. We were attracted to one another, had had a few dates, but I had no sense of direction in our relationship. And I'd thought that was fine with Caleb, which is why I was surprised that he'd come all the way up there.

"I just figured that if Cherry really was in a snit," Caleb was saying, giving her a hard look, "Josie would not be having such a fun time over New Year's."

"Never mind the kind of time I'm having," Sally groused.

"We were having a grand time without you men!" Cherry said.

"Cherry?" Dean looked hurt.

It was my birthday, so I allowed myself an eye roll. "Yep, this has been a blast."

"Anyway," Caleb went on, "I didn't have any plans for

New Year's so I thought I'd just come up. Besides, the Great Walleye Drop might make a quirky travel feature. I left in the wee hours of the morning, and got here about an hour ago. Couldn't believe my luck when the desk clerk said she had a room—if I didn't mind that it was nonsmoking and the previous occupant had been kicked out for smoking after another customer complained."

Everyone looked at me. They all know how fussy I am about no smoking in my laundromat. "What?" I said, not feeling the need to confess.

"Then I asked if there was a Cherry Feinster registered here, and she gave me the room number," Caleb said. He grinned at us, then said, "Ta da!" which was perfectly timed since Hester arrived right at that moment with our food.

We all tucked into our food, making small talk about the number of people who claimed the Great Walleye Drop was a wild time, and speculating about what "wild" might mean—lift your shirt and I'll toss you a walleye? A walleye eating contest?—but mostly feasting on our breakfast, which was good—just as good, truth be told, as the fare at Sandy's Restaurant in Paradise, although we all knew better than to tell Sandy that.

"Now what?" I said.

"You're not full?" Cherry said, eying my plate and gravy bowl, both clean of crumb and dollop.

"I'm talking about what we're going to do about finding Maxine and learning more about Mrs. Oglevee's past."

Dean glared at me. "You're talking to the Port Clinton police, remember?"

I returned his glare, about to snap back, but just then Hester came by.

"You going to the big celebration tomorrow night?" Caleb asked her, to fill the awkward silence as she removed our dishes and refilled our mugs.

"No," Hester said. "Went a few years ago. Too wild for me. I'll just watch the New York City ball drop on TV. But you kids are going, eh?"

I told Hester I wanted to keep my paper place mat. After she left, I flipped the mat over, and pulled a pen out of my backpack purse.

"Item number one," I said, "is to find Maxine and talk with her." I wrote that down.

"Josie—" Dean started, then winced as Cherry pinched his arm and said: "It's her *thirtieth* birthday. She's a mite touchy."

"Number two," I went on, choosing to ignore both Dean and Cherry, "is to find the Butt-Hut man."

"What? Why?" Cherry asked.

"'Cause Sally needs a date?" Dean joked.

"She looks like she's doing just fine on her own, buddy— and I wouldn't rile these women up if I were you. You're off duty, you're surrounded, and we're outnumbered," Caleb said. I was liking this man more and more.

Dean sighed.

"We need to find the Butt-Hut man because I think he's following us," I said.

"Why would you think that?" Sally asked.

"He was at the Butt Hut—pulled in after us, and was starting across the parking lot when we stopped him for the photo op." Sally explained that to Caleb, who burst out laughing, even though Dean glared at him and muttered that he found nothing funny at all about it. "Then Butt-Hut man and Cherry exchanged numbers."

"What?" Dean growled, glaring at Cherry.

"I love you, honey-bunkins," she said, making her eyes wide as she stared at him.

He looked appeased. Caleb rolled his eyes.

"But, you gave him your home number?" Dean pouted.

"No, of course not," Cherry said brightly. "I gave him Josie's cell number!"

"Cherry," I said, "I'm going to hurt you."

"Well, it would be dangerous to give him my home number, and I forgot my cell phone in the rush to pack—"

"Ah, that explains why you never answered!" Dean said. Cherry kissed him on the cheek, and he nearly purred.

Sally looked at Caleb and me. "Who wants to run puking to the bathroom first?"

Caleb raised his hand. I elbowed him. "Stop it. You gave him my cell number and he gave you his number?" Cherry nodded. "Either of you notice that he went back to his car without buying cigarettes?"

"But he was kicked out of his room for smoking," Sally said.

"Actually, some woman was in there with him, and I saw her in the doorway smoking when I left to go to Eileen's," I said. "Who knows whether or not Butt-Hut man smokes? But he did show up at the diner where we had dinner—"

"He did?" Cherry said. Sally looked surprised, too.

I looked at Dean. "For an amateur investigator, I'm pretty observant," I said. "Yeah, he was there. And then in the room next to us. And wanna bet he gave you a fake number, Cherry?"

She frowned. "What? That old trick?" She looked horrified, but Dean was looking happier by the second. I fished my cell phone out of my backpack purse. "Here," I said. "Call him."

Cherry stared at me a long moment. "Go ahead, honeybunkins," Dean said, an edge to his voice. Sally stifled a giggle and I looked at her. We exchanged looks that said, hmm. Maybe this guy will be okay with—and for—Cherry, after all.

A very contrite Cherry took my cell phone, dug a slip of paper out of her purse, and punched in a number from the paper, her hand shaking. I felt sorry for her—almost. She'd given my cell phone number to a complete stranger!

She listened for a moment, then snapped my cell phone shut and tossed it to me, and wadded up the paper scrap and tossed it on the table. "Disconnected," she said.

"What I thought," I said. "I can't prove Butt-Hut man is following us—but it sure looks that way. So second on the list, after find and talk to Maxine, is find and talk to Butt-Hut man.

"After that, we need to find out as much as possible about Mrs. Oglevee's past—especially her past as an exotic dancer, and about the VanWort family." I jotted those items down as numbers three and four on the back of the paper place mat. "And if there's any way Winnie can put us in touch with Mrs. Oglevee's attorney who worked with Eileen—" I paused, trying to remember his name, "—oh, yeah, Morgan Holloway. That was his name. Anyway, that's number five on this list."

"An attorney is not going to violate client confidentiality, Josie," Dean said.

"What, all attorneys are ethical, perfect, never violate their own rules?" Sally said.

"Not for ordinary Janes and Joes who call them up out of the blue—"

"How about for a crackerjack investigative reporter who might be able to work some connections?" Caleb asked, waggling his eyebrows.

Yep, I was liking this man more and more.

"You have a connection for this Mr. Holloway?" I asked.

Caleb shrugged. "Not off the top of my head. But everybody knows somebody who knows somebody," he said, "even ordinary Janes and Joes."

I smiled. "Thanks. Okay, that's your assignment," I said, tearing off number five and handing it to him.

Then I ripped off the top two items, tracking down Maxine and Butt-Hut man, and thrust the paper at Dean and Cherry. Dean didn't budge. Cherry took the paper eagerly, and gave Dean a "sorry" look. She wanted to make up with everyone, even if some of us had conflicting interests.

I looked at Sally. "That leaves numbers three and four for us—which I think means a trip to the library."

Sally moaned.

"Josie," Dean started.

I gave him a long look. "Number six on the list is to get back together for lunch, and—"

"How 'bout at the Cut Bait? We just had drinks, but from what I saw, looked like they had pretty good bar food," Sally said.

Caleb and Cherry said that sounded good. I went on, "—and at lunch we'll compare what we've learned and then, Dean, if . . . if . . . it seems like it makes sense, and the events of yesterday aren't just a weird bunch of coincidences, I'll go back and talk to the Port Clinton police."

"Josie," Dean started again.

Cherry's hand slipped from the table top to, I reckoned, his thigh . . . or parts nearby . . . because Dean's expression slipped toward dreaminess as Cherry said, "You know, Dean, we'll have to go back by the motel to see if the desk clerk can tell us Butt-Hut man's real name . . ."

Dean shook his head, as if to clear it. "Josie—" he tried again.

"Dean," I said, standing up, and putting down a big tip, "it's my birthday, and I'll investigate if I want to."

18

And so I found myself in a place just like where this whole mess started: in a library.

Normally, I love libraries. I feel at home in them. I feel embraced, even, by the sight and smell of books. The chattering and murmuring of people looking for just the right book or article or bit of information—libraries have their own rhythm and hum, contrary to the hush-hush stereotype.

All right. I admit it—I go all lyrical and poetical and mushy about libraries.

But that morning, at the Port Clinton library, I was even more uncomfortable than Sally.

It wasn't the library's fault. The library was very nice, built in the 1950s, well maintained, on the edge of town. The librarians were very helpful, directing us to the microfiche readers so we could dig through old articles and into the past.

And, truth be told, Sally was doing just fine, staring in concentration at her reader, jotting down notes. She'd taken on the "researching the history of the VanWorts" task. I smiled, watching her. She'd never been one for studying in school. But since she had triplets—and wanted opportunities for them that she'd never had—she'd slowly gotten more comfortable with libraries, making sure to take her boys to the bookmobile every Tuesday, when Winnie rolled into Paradise and parked at the back of my laundromat's lot.

Hester had given us directions to the library, and then we'd all walked back to the Perry Inn. Cherry and Dean had gone into our room to "plan their research," they'd said. Uh huh.

After an awkward moment, Caleb had shrugged, and gone to his motel room, planning to make phone calls to see if he'd have luck in learning anything from Mrs. Oglevee's attorney. I'd thought about suggesting he might want to fashion toilet-paper earplugs, but then I reckoned he was a big boy and could deal with the Hallelujah Chorus of Hot Motel Sex in his own way.

Then Sally and I drove over to the library. She took a few minutes to use her cell phone to call and check on Harry, Barry, and Larry and how they were doing at their grandparents' house. The bottom line was that they were being spoiled rotten by their grandparents, which meant they were just fine.

I took a few moments to call Stillwater Farms. Guy was also just fine, Mary Rossbergen (the assistant director) assured me. Then she asked me if the next Wednesday would work for me for a meeting to discuss the new candidate for director—Levi Applegate. There was considerable interest, she said, among the other committee members, in adding him to the interview slate.

Oh, him, I thought. I felt uneasy about him, just based on his file, but I reckoned that maybe some of the other committee members had different views I should listen to, so of course I said I'd be at the meeting the following Wednesday. Mary wished me a happy birthday, and I thanked her and then called my laundromat.

Chip Beavy answered eagerly, on the first ring. He was all alone, he said, which was fine, because he was reading a really good novel just for pleasure—an old one, he said, called *My Petition for More Space*—which was really thought provoking, and maybe next semester for his community college English class he'd do his paper on the author, John Hersey. We chatted for a minute about the author's work—I'd read several of his novels at Winnie's urging—and then Chip said, oh yeah, there had been one customer, Becky Gettlehorn, who couldn't remember what I'd told her about how to remove candle wax, and at Christmas dinner, she'd gotten some on the tablecloth she'd inherited from her grandmother, and Chip couldn't remember, either.

I told Chip the trick—freeze the cloth and peel off as much of the wax as possible. Then, put the stained side down on paper towels, and press the clean side with a warm iron to melt the wax into the tissue. Then launder as usual.

Chip took notes, and said he'd call Becky.

By then, we were at the Port Clinton library and a half-hour later, settled in front of our microfiche readers.

My task was to find out as much as I could about Pearl Oglevee's life in Port Clinton. Given that she was from a well-to-do family, and that I already had the article she'd sent to Eileen (God rest her soul) about Femmes of Iniquity, I figured that finding more details wouldn't be difficult.

But I stalled, suddenly fascinated by articles about fishing derbies or Little League baseball stats from the early 1950s. I told myself I was just uncomfortable finding out more details about Mrs. Oglevee.

Until a few weeks before, when I'd agreed to give that dedication speech, my view of Mrs. Oglevee had been simple: the crabby, loner junior high teacher, passionate about history.

A simple identity, and one that Mrs. Oglevee herself seemed quite comfortable with wearing. I was uncomfortable with that identity being peeled away, revealing this much more complex view of my old teacher . . .

No, you're uncomfortable—the voice of we-don't-do-denial whispered at the back of my mind—*because the young Pearl Armbruster had, for some reason, been on one path . . . creating an identity as an exotic dancer . . . and suddenly changed paths completely for a reason, or reasons, you don't know yet. She questioned her identity . . . and you are questioning yours.*

The revelation startled me, and then I took another look at what I'd written at the top of my notepad. "What do I want?" was at the top of the page, followed by stars-n-curlicues doodles.

I'd meant the question to trigger a list of what all I wanted to find out about Mrs. Oglevee's steamy past, but I started jotting notes that answered the question in a completely different way:

1. Succeed with my Stain-Busters column
2. Overcome fear of public speaking
3. Expand column to include more household hints?
   Go national?

I gulped as I wrote that one. I'd always been fine with my quiet status as the regional go-to gal for removing mustard from Sunday-go-to-church shirts . . . nothing more, nothing less. After all, just getting comfortable with running a business after I inherited it at nineteen—and being my cousin Guy's legal guardian—had been enough for me. I hadn't expected to take on the guardianship quite so young, and I hadn't expected to inherit the laundromat at all.

I'd been helping at the laundromat and attending a few classes at Masonville Community College when Aunt Clara died. Then I spent quite a few years growing into being comfortable with both being Guy's guardian and owning the laundromat.

But, truth be told, I'd been comfortable with both for quite a few years now. So I was starting to want more challenge with my work life. Itch for a little more. And not just for me.

Aunt Clara and Uncle Horace had put every penny they

could into making sure Guy would be taken care of, but they couldn't have anticipated budget cuts in public funding for citizens like Guy, or every dip their carefully invested funds might take, or the skyrocketing cost of health care. Truth be told, I needed to increase my income to take care of both Guy and me . . . and expanding on my expertise seemed like the wisest way to do that. And the challenge excited me.

So . . . what else? I wrote down:

4. Study chemistry at Masonville Community College.

That one surprised me even more. What had I been studying ten years ago at the college? I couldn't remember. I hadn't had specific plans, just the foggy notion "someday I'll be doing great!" that every teen just out of high school has . . . before finding out life has a way of making plans for you.

But studying chemistry would help me know more about exactly why all the folk remedies for stains that I'd learned from Aunt Clara or that I'd stumbled on myself worked.

I shifted in my chair and glanced over at Sally. She was mumbling to herself, swiftly jotting notes, looking by turns surprised and amused.

I had to smile at that. Talk about changing identities. At this rate, Sally-who-hated-school-projects-and-bribed-Josie-to-do-the-research was going to become a research librarian.

I looked back at what I'd written, about what I wanted from life. It was all work related. What about friends? Family?

Well, of course I loved Guy deeply and wanted to keep being the involved, loving caretaker that I already was. But I didn't need to write that down. That was a given.

And I wanted to stay close to my friends, and keep being

a good friend to them—something else I didn't need to write down.

Then my mind wandered back to the mom and her daughters at Jerry's Drive-Thru in Bucyrus, just the day before. Sure, the mom seemed harried, the little girls had been squabbling, but . . .

5. I want a family of my own.

I stared at that last item, stunned . . . and a little appalled. I wasn't going to go get married just for the sake of having kids. If I ever did marry, I knew it would have to be because I just couldn't imagine life without the man, and I'd have to know he couldn't imagine life without me.

Kind of like the couple in the *Saturday Night Live* laundromat skit. I thought about the cable TV ad for an online matchmaking service. Could one purposely go fishing for— and catch—the let's-let-our-undies-tumble-dry-together-forever kind of love? Or did it just have to . . . happen?

I thought it just had to happen. And I wanted it to happen to me. Not the shining white-prince-charging-in-to-save-me-from-my-loneliness kind of love of school girl fantasies . . . the kind I'd experienced with Owen.

But the "ah . . . *there*-you-are . . ." kind of love that had taken Cherry and Dean by surprise. The down-to-earth undies-tumbling-together kind of love that would last through the twists and turns of life.

And, yeah, I wanted those twists and turns to include kids.

The image of the big clock on the countryside billboard popped in my head, and it was ticking—not with Jesus about to appear and holler ta-da! (I reckoned the cosmic clock was a little more sophisticated than a stopwatch) but with my own internal instincts.

Was Caleb my "ah . . . there-you-are . . ." love of my life? That would be awfully convenient, I thought, but no, as much as I enjoyed his company and verbally sparring and even physical closeness, I hadn't been hit with that feeling about him yet.

Randy?

I felt a stirring at the thought of the guy—biology does what biology does, and the guy was every woman's dream hunk, physically at least—and then half-laughed, half-snorted aloud.

Sally gave me a hard look, and cleared her throat.

Look who's a goody-goody about homework now, I thought.

But I ripped the page of "What I Want" off the top of my notepad, started to wad it up to toss away later, but instead folded it carefully and tucked it into my backpack purse. A memento of my hopes and dreams on my thirtieth birthday.

Then I took a deep breath and got down to my real work at the Port Clinton library—finding out what I could about Mrs. Oglevee's past.

"Josie? Josie!"

I looked up from the microfiche reader, taking a few seconds to pull my mind from 1952 and recognize Sally, who was repeating my name in a harsh whisper and poking my arm.

"I just got a call from Cherry," she half-whispered.

I rolled my shoulders and then my head, blinking as I readjusted my field of vision to greater than three inches. That's right . . . we were in the Port Clinton library . . . and it was nearly fifty-five years after the time period I'd been reading about . . .

"They've got information, and a pizza waiting for us at the Perry Inn," Sally said. "Decided it was better for us to all share what we learned in private, instead of at the Cut Bait. You about ready to go?"

I nodded, cleared my throat. "Yes. I just have a few things to print out."

"Well, I found out some interesting stuff about the Van-Worts. You get what you need about Mrs. Oglevee?"

"Oh yeah," I said. "I did. I sure did."

Sally grinned. "Sounds like there's a story."

"Oh yeah," I said again. "There's a story, all right. It's no wonder Mrs. Oglevee never talked about her past."

19

"You first," I said to Caleb just as he took a bite out of the last slice of the sausage-mushroom-extra-cheese pizza that Cherry and Dean had picked up from Papa's Pizza on the town square. The extra cheese—stringing from his bite to the rest of the pizza—made him pause.

We were back in the room that I shared with Cherry and Sally at the Perry Inn—Caleb and Dean's room next door was still being cleaned. We could hear the vacuum cleaner through the thin walls. Our room remained a mess, mostly from Cherry's clothes and makeup that were still spread everywhere.

Cherry was sulking a little, because we'd all made it clear that, no, now that we had two rooms, Caleb wasn't going to bunk with Sally and me just so she and Dean could explore variations on sweaty snuggle-bunnies while the rest of us stuffed tissue in our ears and pulled pillows over our heads.

Dean had taken it well, even looked a little tickled, I reckoned because he found reassuring every sign that Cherry couldn't get enough of him.

"Why don't you go first," Cherry said to me. The rest of us had finished our pizza. Cherry, I'd noticed, had plucked sausage bits off her pizza slice and carefully put them on Dean's. She'd decided that her New Year's resolution—for the third year running—was to become a vegetarian so she'd lose some weight. And this time around, she wanted to get a jump start on her goal. Of course, then she'd requested extra cheese for the pizza. "You have the juiciest bit of news— Mrs. Oglevee's past."

I shook my head. "I'm going last. First Caleb needs to tell us what he learned from Mrs. Oglevee's lawyer, then you and Dean can fill us in on tracking Butt-Hut man and Max-inc, then Sally can tell us what she learned about the Van-Worts, and then I'll share what I found out about Pearl Oglevee's past."

"And then?" Dean said, giving me a hard look.

I returned his look. "And then, we'll see if it all adds up to something that's worth a trip to the Port Clinton police."

Dean didn't look too happy about that, but it was the best I was going to give him at the moment.

"My news is fairly straightforward," said Caleb, wiping his mouth with a paper napkin. He'd finished the pizza and stuffed the box into the trash can. We all had sodas from the cooler Sally'd packed. "I got a hold of Winnie—she says happy New Year to everyone, by the way. She told me Mr. Holloway, Pearl Oglevee's attorney, had contacted her a few months ago with the happy news of Pearl's bequest to the Mason County Library. Seems Winnie had been helpful years ago with helping Pearl get books she needed to teach a regional history unit at the junior high.

"So, she'd directed Mr. Holloway to contact Winnie, although it would have made more sense to contact the director of the library, first."

"That was Mrs. Oglevee, though," I said. I still couldn't bring myself to call her Pearl. "Always did things her way."

"So does Winnie," Caleb said. "I told her all about the note Eileen received from Pearl, how that had apparently been triggered by the dedication of the Pearl Oglevee Regional History Collection, and about what's happened up here in the past—" Caleb looked at his watch—"well, less than twenty-four hours.

"Winnie insisted she'd call Mr. Holloway herself and see what she could find out. A half-hour later she called me back. Said she'd told Mr. Holloway that she'd had a long conversation with Eileen before Eileen was murdered, and that Eileen told her she'd gotten a note from Pearl, through Mr. Holloway.

"Apparently Mr. Holloway was so shaken up by the news of Eileen's murder, that he admitted that, yes, Pearl had instructed him to send two notes—one to Eileen and one to Maxine—once Mason County library received her bequest."

My eyebrows went up. A note to Maxine, too? Now that was interesting. I was even more determined to find her.

"And Mr. Holloway did just as Pearl had requested years ago. But he said he had no idea what was in the notes, and even if he had, he wouldn't share that information—client confidentiality, and all."

I grinned. I could always count on Winnie to find out what I needed to know.

"But he did tell Winnie Maxine's address and phone number, since he said that was a matter of public record anyway—"

Cherry cut off Caleb. "Hey, that was one of our assignments! And we found out, too. She lives year-round at 549 Lake View, one of the waterfront condos. And we got her phone number, 555-6794."

Cherry looked proud, until Dean said, "All that was in the phone book."

She swatted him, and he just laughed. "We also went over to her condo," Dean said. "No one home. In fact, very few people home. Most of those condos are just used in-season, by sport fishing fanatics. Wealthy folks, for whom it's their second—or third—home. Some come up just for a week or two, and then rent out the condos.

"Anyway, a few people live there year round, and Maxine

is one of them. We met one of her neighbors, an older
man—"

"Dell Stoker," Cherry said. "He lives about four condos
down. He said he hadn't seen Maxine for several days, which
bothers him, because normally she asks him to come feed
her birds if she's going to be away. He has a spare key to her
condo and did so anyway when he realized she was gone.
He didn't see anything out of order in the condo."

Cherry shivered. "What if she's been killed, her body
dumped in the lake, and already floating out to sea . . ." She
frowned. "The lake does end up dumping into the sea, right?"

"Eventually," I said. "But Cherry, I think that's a pretty
big leap, don't you?"

Or was it? After all, Eileen had been murdered—suppos-
edly by burglars, but now Maxine was apparently missing.

My stomach flipped. Oh, Lord. We were already in over
our heads. Dean smiled, giving me a look that said, see?
Isn't it better to leave this in the hands of the professionals?

He passed me a framed photo and I studied it, a picture of
an older man and the woman who had, just the day before,
pretended to be Eileen and passed that note to me through
Winnie. She and the man were holding up a fish between
them, proudly, apparently a prize catch.

"That the same woman?" Dean asked.

"It is," I said.

"That's Maxine," he said. "Dell was really worried about
her. I reckon they've become friends over the past few years,
being among the few year-round residents. That photo was
from his seventy-fifth birthday a few years ago. They went
fishing to celebrate it, he said."

"I think he's like a father figure to her, and she's like a
daughter to him," Cherry said. "Not that he said that. But
that was just the sense I got."

"Now, Cherry, that's not a fact we know," Dean started.

She playfully swatted him again. "Intuition, sweety-buns,
can be just as useful as facts. Anyway, he said she has a
houseboat, which she christened the *Crying Cormorant*—"

"Whoa," I said. "He really said that was her boat's name?"

"Yes," Cherry said.

"Wow. This is one woman who doesn't care if she rubs people the wrong way," Caleb said.

"Well, he did say that with her politics, he was one of her few friends," Cherry said, "and that she was lucky to work for her brother's company as an accountant, or she'd probably be unemployed in this area. And she's passionate about protecting cormorants. Anyway, the boat is at her brother's company now, in storage until it can get fixed. Apparently, someone vandalized it, ramming a small hole in the hull so it's not lakeworthy. She has more than a few enemies, I reckon."

"Let's get back to the point," Dean interrupted, ignoring the frown that Cherry gave him. She didn't even follow it up with any eyebrow lifts. Uh oh. Another fight was brewing. "Dell hasn't seen Maxine around in more than two weeks. He's called and left messages on her home phone and cell phone. He even gave us the cell phone number."

"And yet, she showed up yesterday in Paradise," I said. "Just to give me that note. Is she on the lam for some reason? Scared? Hiding?"

"Sure looks that way," Cherry said.

"Although we can't know—" Dean started.

"But we do know," Cherry interrupted, "about the Butt-Hut man. That was fairly simple to research, too. Dean flirted with the check-in clerk, Rhoda—"

"I just asked her if she knew who had the room before us—meaning Caleb and me—because we'd found a Zippo in the room—"

"We did?" Caleb asked.

Cherry snorted. "Dean bought it at a smoke shop on the way back from Maxine's condo, showed it to Rhoda, batted his big brown eyes at her, and came up with this story about how his grandpa always had a Zippo, and now he was a

Zippo collector, and he'd like to talk with whoever had left this behind because it was a valuable item."

Dean chuckled. "And she fell for that? With you holding a new Zippo?"

"Trust me, she wasn't looking at his Zippo," Cherry said.

Sally smiled, mischievously. "Or . . . was she?"

I poked Sally and shook my head.

"I assumed Rhoda wouldn't be a Zippo collector," Dean said, with so much seriousness and dignity, that I almost laughed. "And I was right. My simple white lie worked. She told us who Butt-Hut man really is." He paused, and gave Cherry a long, hurt look, and she finally glanced away, apparently figuring out on her own she didn't have much right to be mad at him for flirting with Rhoda. "He's Martin Joubert, a local fisherman who used to work in-season for the Perry Commercial Fishing Company—"

"—which Maxine's brother, Tanner Jr., owns, and which Maxine works for as an accountant, and which Mrs. Oglevee's dad—Eileen's grandfather—and Richard VanWort, Tanner Jr.'s grandfather, started together years ago," I started excitedly.

"—until he was found out as part of a racketeering ring that illegally caught tons of walleyes in excess of the company's quota. He used the company's boats and equipment in the middle of the night—Martin has a reputation of being able to navigate a boat under pretty much any circumstances. He swears, though, that the company didn't have any knowledge of his illegal activity."

We all thought about that for a moment. "Anyway," Dean said, "Rhoda gave me Martin's address. He lives in town."

"Kinda odd that he's here at the motel, then," I said.

"Not really. The woman you saw smoking in the doorway is Sheila Dee—a local hooker," Dean said. "And given his illegal activity, Martin can't get a job as a fisherman any more, plus he recently hit some hard times financially, gambling, and is living back at home with his mom."

Ah. So Martin, a.k.a. Butt-Hut man, just wanted to have some illicit fun, but—understandably—not under his mama's roof.

"And it's Sheila Dee who smokes—not Martin," Cherry said. "Not that Rhoda told me. She told Dean. But I got to overhear the whole conversation. And Rhoda really kicked them out because she doesn't want the likes of Sheila at the motel."

Also understandable. But something else was not. "So . . . why was Martin Joubert at the Butt Hut in Bucyrus, then? I still say he was following us."

Dean looked at me. "You don't know. You're just assuming."

"It's not a bad assumption, you know," Caleb said.

I gave him a grateful look. "So let's see. We know where Maxine lives and her phone numbers and that she's missing—except she showed up in Paradise yesterday to pass along a note that says she's Mrs. Oglevee's daughter and that Mrs. Oglevee was murdered. We know that someone else who used to work for her brother's company, this Martin Joubert, is maybe following us. We know that Mrs. Oglevee"—I was never going to be able to call her Pearl— "sent a note to Maxine, probably similar to the one she sent Eileen."

I looked at Dean. "Still think I ought to talk to the Port Clinton police about all this? That they're going to think any of it relates to Eileen's murder?"

"Why don't you and Sally tell us what the two of you learned first," he said.

"Well," Sally started, rubbing her hands together, "I never thought I'd say research was interesting, but—"

Suddenly, the door clicked and swung open. We all startled, and stared at the middle-aged woman standing in the doorway, a cleaning cart behind her. A shot of cold air filled the room.

"Housekeeping," she said.

20

We went to the Cut Bait, settling in a booth with drinks. It was still midafternoon, so Dean, Sally, and Cherry nursed beers, and Caleb and I had colas, while Sally and I shared what we'd learned at the Port Clinton library about the Van-Wort family and the young Pearl Armbruster.

What we shared—starting and stopping, interrupting and tripping over each other's words, piecing together from what we'd each learned earlier that day and from what we already knew, including what Eileen had told me the night before—we later ended up calling, Part I of the Incredible, but True, Story of the Real-Life Pearl Oglevee: Before She Became the Junior High Teacher from Hell.

In 1926, Cecilia Houser and Clayton Armbruster marry. They're from modest backgrounds, although Cecilia's claim to fame is that she's a distant descendant of Commodore Oliver Hazard Perry.

Clayton and Richard VanWort started out as fishermen and joined forces to start the Perry Commercial Fishing Company, playing up on the fact of both Cecilia's kinship—thin but traceable—and the amazing coincidence of Richard also being descended from Perry, the only difference being that Richard's kinship was based solely on family lore (a great-grandmother who had Richard's grandfather out of wedlock, allegedly with a Perry descendent . . . so she'd claimed). Richard makes a point of telling everyone about his blood connection to the wartime hero. (This from an in-depth article about the War of 1812 and Perry's significant role in it.)

Richard and his wife (Beatrice Teeter), a few years older than Clayton and Ceclia, have their only child, Tanner Van-Wort, ten years before Cecilia and Clayton produce Pearl.

Just one year later, they have Rose.

As Clayton becomes more and more successful, Pearl and Rose are reared with every possible advantage. They win spelling bees, take voice lessons and win singing contests, attend ballet class and dance in recitals, star in high school dramas (all documented in the local newspaper, with—as Caleb puts it—the carefully composed, effusive prose that only a mama could write—and that a harried editor would leave unedited.)

And in early 1947, when Pearl is twenty-one, she and Tanner VanWort (age thirty-one) are engaged to be married.

(Exhibit A: a printout of the couple's engagement photo, fuzzy but still showing clearly enough the confusion in Pearl's reflection; she's smiling, yet tilting her face away from his, while he leans his shoulder into hers, and turns his gaze ever so slightly toward her. Pearl, so young and tender that you just want to say, "Oh." Tanner, older and a little preoccupied even as he edges into her space.)

Fast-forward to late 1947. Pearl and Rose in New York City! Small dancing roles in musicals! Pearl with a small singing part; Rose with a small dramatic part! (All documented in the local newspaper, with the carefully composed, effusive prose that only two young women, aching to break free of their small, Midwestern roots, could write . . . and in fact, the articles are dubbed, "submitted by Pearl Armbruster.")

In 1948, one terse article—by an actual reporter—about Rose Armbruster returning to Port Clinton to help her mama, Cecilia, take care of her daddy, Clayton, who is ailing from . . . something. Only vague references to the illness that (we reckon) is the reason Cecilia would want her daughters to return home. (A few articles and photos soon after that show Clayton in various civic roles—at the dedication of a new fire truck, at a fishing derby for a charitable cause—so we also reckon, but don't know for sure, that Cecilia perhaps exaggerated Clayton's illness—whatever it was—for her own purposes, and that he recovered— a miracle! Prayers answered! shortly after Rose's return.)

But no mentions of Pearl at all, until 1950, when a full-page article detailed the return of Pearl Armbruster to the area, with her "business partner" Sol Levine, and the controversial opening of their Femmes of Iniquity nightclub, at which Pearl would be the featured exotic dancer.

(Exhibit B: several photos showing protestors at the site of the club. Especial outrage because the club is in a building that was formerly an Anabaptist meetinghouse—the congregation's leader swearing they were duped in the sale to Sol Levine, who claimed the building would be converted to office space for an insurance company. No comment from Sol. But is that Rose, leading the protestors, in one of the photos? And that's definitely Pearl—looking defiant and proud and quite lusciously beautiful—in another photo.)

The Femmes of Iniquity opens anyway, despite protests from church and civic groups (with more photos that have Rose in the forefront) that continue on a regular basis.

In 1952, several announcements of note appear in the newspaper: Tanner marries Pamela Greene and is elected to the state senate of Ohio; Rose marries Grier Patterson and appears less often in the protest photos.

But a few months later, Tanner is busted on gambling charges at the Femmes of Iniquity.

And three weeks after that, Sol Levine is found murdered—shot in the back of the head—at his office at the club.

No one is ever brought up on charges. In fact, from the newspaper accounts, it seems that everyone is just plain relieved to have Sol out of the picture. The Femmes of Iniquity abruptly, finally shuts its doors, once and for all.

The newspaper announcements after that are few, far between, and much more mundane.

Birth announcements in 1953 for Tanner VanWort Jr. and in 1955 for Eileen Patterson and Maxine VanWort.

A college graduation announcement—Bowling Green State University, bachelor's of education, for Pearl Armbruster in 1958, followed by a wedding photo of Pearl and Millard Oglevee (and the accompanying announcement that they will make their home in Paradise, Ohio, where Pearl will teach at the Paradise Junior High, and Millard will work in the quarry.)

In 1959, an article about Pamela VanWort—Tanner Jr. and Maxine's mother—being found by the housekeeper, dead of an overdose of sleeping pills.

Millard and Pearl divorcing in 1961 (not documented in the newspaper, but information we already knew.)

An obituary in 1963 for Clayton Armbruster (who had managed to live in apparent good health a whole decade and a half since his daughters' move to and return from New York).

Tanner's buyout of Perry Commercial Fishing Company right after that.

Cecilia's obituary in 1965.

Eileen's and Harvey Russell's wedding announcement in 1976, with birth announcements for their kids in 1978, 1982, and 1987.

Obituaries for Grier Patterson (Eileen's dad) in 1992, Pearl Oglevee in 1996, and Tanner VanWort in 1997—also of a heart attack, but then, that was the official reason Pearl died . . . and of course she'd been haunting my dreams, wondering if maybe Maxine's claim that she was murdered was really true. Which is partly why I was trying to sort out this whole complex timeline, with the help of my friends.

To see if any glaringly obvious clues or leads popped out . . .

"So, any glaringly obvious clues or leads pop out to anyone?" I asked eagerly, then took a sip of cola, now watery from melted ice.

Silence all around.

"It's depressing," Cherry said finally. "Everyone in the story is dead." She sniffled.

"Aw, sweetie pie," Dean said. "Don't go getting despondent, like you do with your stories." Cherry tapes soap operas during the day, then catches up with them at night and on the weekends, and it's true, if a favorite character passes on or gets cancer or is in an accident that gives her amnesia, Cherry gets depressed as if the person were a real-life family member or friend.

"Besides," Sally said. "It's a story that covers a lot of years. And not everyone dies. Tanner Jr. is still around, and Maxine—though we haven't found her yet—and Millard Oglevee is probably alive and kicking somewhere."

"That's true," I said, "maybe we could talk to Millard. And somehow get in touch with Tanner Jr. and just flat-out tell him about the note Maxine brought to me in Paradise—"

"But what does any of this have to do with Eileen Van-Wort Russell's murder?" Caleb said. "It's interesting history—we have a much fuller picture of Pearl Oglevee's life before Paradise, but there's nothing in it that supports Pearl having actually been either Maxine's or Tanner Jr.'s mother. By then, Pearl had left the whole exotic dancer business behind and gone off to Bowling Green."

"Caleb's right," Dean said. "I don't see any connection between what we've dug up so far and Eileen's murder."

"So you don't think I should talk to the police about the fact I was at Eileen's house last night right before her murder?" I asked, confused.

"Of course you should," Dean said. "For one thing, you

filed a police report about being mugged right after your visit with Eileen—and right before she was murdered. Sooner or later the right hand will know what the left is doing, and the police will want to talk with you, just to find out if Eileen said anything that might help—for example, if she was afraid of being robbed, if she'd gotten any threatening phone calls lately—"

"Why would she share anything like that with a perfect stranger?" Sally asked.

"Well, she shared a whole lot of personal history with a perfect stranger," Dean said.

"Because I had the note from Maxine," I said.

"And because Josie's good at getting strangers to open up," Caleb said.

"The point is," Dean went on, getting a little perturbed, "that out of civic duty, Josie should share with the local police what she talked about with Eileen, just to save them the trouble of tracking her down."

"I agree," Caleb said. "And from what I've heard, Maxine is as loony as her precious double-crested cormorants—"

"You can only be as loony as a loon," I said grumpily. "You're mixing bird metaphors. Assuming there is a double-crested cormorant metaphor . . ." I trailed off, realizing no one was really listening to me.

"—and so who knows why she came down to Paradise to bring you that note. Maybe just hoping you'd get things stirred up somehow," Caleb went on.

"But that doesn't make sense," I said. "I still think it's odd she went to the effort to bring me the note and then just disappeared, or seemed to, from her apartment and her life . . ."

"Exactly," said Dean—not in response to what I was saying, of course, but to Caleb's commentary. "What we've learned is fascinating, but I don't think it has anything to do with Eileen's death. Entirely circumstantial and coincidental and—"

Suddenly, Cherry stood up and stomped her foot. "I'm

going to the ladies' room," she announced, a little too loudly, so that other people stared over at her. If she noticed, she didn't care; she just scooted her chair back and stomped off in her high-heeled hot-pink ankle boots (which matched the hot-pink Stetson appliqués on her very tight jeans' back pockets and her hot-pink sweater and matching tam) toward the doorway leading to the restrooms at the other side of the bar.

"Me, too," said Sally. It was harder to stomp in sneakers, but she did her best.

The two men were too preoccupied with watching Sally following Cherry to notice the glares I gave them. "And me!" I snapped. That got their attention.

In my rubber-soled snow boots, I stomped away from the table with even less drama than Sally, but I gave it my stomping best shot.

Not so loudly, though, but what I could hear Caleb say, perplexity lacing his voice, "Why do women always go to the bathroom in flocks?"

"I have no idea," said Dean, just as baffled.

"Why are men always like that? Wanting to come to conclusion as fast as possible?" I asked, truly perplexed.

"I have no idea," said Cherry, as baffled as I was.

"Actually, that's a pretty good description of my entire marriage," Sally said, dryly.

Cherry and I snickered, but otherwise let that comment go.

We were in the Cut Bait's women's restroom (the door was marked SEA-GALS, while the men's door was labeled SEA-GUYS), each leaning against the sink counter. We'd made sure we were the only Sea-gals in the restroom before we started yapping.

"Maybe if you told Dean and Caleb about your dream-visits from Mrs. Oglevee and how she herself is all perplexed about just how she died and how you want to figure it out so you can tell her to go away, then—" Cherry started.

"No!" I said. "I—I'm not ready for anyone but the two of you to know about my Mrs. Oglevee dreams."

And truth be told—though I wouldn't want to tell Cherry or Sally, as it would hurt their feelings, I wasn't too sure that it had been a good idea to tell them. Cherry reckoned I was being visited by Mrs. Oglevee's ghost and now and then asked me to ask Mrs. Oglevee about the future, for some reason assuming that wherever she was, she had access to such knowledge.

Sally's theory was that Mrs. Oglevee showed up as a nagging part of my subconscious whenever I was stressed, a theory that I found more comfortable, but that didn't work perfectly. Mrs. Oglevee had showed up several times when I was feeling perfectly relaxed. Of course, after her "visits," whatever their nature, I always felt stressed.

"Well, Dean and Caleb have pretty much decided," Cherry was saying, "that what we've figured out about Mrs. Oglevee's life so far probably doesn't have a thing to do with that poor Eileen's murder. And they're going to make it mighty awkward to investigate. So now what?"

I thought about that for a minute. Then I said, "So now we let them think they're right."

"What?" Sally protested, nearly shrieking. "We're going to tell the guys they're right, and not keep digging? Why, we haven't even talked to Mrs. Oglevee's ex-husband, for example. Maybe he knows something about her past that would fit Maxine's claim. And we haven't even talked to Maxine or Tanner Jr. or . . ."

"Exactly," I said. "And how are we going to accomplish any of that with the guys going on about how this is all for naught? So, here's what we're going to do . . ."

And then I told them the plan. At least as much as I knew at that moment. I'd make up another one, just as soon as we finished gathering up the last bits of information that we were likely to find about Mrs. Oglevee's past—at least, as part of public record.

* * *

The three of us went back to the table and were all sweetness to Dean and Caleb. They didn't see through it, not one itty-bitty bit.

First, we told them we'd chatted it over in the Sea-gal's room, and we thought they were right—Mrs. Oglevee's past was fascinating, but there was nothing in it that seemed to connect to Eileen's murder.

Then I said, "I think I should go with Dean to the Port Clinton police and tell them all about my meeting with Eileen from last night."

Before Dean could shout for joy, though, Cherry made big eyes at him and proclaimed, "Dean, honeybun, I was hoping to spend a little alone time with you this afternoon, but I'm sooo weary. Maybe I should go back to the motel room for a little nappy-poo?"

Then she gave a kittenish stretch and delicate little yawn, and poor Dean practically drooled in his beer.

Cherry had been more than happy to implement her part of the plan—distract Dean.

Dean—staring the whole time at Cherry—said to me, "Uh, Josie, I think a phone call to the police would do just fine, and if they want more details from you, they'll let you know. You don't need me around to make that call, do you?"

"Nah, I can handle that on my own," I said.

Now it was Sally's turn. "You know, a nap sounds good, Cherry. I think I'll go back to our motel room, too."

Poor Dean looked so dismayed, his face sagging with disappointment, that I had to stifle a chuckle. Of course, what Sally really planned on doing in our motel room was call our buddy Winnie and enlist her help in tracking down Mrs. Oglevee's ex-husband to see if she could learn anything more about Mrs. Oglevee's past. This meant we needed to set up a chance for Sally to be alone.

"Oh, Sally, you snore when you nap in the afternoon!" Cherry protested.

"I do not," Sally said, truly sounding offended. Although,

if the men thought about it, when would Sally have time to nap as a single mom of triplets . . . and when would Cherry have been around when Sally was napping?

But Dean was busy looking so disappointed at losing his opportunity to, well, rock Cherry to sleep, that he was never going to think of that.

Caleb was starting to look a little suspicious, though.

Which meant it was my turn to pipe up.

"I'm not tired at all," I proclaimed perkily. "In fact, after I call the Port Clinton police, I was hoping to take a drive in the countryside . . . and I'm hoping Caleb will go with me."

I put my hand on his arm for good measure.

"So . . . maybe Sally could nap in your room?" I said to Caleb.

He looked startled for a moment, then saw the desperate look Dean was giving him and—I reckon—considered the alternative . . . Dean and Cherry in his room.

"I mean, it is my birthday, and you did come up here to celebrate it with me—"

"Fine," he said, a mite snappily. "I'd love to escort you about the countryside of northern Ohio on December 30."

So our plan to give Sally some alone time to do a little more investigating was working. Although we still weren't sure—after all, you can figure out only so much leaning against the counter in the Sea-gal's room—how we were going to track down Maxine or Tanner Jr. or both.

But that got resolved when a big fish walked into the bar.

21

Of course, the big fish was really Henry Steinbrunner, who would dress up as the Great Walleye Drop's mascot—Wylie the Walleye—for the next night's festivities. Not to be confused with the six hundred-pound fiberglass walleye—also Wylie—which would be suspended from a crane until it got lowered right at midnight.

Anyway, Cherry and Sally waved Henry over, and made introductions all around. Henry was fifty-something, a little balding, a little paunchy, a little short, with a bewildered look. He looked so despondent, stumbling all over himself to explain that, really, he was really just a regular guy who liked to lead fishing charters, a guy who liked to go hunting and drinking, a guy who made a little off-season cash snow-shoveling, a sensitive guy, really, who also liked to play blues guitar at gigs around town, whenever he got the chance, not a guy who dressed up as fuzzy versions of a fish, which made no sense, see, since fish are scaly . . .

We hung out for a little while, until Sally gave Cherry and me the "eye" to indicate: go away.

Cherry and Dean took off quickly.

I gave Sally a little frown—a reminder that she was supposed to call Winnie, start tracking Mrs. Oglevee's ex.

But Sally gave me a quick wink and a nod, and I realized she hadn't forgotten—she was just taking the chance appearance of Henry/Wylie walking into the bar to see if she could learn anything else. (Well, maybe his appearance wasn't such a coincidence; after all, the start of the next fishing season was three months away, and clearly the poor guy was looking for any chance to douse his sorrows.)

Sally said she'd be fine—the motel was a quick walk from the Cut Bait—and she'd see herself back after she had another beer with Henry. Caleb gave her his motel card key—gave Henry a reassuring "it's not what it looks like" look but left the explanations to Sally—and we left.

"So," Caleb said, "what are you three really plotting?"

"What?" I asked as innocently as possible. We were in Caleb's room. We'd walked back to the motel, and he'd requested an extra key card, and then we'd hurried to the room. There still wasn't snow, but the temperature had dropped to the teens, and the wind had picked up. While mild for that part of Ohio on December 30, the conditions were still plenty bone-chilling.

Once back in the room, I'd perched on the edge of the bed, and called and talked to an officer at the Port Clinton police department, who said "um hum," a lot, while (I reckoned) taking notes. This was good information to have, she assured me, and if anything came up in the investigation that warranted asking for an official statement, they'd get back to me.

Which meant that they were still operating on the theory that Eileen's murder was the result of a burglary.

"I've known you, Cherry, and Sally long enough," Caleb was saying, and giving me the evil eye from his chair across the room, "to know that the three of you aren't going to just let something go like that, not that easily. Especially not because a pair of men tell you to. Dean might be too smitten by Cherry's charms to see it, but I'm not that easily swayed."

I'd been glancing around Caleb's motel room as he yammered on. My goodness, but he was a neatnik. His overnight bag was to the right of the front door. No clothes in sight—I reckoned he'd taken advantage of the dresser to put his clothes away. Of course, the bed was still made, because he'd just checked in late that morning. One novel—a thriller—was on the nightstand next to the bed. His keys were on the dresser. I'd have to ask to use his bathroom to see if he was just as neat with his toiletries.

But for the moment, I looked at him. "Caleb," I said, "I'm rather hurt. I was starting to think my charms might just sway you from your senses . . ."

Caleb wasn't amused, and I reckon that spoke well of him. "Don't tease me just to tease," he said. "You're not Cherry."

I sighed. "True. But I still like to think my charms . . ."

He stood up from the chair, and crossed the room before I could finish the sentence, and sat down again, next to me on the bed. He pulled me into his arms.

"Your charms are sweet, simple, and down-to-earth . . . and that's a compliment, if you don't know it," he said, his voice going a little gruff. "Plenty to sway a man."

I was just starting to think hmmm, Sally could possibly spend a long time at the Cut Bait with Henry, before walking back to the motel and letting herself in with the key Caleb had given her, long enough to . . .

My thought was cut off by Caleb's kiss, which was warm and just a little tangy, and—I blush to admit it, but it had been a few months since Owen had walked out of my life—plenty to start swaying me toward a giddy sense of abandonment, which I indicated by responding with a little heated kissing myself . . .

But just as we were tilting back on the bed, we heard from

the next room—Sally, Cherry's, and my room—a "Whoop, whoop!"

The effect was kind of like the old saying about fighting fire with fire. And Cherry and Dean's sudden whoops—muffled as they were through the wall—had definitely snuffed Caleb's and my flame. At least for the moment.

We disentangled, and I stood up, shuddering at the next "whoop." I wasn't about to stay for the whole Hallelujah Chorus of Motel Sex, Part II. Caleb and I would have to see if we could rekindle our passion another time. And I'd have to find out some other time and place about his bathroom habits.

"Ready for that drive?" Caleb asked, sounding bemused.

"Yes," I said. He helped me with my coat. Hmmm. Neat, gentlemanly, and a good kisser.

And to think that just the night before I'd been bemoaning my loneliness while watching the *Saturday Night Live* laundromat skit.

We headed out, Caleb slamming the motel door a little harder than necessary, I noticed, which made me snicker.

"I doubt Sally's going to get much of a nap," Caleb said.

"I wonder if I can get the maid to bring new sheets later," I said.

Some stains, I just didn't want to deal with.

About forty-five minutes later, Caleb and I were sitting in his car in the mostly empty parking lot of the Living Waters Christian Church.

It was an odd building, I must say. Maybe I just felt that way because my Methodist church back home was of the traditional, white clapboard, here's-the-church, here's-the-steeple variety.

This one looked like a crown descended from the heavens, settled itself down, and then spread out a bit at the bottom. Instead of the usual steeple with a cross, a tall column arose in the middle, festooned at the top with crosses. The rest of the building billowed out at the base of the column, in a hexagonal shape. A large cross—the kind that would light up at night—hung over the church's door.

"Nineteen-sixties architecture," Caleb said. "You gotta love it." He sure didn't sound like he did, though.

I, for once, didn't say anything. I was mentally reviewing the history we'd put together at the Cut Bait. In 1950, Pearl had returned to the Port Clinton area with her shady lover, Sol Levine, and opened a shady night club—the Femmes of Iniquity—with Pearl as part owner and exotic dancer.

They bought land that included a small, no longer functioning church—of the here's-the-church, here's-the-steeple variety, I was guessing—and then committed what folks in the surrounding area would consider the ultimate sin: they tore it down to make space for the inelegant, flat cinder block Femmes building, with its twitching neon female dancer sign.

I pulled my notes and newspaper photocopies from my backpack, double-checked. Yep. We were at the same address.

Long gone were the Femmes building and its gaudy neon dancer. What color had she been? Red? Purple? It was impossible to know from printouts from microfiche of old black-and-white newspaper articles.

But in her place was this building and a neon cross.

"Ironic, huh," Caleb said, perfectly guessing my thoughts.

"Yes," I said.

"So why did you want to come here?" he asked. "We never did finish that conversation about the fact you and your buddies are still digging into old Mrs. Oglevee's past, no matter what Dean would like to think. Why is it so important to you?"

"It just seems too much of a coincidence to me that Maxine, whose family has close ties with Mrs. Oglevee's family of origin, decided to show up and give me a note that Mrs. Oglevee was murdered, and then later that night, after I've shared that note with Eileen, Mrs. Oglevee's niece, I'm attacked and Eileen's murdered and meanwhile, no one can seem to track down Maxine. Plus it seems as though we were followed all the way up here by Butt-Hut man—"

"Martin Joubert," Caleb corrected.

"Fine, Martin Joubert, then, who worked for Perry Commercial Fishing Company, which is owned by Maxine's brother—"

"—and got busted for illegal fishing. I know." Caleb said. "You didn't really think the Femmes of Iniquity would still be here, did you?"

I shrugged, stared out the window.

Why had I wanted to come here? Caleb was right; I knew there was no likelihood of the Femmes building still being there. I wasn't so naïve that I really thought I'd walk into an old, shuttered nightclub, and conveniently stumble across some clues that would neatly fit together all the bits and pieces we'd dug up, into some picture that would help me understand Mrs. Oglevee and whether or not her surprising past had anything to do with her death . . . or with Eileen's death . . . or with Maxine's shenanigans.

But I reckon I was naïve enough that I'd thought . . . or at least hoped . . . that somehow, I'd find a spiritual connection to the real Pearl Oglevee, a sense of how the Mrs. Oglevee of my dream visits, and the Mrs. Oglevee of my junior high school days, and the Mrs. Oglevee who had once been Pearl Armbruster—child of privilege, woman of rebellion—all added up.

And what I sensed was . . . nothing more than the fact that I was getting overly warm, between my coat and scarf and gloves and Caleb's car heater being set too high.

Showing, again, that he could be sensitive to my feelings, Caleb turned off the car. There was plenty of ambient warmth to last us for a while.

"There's something you're not telling me," Caleb said, "about why this is so important to you."

"Mrs. Oglevee was my school teacher," I said, as if that explained my—and Sally and Cherry's—frantic investigations of the last few days.

"Nope, that's not it. From everything I've ever heard about her, Mrs. Oglevee was not beloved by anyone in Paradise—especially her former students. Especially, probably, you."

I was silent.

"You're not going to tell me why this matters so much to you, are you?" Caleb asked.

"Not yet," I said. Maybe not ever. I didn't want to come off as a nut job. On the other hand, Caleb was displaying enough sensitivity that I figured I probably could tell him about the Mrs. Oglevee dreams, and he'd listen with an open mind.

I thought about it—just for a fleeting second—and opted to instead talk about something else that was eating at me.

"Here's what I can't piece together," I said. "The Pearl Armbruster we've learned about and the Mrs. Pearl Oglevee we all knew. How do you go from proper, privileged upbringing, to exotic dancer, to prim, buttoned-up teacher with no friends? It's like three identities in one lifetime."

"People change," Caleb said, with enough quietness in his voice that I thought . . . uh oh. My ex-boyfriend Owen had carted around a heavy past. I didn't know Caleb that well—just that he did a fine job with my columns, and I clicked with him.

But I didn't know if he, like Owen, might have issues that would end up with me having a broken heart.

Better to refocus on the topic at hand, and move slowly.

"People do change," I started, "but there has to be something that motivates them—"

I stopped because my cell phone rang.

"Let it go," Caleb said. "This is interesting—"

I snatched the cell phone out of my backpack purse, and flipped the phone open. "Can't. It might be Stillwater," I said.

"Ah," Caleb said.

"Hello, this is Josie!" I perkily announced into my cell phone, not bothering to check the caller's number on the tiny display.

I felt the relief I always do when I get any phone call, and it's not Stillwater calling to tell me something's happened to Guy. Then I immediately felt annoyed . . . because it was Randy Woodford, hunky general contractor.

22

"I heard Caleb came up there to Port Clinton for your birthday," Randy said, clearly pouting. "And I was thinking—"

"No!" I barked into the phone.

Caleb looked at me, eyebrows lifted.

"I mean, no, Randy, that's sweet, but really, by the time you get up here, it will be really late, and—"

Caleb's eyebrows went higher, and his lips twitched into a bemused smile.

"But, Josie, I want to do something special for you for your birthday! Maybe I could just finish up the renovations—"

"No!" I barked again.

Caleb snorted with barely suppressed laughter, and I elbowed him. He winced, but was clearly pleased at my distress.

"Randy," I went on, "if you want to do something nice for me, then *please* wait for my return to start up again on the renovations, Okay?" Randy was a good worker, but he kept coming up with ideas about how to improve the project— ideas that I didn't want to see implemented in my simple conversion of two-tiny-apartments-to-one-big-one. All I wanted was more space, a bathroom with a Jacuzzi tub, and lots of bookshelf space.

"Oh, okay, Josie," Randy said, with such a little-boy-disappointed voice that I almost told him to go ahead with the kitchen "garden window" he'd enthusiastically endorsed the week before, for an indoor herb garden. Never mind that my one plant—a pothos ivy optimistically named Rocky—clings to life despite my severe neglect of him. Her? It. Anyway, I could just imagine how little pots of thyme and sage and basil would do under my care. Gives a whole new meaning to the word "herbicide."

"But, Josie," Randy was saying, "I really do miss you. So much, in fact, that I think . . . I think I might love you."

I was stunned. Utterly stunned.

Caleb, who had overheard Randy's proclamation, was turning purple from suppressed laughter.

"Randy," I said firmly, "do not do anything to my apartment while I'm gone. We'll discuss . . . everything . . . in a couple of days, okay?"

I clicked the phone off and dropped it back in my purse while Caleb laughed so hard that his warm breath steamed the cold windows.

"We are not," I said, "discussing what you just overheard."

He finally caught his breath and stopped laughing. I gave him a hard look, and he had the good sense to look contrite.

"I guess it's not cool to laugh at one's rival?" he said.

I almost did a double take at that. Caleb saw Randy as his rival? I had two guys vying for my affection?

My prim, Methodist, moral side whispered "naughty, naughty!"

My, um, other side yelped "Whoop! Whoop!" . . . in a call that was uncomfortably like the sounds we'd heard coming from Cherry and Dean in the motel room.

I felt myself blushing and tried to look serious and stern as I stared at the Caleb-steamed windshield.

"Now, what was I saying? Oh, yes. People do change . . . but for such a strong identity shift, something has to motivate them. People don't just say, oh, I think I'll change now."

"True."

"So . . . I can see the motivation for Pearl Armbruster wanting to go to New York, to try to find her way as an actress. Young people—" I suddenly felt old as I said that. On the day I turn thirty, I'm suddenly a philosopher who can wax lyrical about young people's motivations. But I went on. "—young people's identities aren't set. They want to rebel, fight against whatever is expected of them . . ."

"Did you?"

I frowned at the question, and then did a few Cherry-inspired eyebrow lifts to compensate as I thought that over. "In some mild ways," I said. "I had my moments of youthful . . . wildness." And a hangover at age sixteen that would forever make me nauseous at the merest whiff of rum—even in Christmas-time rum balls. Thank goodness Aunt Clara and Uncle Horace had been quietly helpful and nonjudgmental. I guess they reckoned that in that case, the punishment was inherent in the sin.

"But not like Pearl Armbruster," I said. "Of course, my aunt and uncle who reared me were very loving and supportive, and Guy meant so much to me—and still does. It sounds like Pearl—and her sister, Rose—had a staunch upbringing."

"Expectations they didn't feel like meeting," Caleb said. "That made them chafe. I can relate to that."

Really? I thought. Hmmm. Sometime, sooner or later, I'd have to ask for more detail about that.

"Plus," he was saying, "they had all that drama and dance training as young ladies. Maybe going to New York to try for careers in theatre was a sort of safe rebellion for them. But it didn't work out, so Rose came back and settled into the identity she was always expected to have all along."

"Pearl, on the other hand, stayed," I said, "and became an exotic dancer. She didn't have to do that. She could have come home, too."

"I'm guessing, from the photos and articles, that she actually liked the role," Caleb said.

"Exactly. But then, abruptly, she morphs into Pearl Oglevee," I said.

"Her lover was found dead. The father of her old beau was found guilty of establishing a gambling racket at the club, which was then closed. I'd say that was motivation enough to go back to her prim and proper identity," Caleb said.

I shook my head. "Mrs. Oglevee wasn't just prim and proper. She was angry and miserable and closed . . . and feisty. Feisty. That's the one characteristic that pops up in all her various identities." Even the one(s) she assumed in my dream life, I thought—but didn't say. "All that happened here—" I gestured toward the crown-shaped church we could no longer see through the steamy car windows—"was upsetting, but not enough to motivate her to become a teacher and stay in Ohio. Why not just leave the area entirely? Keep being her exotic-dancer self . . . but elsewhere? She'd already 'showed' her family, so why not just take her act as far away from here as possible?"

Caleb was silent. Finally he said, "That's a good question. And the answer is . . . I don't know."

"The answer," I said, "is that something had to motivate her to revert to being prim and straitlaced . . . and to stay in Ohio. I mean, she went to the opposite edge of the state, but she still stayed close, even though she never became close again to Rose or the rest of her family of origin."

"And you think that whatever that was is connected somehow to her being murdered and also maybe to Eileen's murder."

"Exactly."

We were silent again for a bit.

"So how do we figure that out?" he asked.

I grinned. He wasn't as completely convinced as Dean was that Maxine was just a nut job and Mrs. Oglevee's past had no bearing on current events.

"I don't know," I said, which took my smile away.

"Josie, you ever think about leaving Ohio?"

I looked at Caleb, startled by the question.

"I mean, you could really go places with your expertise, build a real career—"

"Then I'll have to do it here," I snapped.

"Guy," he said, knowing better than to make it a question.

"Exactly," I said again.

He nodded, and looked understanding—but was that a look of sadness that just flitted across his face?

My cell phone rang again.

Caleb opened his mouth, and then shut it again.

"Just so you know," I said, "I always answer my cell phone—or at least flip it open to see the caller's number—no matter how inconvenient it is when it rings."

"Stillwater," he said, again with no question in his voice.

I nodded as I flipped my phone open. This time I looked at the number, and recognized it as Randy's. But I answered anyway, since he did, after all, have the fate of my apartment renovations in his leather-gloved, hammer-wielding hands.

"Hey, maybe when you're back, to celebrate all private-like, I could take you out for dinner and a movie," Randy said. "I pondered it a while and just came up with that!"

It took him the whole length of the conversation I'd just had with Caleb to come up with something *that* original? On the other hand, he was cute . . . and he'd never leave Paradise, either.

I sighed. "Sounds great, Randy," I said, "but I gotta go. Please don't call back."

"Why?"

"The fish are biting, Randy," I said.

Caleb snorted. I swatted his thigh. "Ohhhh," said Randy, with grave understanding. I hung up.

"Don't even comment on that conversation," I said.

"Okay," said Caleb, snickering, which was commentary enough.

I frowned—wrinkles be damned—not liking Caleb's belittling attitude toward Randy.

"You know," I said, "I do think Randy is awfully sexy. And charming, in his own way."

"Oh," said Caleb, no longer snickering. He cleared his throat. "So, you were saying, you think Mrs. Oglevee had some other motivation, yet to be discovered, for staying in Ohio and reverting to a laced-up, but angry, approach to life, because people just don't change whatever they see as their identity without motivation. And if we could only find out what that motivation was, maybe we'd discover there is some truth to Maxine's claims, even some connection to Eileen's death."

"Pretty much," I said.

"Hard to do."

"Sadly, yes."

"Josie, do you always spend your birthdays in such dramatic fashion?"

I smiled at that. "No. I have to say, I'll remember my thirtieth birthday as the most unusual—"

"What? You're thirty? Why, you don't look a day over twenty-four!"

I laughed. "Caleb, you're a tease." He pulled a pouty face. "Which I kinda like, by the way."

He smiled at that, and reached into his coat. "On your thirtieth birthday, you should get to have some of the traditions of celebration. So I brought you this."

Out of an inner coat pocket, he pulled a small, silver-wrapped box, tied with a tiny lavender ribbon. I pulled in my breath sharply. Oh my. No way was I ready for anything serious with Caleb just yet—never mind my list including wanting a husband and family some day. I mean, I thought I could feel that way, possibly, someday about Caleb, but . . .

"Open it," he said. "It's just to let you know I like you, and want to get to know you better."

I pulled off my gloves—the better to unwrap the gift—and accepted the package from Caleb. For a second, I admired the lavender ribbon. I liked that. Lavender. Not leftover Christmas green or red, as I was used to getting on my birthday gifts.

Then I carefully pulled off the lavender ribbon and pulled off the paper to reveal a jewelry box. I opened it, and gave a little gasp of pleasure when I saw what was inside—a pearl, inside a silver heart, on a silver chain.

"It's so pretty!" I said. "Thank you."

"My pleasure," Caleb said, with enough throatiness to his voice that I thought the inside of the car was getting plenty toasty, despite how long we'd been sitting there. He pulled off his gloves. "Here, let me help you."

I pulled the scarf from my neck, and unbuttoned the top button of my coat. Expertly and swiftly, Caleb removed the necklace from the box, and then put the necklace around my neck.

"How does it look?" I asked, a little throatiness in my voice, too.

His gaze locked with mine. "Perfect," he said. "I know it's an odd place to give you a gift, but I wanted to be alone with you when I gave it to you, and I wanted to give it to you on the actual day of your birthday, and with Cherry and Sally and . . ."

I had to kiss him to shut him up. He didn't seem to mind.

But then two things happened at once.

My cell phone rang, again.

And someone started knocking on the steamed window on Caleb's side.

We pulled apart. I pulled out my cell phone and snapped it open, while Caleb rolled down the window.

"May we help you?" Caleb said to the angry-looking woman, leaning down to glare in at us.

"Randy, I told you not to call again," I barked.

"Randy's been calling you?" Sally asked, surprised and a little gleeful.

"Sally! What do you want?"

"Who's Sally? Who's Randy?" The woman craned to look

around in Caleb's car, as if perhaps Sally and Randy were yet another couple, making out in the backseat.

"Who are you?" Caleb asked calmly.

"Who's in the background screaming my name and Randy's?"

Caleb grabbed the phone from me. "Not to worry, Sally. It's just Josie and I are in a church parking lot, kissing in my car—a nice, tender, romantic kiss, I might add, no groping—and it seems to be upsetting one of the locals, which I don't particularly understand since the car windows are fogged up—"

I grabbed the phone back from Caleb.

"You're fogging up windows?" Sally asked, slowly.

"I'm not just a local! I'm the secretary at this church, and the two of you have been sitting out here a mighty long time, and we don't appreciate this kind of philandering in the Almighty's parking lot, and if you must sin, you ought to at least get a room—"

"The windows were fogged from us talking," I said. "Look, I'll explain later—"

"Excellent idea," Caleb said to the woman as he restarted his car, and wiped at the inside of his windshield with his glove. Then to me: "Josie, let's go get a room and have wild, crazy sex, shall we?"

The poor church secretary gasped.

"Ma'am, if you could please step back from the car—your suggestion has put me in something of a mood to hurry."

She stepped back, as if from the very gates of hell.

"Dear," Caleb said to me, loudly, "I believe I have condoms in the glove compartment. Red. Glow in the dark."

Then he backed up and pulled out of the lot, and turned the defogger on full blast.

Sally was struck silent. So was I.

We were on the road again before I was able to say softly, "Sally, you still there?"

"Um . . . yeah," she said. Then giggled.

"Don't you dare start laughing." I glared at Caleb, who was trying not to smile. "That lady was right, we had no business, and he . . . he's just going to burn in hell for that."

Sally was laughing full throttle, now.

"Caleb," I said, while waiting for Sally to calm down. "You are the devil himself."

"That, my dear, is why the condoms are red."

Which set me to giggling.

But not so much that I wasn't able to hear Sally, when she finally calmed down enough to speak.

"Josie, I talked to Ron Oglevee—the son that Mrs. Oglevee's ex had when he remarried, after leaving Paradise and moving to Lexington. And I have some very interesting information."

"Really? What's that?" The prospect of news calmed me.

"I'll tell you when you get back here. But there's something else. It's a good thing we packed your nice black pants, because Maxine turned up at our motel room. We're invited to a party tonight—at Tanner Jr.'s house."

23

"Josie, really now, you ought to undo just one more button," Cherry said, reaching toward the top of my silky, pale blue blouse.

I swatted her hand away. "Stop it, Cherry. We're going to a fancy party, and I'd rather not look indecent."

We were both standing in front of the mirror in our motel room. Cherry rolled her eyes at my reflection; I stuck my tongue out at hers.

"Nice," said Sally, behind us on the bed, already dressed in khakis and a red turtleneck. That's as fancy as she gets.

That's usually as fancy as I get, too, but I was glad Cherry had thought to pack my one dressy blouse, which looked sharp over my black pants. And, I thought, the necklace from Caleb looked very nice with the blouse, too.

"But Caleb's going with us," Cherry said. "And since Sally said she overheard Caleb talking about making out and red glow-in-the-dark condoms in his glove compartment—"

"He doesn't have any such thing in his glove compartment," I said, blushing.

"You checked?" Sally asked.

"Well, no, but—"

"Just in case—" Cherry reached again for my button.

I started swatting, again, as Sally said, "Just in case, she might want to leave something to Caleb's imagination—like the pleasure of *him* doing the unbuttoning."

Cherry's hand did a sudden U-turn away from my cleavage and back to her own. She buttoned another button.

I snickered.

"What?" she said, frowning at me in the mirror, and then immediately doing another eyebrow lift. "Dean has an imagination, too."

"I can only imagine," I said, waggling my eyebrows.

"Uh huh," Cherry said, buttoning one more button. "You weren't supposed to be imagining us, you were supposed to be distracting Caleb—while I was distracting Dean"— she paused, and gave a little kittenish grin—"so Sally could see if she could learn anything more about Mrs. Oglevee's past."

"Right," I said. We hadn't had a chance to talk about it yet. "Hurry and tell us, Sally. The guys are waiting for us."

Cherry kept preening before the mirror, while I sat in the chair.

"It's pretty simple," Sally said. "I called Winnie, and she said she remembered something about Millard Oglevee— Mrs. Oglevee's ex—moving to St. Louis after the divorce. She did some Internet research through an online 'people search' company called Inteligus and found just two Oglevees in the state of Missouri—and only one hundred thirty-eight in the U.S."

"Isn't it a little creepy how easy it is to track people down these days?" Cherry said, though her words were coming out garbled, as she was reapplying her lip liner for the third time.

"Isn't it marvelous that Mrs. Oglevee didn't marry someone named Millard Smith?" I said.

"Anyway," Sally said, "the Oglevee that Winnie found wasn't Millard—"

My shoulders slumped. How disappointing.

"—but someone named Ron. So I called him—three times. Third time, he answered. I told him I was trying to find Millard Oglevee, that I was a former student of Pearl Oglevee, Millard's ex-wife, and wanted to know how to get in touch with Millard because my beloved former teacher had passed away and asked me to send Millard a gift in a small box, and that I wasn't sure what was in the box, but I knew she felt badly about how things had turned out and that she'd had deathbed regrets and that I was pretty sure the gift was pretty valuable."

Sally smiled, pleased with herself.

"Sally," I said, "you are as bad as Caleb. Maybe the two of you should get together."

"Thanks—not interested—though I'll take that as a compliment."

"Oh, Josie, c'mon, admit that was clever," Cherry said, now re-teasing her hair.

I ignored her. "Aren't you worried about what will happen when he doesn't get a box from you?" I asked Sally.

"Nah," Sally said. "I said I was Cherry Feinster."

"What?" Cherry said, whirling away from the mirror, hands on her hips, comb stuck in the top of her hair.

"Oh, look who has morals now," I muttered.

"Stop worrying," Sally said. "We'll send him something later, some cheap jewelry, and you can claim Mrs. Oglevee made you think it was valuable, and he can go back to hating her."

"But why'd you say you were me?" Cherry demanded.

"It was a sudden inspiration. When the guy answered the phone, it was on the first ring, and he sounded kind of lonely, like maybe he'd been out, and was hoping for a call from someone special. So, I found myself saying I was you, talking like you do when you want to manipulate a guy, all husky-like . . ."

"Why couldn't you do that as you?" Cherry wanted to know.

"I'm a tired, single mother of three," Sally said. She sighed. "I've forgotten how to do husky as myself . . ."

"That's identity theft of . . . of . . . my persona—" Cherry wailed.

"Please!" I hollered. "Sally, did you find anything out, or did you just torment the poor guy?"

"Oh, I found out plenty. Not sure if it was my husky-Cherry voice, or the lure of the gift. He said he knew his dad had been married before moving to St. Louis and marrying his mom and having him. They all had a nice life together, although his dad has passed on and his mom has remarried.

"All he really knew about Pearl Oglevee was from one conversation he'd had with his dad when they'd gone fishing. Apparently, Millard was trying to warn him about certain kinds of women—" Sally shot Cherry a look, and Cherry glared at her. "—because he didn't like the girl Ron was dating at the time. Said she was needy and just trying to escape a broken heart, like his first wife Pearl. Said they'd met in Chicago—"

"Wait, what?" I said. "Where does Chicago fit into this?"

"Would have been around 1952. Ron and I figured it out as best we could. Pearl was living in Chicago with a great-aunt from her mother's side of the family, working at a hat shop there. Millard was a working-class guy, just went in to get a hat for his mom for Mom's Day—"

"Aw. Nice guy," Cherry said.

"Yeah, sounds like it. Anyway, he was smitten with Pearl. And apparently, she was honest with him. Said she'd just given up a baby for adoption—"

"A baby!" Cherry and I both said.

We stopped, took that in, while Sally smiled at us.

"I was shocked, too, but I've had time to think about it. Maxine said she was Pearl's daughter. But that timing doesn't work. For one thing, from the timeline we figured out earlier, Pearl was already back at Bowling Green, working on her teaching degree by the time Maxine was born.

"But there's nothing in the newspaper articles about Pearl's life between Sol's death and the closing of the Femmes of Iniquity in 1952 and Pearl going to Bowling Green in 1954. What if she was pregnant by Sol at the time of his death, and just felt she couldn't handle rearing a child on her own . . ."

"Or," I jumped in, "what if she was pregnant by Tanner Sr. . . . the original love of her life that she dumped because she didn't want the conventional life—or so she thought when she was nineteen. And, again, gave the baby up . . . or to Tanner Sr. and his wife? After all, Eileen said that at first Tanner Sr. and his wife had trouble conceiving."

"But why would Mrs. Oglevee do that?" Cherry said. "And how do you explain Maxine coming along?"

"I have no idea why Mrs. Oglevee would do that," I admitted. "But I have heard that sometimes if a couple can't have a child, and they think it's because of infertility issues, they adopt, and soon after the wife becomes pregnant after all."

"I've read stories like that, too," Sally said. "Anyway, Ron said his father told him that Pearl wanted to get her teaching degree before getting married. They corresponded while she was in college and on her graduation day, he showed up, and asked her to marry him, and to his surprise, she said yes. They tried to make a life together, but Pearl was always uptight, picked fights with him. He figured she had issues, and she wasn't about to let him help her work them out.

"So, they divorced, he moved to St. Louis because a cousin of his knew of work there, and he remarried and lived happily-ever-after until a few years ago. Lung cancer got him."

We all had a moment of silence, in honor of Millard Oglevee. His story was, I thought, kind of inspiring. He'd had a rocky marriage with our old teacher, probably a broken heart, but still pulled himself back together and made a happy life for himself after all.

"Anyway, Ron said the point of the story was that his dad didn't want him to idealize the girl he was dating, and love her just for his image of her, like he'd done with his first wife."

"Did Ron say if he'd listened to his dad?"

Sally shook her head. I hoped so, although I felt a pang of worry for him, considering that Sally said he'd answered the phone so eagerly.

"After that, I got his address and promised I—well, you, Cherry, really—would send him whatever it was Mrs. Oglevee had left for his dad," Sally said.

"He hadn't heard of Mrs. Oglevee's death?"

"No," Sally said. "I guess this conversation with his dad took place a few years ago, and as far as Millard was concerned, all ties were cut with Pearl and he liked it that way."

We all thought that over, gave each other looks, and each knew what we were all thinking: nope. Ron had not listened to his dad.

"We're gonna have to buy a nice pinky ring or something to send the man," I said.

"Yeah," Sally said, sighing. "Sorry about that."

"Now, wait, I don't think I should have to chip in, considering—" Sally and I gave Cherry withering looks, and she stopped. "Fine. Pinky ring. I'll chip in. Wouldn't want my name to have a bad rep in St. Louis, just in case I end up visiting there someday."

Her face lit up.

"Ooh! The arch! I've always wanted to see the Golden Arches! That would be great for a honeymoon, wouldn't it?"

"It's the St. Louis Gateway Arch, Cherry," I said. "*One* arch. Silver. A monument to westward expansion, not to—"

"Did Dean pop the question?" Sally asked.

"No," Cherry said, her expression dimming a little. "Not yet, but—"

There was a knock at the door.

"You ladies ready yet?" Caleb hollered.

"Let's go," Cherry said, grabbing her faux fur coat.

"Um, Cherry," I said.

"What?"

"You might want to take the comb out of the top of your hair."

"I'd have just let her go out like that," Sally said, with a snicker.

24

And so, off we went, all piled into Caleb's car, on the short drive to Tanner Jr.'s party.

We were quiet on the way, none of us quite sure what to expect. After all, we weren't even in the congressman-wanna-be's voting district, and if we had been, it wasn't like we ran in influential circles.

But as Sally had explained to us, after Caleb and I returned to the motel, and then Cherry and Dean returned (having left for a brief walk along the shoreline while the maid thankfully changed the sheets again without asking why), Maxine just showed up at the Perry Inn Motel, asking to see me.

Rhoda, the beleaguered clerk, tracked Sally down instead, and Maxine handed Sally an invitation, saying that her brother was hosting his annual New Year's Eve party that night—always held a night early on the thirtieth, since most people wanted to go to the Great Walleye Drop and, besides, he'd be working the crowd this year as part of his campaign.

According to Sally, Maxine had said she was sorry for upsetting me before my speech at Mrs. Oglevee's dedication

ceremony, and the invitation—with her brother's blessing—
was her way of making up for it.

And I didn't believe it for a minute.

For one thing, where had Maxine been since the morning
before? Her neighbor, Dell, had been worried about her. It
wasn't like her to be gone overnight without making arrangements with him for the care of her pets.

And for another, I just didn't buy this sudden change of
heart. I'd only seen Maxine briefly, but she didn't seem like
someone who would apologize for her actions.

And for yet another, why bother to invite us to her brother's party—five people he'd never met before? That seemed
over the top. A simple "I'm sorry" would have done.

Of course, we were going—Sally, Cherry, Caleb, and I—
out of curiosity, Dean because he wanted to be with Cherry.
I kept thinking about what Mrs. Oglevee had said in my
dream: We have met the enemy and they are ours.

Were we going into enemy territory? Or was Maxine just
a flake who'd thought better of her impulsive note to me and
truly wanted to apologize?

It was all very confusing.

But it was better to think about that than the possible contents of the glove compartment, right above my knees . . .

Caleb had to have been joking . . . right?

We pulled past Eileen's house—I felt a jolt of pity for
her—and past numerous cars lining the street, all for Tanner
Jr.'s party, I reckoned.

Caleb pulled alongside the curb seven or eight houses
down from Tanner Jr.'s.

"We're going to get chilly on that walk," Cherry whined.

"Don't worry, baby-cakes, I'll have my arm around you,"
Dean said.

"Aw," said Cherry. "You're so sweet! I miss you!" And I
heard her blow him a kiss.

"Miss him? How can you—" I unbuckled and turned
around in my seat, and saw that Sally was sitting between
Dean and Cherry.

She said, "You didn't think I was getting in the backseat with these two if they had access to each other, did you?"

"Okay, enough of that," Caleb said, "let's go to the party, have a few munchies, let this kooky Maxine give her apologies, and then head back over to the Cut Bait."

We had barely walked in the door when Maxine greeted me like we were old friends.

She'd cleaned up well, I had to admit. No coffee stains. Bright red tunic over black velour long skirt. Only the faintest whiff of tobacco odor. Gold dangly earrings and matching bracelet and a gold pin in the outline of what I would normally have guessed was a crane, but what I realized—based on what I'd learned over the past two days—was supposed to represent a double-crested cormorant. Nicely done makeup.

She didn't, I realize, look a thing like Mrs. Oglevee.

Cherry, Dean, Sally, and Caleb all looked at me like—this is the woman you described as a scary nut job? Who passed you a note claiming to be Mrs. Oglevee's daughter? Claiming Mrs. Oglevee was murdered?

I felt more than a little annoyed. I wasn't prone to embellishing my stories—or my intuitive reactions. Maxine looked like a well-to-do, middle-aged woman, no hint of her rebellious nature—except for that pin, of course. And everyone seemed to be more than willing to ignore that, or at least react to her politely, when she introduced us around.

Even her brother—tall, handsome, and bearing no direct resemblance to Mrs. Oglevee, either—greeted us graciously, introduced us to his wife (Amelia, a trim, lovely blond) and his children (Zach and Tanya, both home on college break). All of the VanWorts treated us with nothing but delight, as if we were all old friends, and then wandered off to greet other guests.

Martin Joubert—a.k.a. Butt-Hut man, a.k.a., unemployed fishing captain, fired from Tanner's Perry Commercial Fishing Company for poaching—was nowhere in sight, I noted. This was strictly polite company.

Then an older man saw Dean and Cherry and rushed over to assure them that Maxine had called him that very afternoon, to say she'd been staying with her brother to help with this party, and just forgot to call about the pets.

Dean and Cherry introduced the man to us as Dell Stoker, Maxine's neighbor. He'd seemed a little confused and disbelieving of Maxine's claim as he described it to us, but immediately adopted proper meet-n-greet form as introductions were made all around.

Then Dean saw someone he recognized from his summer trips to visit his grandparents, and excused himself and Cherry so they could go chat.

Sally and Dell got caught up in a conversation about pets—she was thinking of eventually getting a dog for her triplets, and Dell was only too happy to start filling her in on all the breeds and which ones might survive three boys.

Caleb and I hung in until "beagles," and then wandered out of the parlor in search of the buffet table, which, as it turned out, was set up in the den.

As we filled our plates with munchies, I glanced around the room. The VanWorts' house was similar to Eileen's, but with more traditional decorating—antiques and muted wall colors, all very classy. Only one fish was in sight—a large walleye, of course, and a fishing rod and reel, carefully mounted behind glass over the fireplace.

Why not, I thought. It was no more odd than a deer's head and rifle mounted on the wall, which is what you'd see in several houses in Paradise.

We carried our plates and worked our way through the crowd so we could study the plaque—both of us immediately curious. CAUGHT BY TANNER VANWORT, SR., 1952.

The year he'd been in the state senate . . . and been caught illegally gambling at the Femmes of Iniquity. The year Sol was found murdered—his death still unsolved—and the year, I now knew, that Pearl Armbruster took off for Chicago, had a baby, gave the child up for adoption, and met her future husband, Millard Oglevee.

A busy year, all around.

"You know," Caleb said softly, "the VanWorts aren't exactly the scary family I'd imagined up from your description of Maxine." He popped a stuffed mushroom into his mouth.

"Remember the last catered event we went to? How I nearly ended up dead?"

Caleb stopped in midchew, which made me smile. Ha! (We'd gotten involved in investigating a murder involving my father's family, and crashed a catered party to do it. Things hadn't gone well right after we helped ourselves to the canapés—but that's a whole other story.)

Caleb swallowed. "That's not exactly fair, Josie. And besides, while I think it's fascinating to try to figure out your old teacher's psyche, I still agree with Dean." He leaned closer to me, and whispered, "I don't think it has anything to do with poor Eileen."

"Well, I don't necessarily, either, but—"

Caleb put a finger to my lips. "You're wearing the necklace I gave you," he said, still whispering, which—truth be told—I found so sexy I nearly swooned. "It looks lovely on you," he added, and rubbed his thumb gently just above the heart pendant, on my chest.

"Thank you," I managed to say. "I really—"

I don't recollect, now, what I was going to say next, because suddenly, above the general chatter, there was a sudden cry.

"Oh no! Oh, Tanner, I'm so sorry!" It was Maxine's voice.

Everyone looked to the dining room entry. There she and Tanner Jr. stood, she looking horrified—and he splashed with a brown liquid. He looked annoyed.

Maxine saw me across the room. "Josie, yoo hoo, Josie, could you come here? We need help with this coffee stain!"

I held my plate toward Caleb. "Do you mind? Duty calls!"

He took my plate and gave me a worried look. "Josie—be careful," he said.

"Oh, why worry? Everyone's concerned first about the stain when they've just been splashed with hot coffee—right?"

Somehow, my sarcastic comment didn't erase his worried look.

25

"Thank goodness it was just lukewarm coffee I'd been carrying around a while!" Maxine said.

I rolled my eyes, not even trying to disguise my disbelief. I stood in the kitchen, which was large and white, sparkling and clean, as if not a dollop of the buffet food had been prepared in it. The buffet, I realized, had been catered. Of course. Took me a minute, because I'm so used to pot luck carry-ins.

Nobody was in the kitchen except Maxine, Tanner Jr., and myself.

"Yeah, it's a good thing you waited until the coffee cooled to slosh it on your brother," I said. "Otherwise, you'd need a medic—not a stain expert."

Maxine frowned, started to protest, but Tanner laughed.

"Josie, you're right, of course. We do need to talk to you, and we wanted to do it with a little privacy," he said pleasantly. "Maxine came up with clever—but messy—ruse."

I gave her a hard look. "She seems to have a thing about coffee stains," I said. "When she showed up yesterday at my speech, she had on a coffee-stained sweatshirt—and gave me a coffee-stained note claiming that Pearl was Maxine's mother . . . and that Pearl had been murdered."

"Yes," Tanner said smoothly. "So I've heard."

Maxine put her cup down on the counter so hard, I was surprised the cup didn't break. She gave a tight smile.

"I've also heard you've been doing a little investigating of your own into these claims, since then," Tanner said. "You're from Paradise, a very small town, Josie," he said. "Port Clinton is bigger. But you know how small-towns are."

I looked at Maxine. "Why did you bring your claims to me?"

Maxine looked at her brother. "Better start from the beginning, dear," he said, again pleasantly.

"I found out about the Pearl Oglevee Regional History Collection dedication from a brief article in the local newspaper," Maxine said. "I assume the Mason County Library sent a press release, since Pearl was born and reared here. You were named as the speaker—"

My stomach did a flip at the reminder. Would I ever get over my fear of public speaking?

"—and as her star pupil," Maxine went on. "The paper made you sound like you'd been close to her, and like you're a rising media star, with your regional column."

She stopped. I stared at her. Tanner Jr. frowned at Maxine slightly, and she looked away.

"Ohhhh-kay," I said. "And this motivated you to come all the way down to Paradise, and pop me a note that said you're really Pearl's daughter and Pearl was murdered . . . why?"

Maxine looked at me. "I wanted to get your attention," she said flatly.

"People usually get my attention by asking for stain-removal tips," I said. I looked at the big coffee splotch on Tanner Jr.'s chest. "Such as how to remove coffee."

Tanner Jr. smiled. "My sister has always had a flare for the dramatic," he said.

"No kidding. So you got my attention with these two little

lies—" I admit it. I was indulging in sarcasm. "Why did you want my attention?"

Maxine cleared her throat. "My father and Pearl were friends when they were younger. I noticed the newspaper doesn't mention it, but she was fond of bird watching—a passion she shared with my father, and which he passed on to me. In fact, I am very passionate about birds." Her voice changed, filled with enthusiasm. She was, at least on this point, telling the truth. The rest of it sounded pretty shaky to me. "I've taken on as my cause a fight against cruelty toward double-crested cormorants—"

"Maxine!" Tanner Jr. snapped. Then he recomposed his expression into calmness. "You can tell Josie about that later, if you like. But for now you owe her an explanation for luring her up here on false pretenses. Go on."

Maxine sighed. "Pearl and my father corresponded until her death about their love of birds. I thought, since you were close to her, if you knew about my cause, you'd be interested in using your media connections to help me get the word out."

I considered what Maxine had just said.

She was trying to flatter me—that was for sure. The kind of media connections I had weren't going to really help her much, unless for some reason she thought a regional columnist had national connections.

I could see where, if I did gain national attention for my column, I would have to figure out a way to deal with this kind of occasional nuttiness—but I filed that away for later thought.

That she was passionate about preventing cruelty in the control of the double-crested cormorant population, I definitely believed. That she'd gained her love for birds from her father, also believable. After all, Eileen had said as much.

That Pearl Oglevee had a hidden passion for birds . . . not so much. I knew what had been her passion. History. Not ornithology.

There were a few other points I found unbelievable, and I voiced them.

"Why in the world would you try to get my attention with a note containing two outrageous lies?" I asked. "You could have just stayed and chatted with me after my speech. And for that matter, why didn't you stay? You just disappeared."

"I went outside to take a cigarette break," Maxine said, "then realized how foolish I'd been to write that note, and took off. Out of embarrassment."

A little smile played on her lips then. "Of course, you found the note compelling enough that you did come all the way up here to talk to me—and on a holiday weekend, at that?"

I glared at her. "I was coming up here, anyway, as it turned out, with friends to celebrate my thirtieth birthday." I didn't see the need to mention that this was, in fact, my birthday. "I would have come up here without your having given me the note."

Maxine and Tanner Jr. exchanged a brief glance, something passing between them.

"But you talked to Eileen last night," Tanner Jr. said.

I looked at him. "Small-town drums beating? About a brief visit at a neighbor's house?"

He smiled. "Eileen and I have long been friends," he said.

"She mentioned you used to date, in fact," I said.

"Yes. We did. And we were friends. Anyway, she called me to tell me about your visit, a few hours before the horrible tragedy."

"Did she always call you to let you know when someone dropped by her house?" I asked. "I don't do that with my friends."

"She felt guilty, because she'd shared so much about our families' histories with a stranger," Tanner said. "And that Maxine has, in the past, claimed I was not really our mother's son and that's why our mother killed herself."

I flinched again, less at his message than at the bland tone he used to deliver it. Maxine looked down again.

"Yes," I said, "she mentioned that."

"Poor Eileen was concerned that you'd talk it up around town, since you apparently alluded to the fact you were more than willing to talk to anyone and everyone to find out about Pearl Oglevee," Tanner said. I lifted my eyebrows. Eileen must have called Tanner, for him to know that. "And she didn't want the old rumors to hurt me, again."

He gave a long look to his sister, who missed it, because she was still staring away.

"Seems to me," I said slowly, "your sister likes to make up wild stories about people."

"Actually, the wild story she told about me not being our mother's son is actually true," Tanner said. I looked at him, startled. "My mother was Pearl Oglevee. She had a child with my father, early in my parents' marriage, around the time she was part-owner of Femmes of Iniquity with some hood—"

"Sol Levine," I said, and immediately regretted it. I hate it when my tongue gets ahead of my brain.

Tanner looked amused. "Yes, you'd know that. Since you've been researching so much."

"Small-town drums?" I said, my mouth dry.

He nodded. "You've been busy."

"Not much to do here."

"It'll be more exciting tomorrow night. The Great Wall-eye Drop is always a little wild. Anyway, yes, I admit that Pearl was my mother, and that she gave me up for adoption to our parents. I guess that had some kind of relaxing effect on our mother, because not long after, she became pregnant with my dear little sister."

"You seem so . . . relaxed . . . about admitting this," I said.

Tanner shrugged. "I grew up thinking my mom and dad were both my biological parents. Our dad shared the truth with us, remember Maxine?" He gave her a little poke.

She looked up, anger flashing across her face. "Yes, I remember our father's deathbed confession all too well."

This seemed to amuse Tanner. "That's right. On his

deathbed, he confessed who my mother really was. And it bothered my sister far more than it bothered me."

"He always liked you more—probably because he was really in love with Pearl all along. Mom probably knew it, and that's why she killed herself—although he said several times, when he was mad at me, that it was postpartum depression after having me! I always knew—"

"Enough!" Tanner said, grabbing Maxine's arm and squeezing hard. I was taken aback at this outburst, suddenly wishing I wasn't witness to this family's dirty laundry, no matter how willingly they seemed to air it. Being nosey has its dark side.

"Enough," Tanner said again, more calmly, putting his arm around his sister. "Dad wasn't perfect, but he loved you. That's why he shared his love of birding with you. He was always disappointed that I wasn't interested."

He looked at me. "Sorry about the outburst. Anyway, I thought you deserved to know the truth—since my sister's note was so disturbing to you," he said, giving me a look that added, she's not quite right. Please forgive her, okay? "I'm not ashamed of the truth of my parentage. Maxine's always tried to use it to manipulate me to see and do things her way," he added, casually, as if to say—eh, what's a little emotional blackmail among siblings? "And I used to be embarrassed when she told people I wasn't really our mom's son, but I've come to the conclusion that I might as well be honest about this. It will probably come out in my campaign, anyway. And if this is the worst family secret we have, well, so? No one has a perfect family history."

Well. That certainly sounded very sane and healthy.

"Oh, Josie, about this coffee stain," Tanner said. "I have shirts aplenty, but this one was a Christmas gift from my daughter."

For a second, I hesitated. I was tempted to tell him: rub it with a bar of soap! Let that sit overnight! Then wash in the hottest water possible! All of which would, of course, set the stain, because coffee makes a pure tannin stain.

That would have been mean, but I felt annoyed at the sense I was being played, somehow.

Which wasn't Tanner's daughter's fault.

So I did the right thing.

I said: "Coffee stains are, chemically speaking, very complex. The little coffee molecules rush, as fast and best they can, away from the original spot where the coffee spilled on clothing or linens. That's why the outer ring of a coffee stain is always darker than the center.

"And coffee is a tannin stain—tannin being an astringent polyphenol—group of chemicals—found in plants such as coffee beans, tea leaves, or berries. The astringent property of some tannin plants—like oak bark—is used to tan leather.

"Anyway, some stains are actually combination stains. Such as wine. That's a tannin/alcohol stain. Or if you'd had milk in your coffee. That's a tannin/protein stain."

"I, um, take my coffee black," said Maxine, looking a little overwhelmed. So did Tanner, to my amusement.

"So your brother's stain is pure tannin stain," I concluded.

Tanner gazed down at his shirt in dismay, as if he'd never get the stain out.

"It's a complex stain," I said. "But a simple enough problem to solve."

He looked up at me. "How?" he asked, impatiently.

"Since it's still wet, just rinse the shirt from behind the stain with very cold water."

"That's it?"

"Yep," I said. "You'll want to pretreat the area with white vinegar or your regular detergent if there is still a spot, and then wash as usual. Retreat and rewash until it's gone, though. Drying sets stains."

I smiled. "Complex problem—when you dig into it—but very simple solution."

Tanner smiled back. "Like many problems in life."

Why didn't I believe it?

26

"I don't believe it!" said Sally. And she looked unhappy about it, too.

"I do," said Cherry, yawning. "Makes perfect sense to me."

Sally, Cherry, and I were all back in our room at the Perry Inn. Caleb and Dean were in the room next door. Sally and I had said "no way" at Cherry's whispered suggestion on the walk back to Caleb's car, after we all left the VanWort party, that the room arrangements should be Cherry and Dean in one room, and Caleb, Sally, and I in the other. Too awkward.

Now we were in our jammies, munching on pretzels and chips and minicupcakes and drinking sodas, even though we'd all enjoyed the fancy treats of the VanWort buffet. Cherry'd said we needed a just-us-girls birthday celebration for me, and she broke out the snacks and the minicupcakes she'd made herself.

Sally and I were sitting, cross-legged, on the water bed, and Cherry was on the chair. I'd just told Sally and Cherry about my odd little conversation in the kitchen with Tanner Jr. and Maxine.

"So what we've learned is that our dear, old, deceased

prim teacher, Mrs. Oglevee, started life as Pearl Armbruster, in a fairly well-off family," said Sally. "She dated Tanner VanWort, the much older boy next door, and liked him, but when it came time to marry him, she ran off with her little sister Rose to New York to chase some dreams."

"Right," said Cherry, popping a cheese puff in her mouth.

"Rose came back, settled down to a conventional life, married, had Eileen," Sally went on.

"Uh huh," Cherry agreed.

"But Pearl came back with a new identity—woman gone wild."

Cherry giggled.

"With her lover, Sol Levine, she opens—and dances at—an exotic dance club, Femmes of Iniquity, but also resumes an affair with Tanner VanWort, who has since married Pamela, who can't get pregnant," Sally said.

"All true, and better than my soap operas," Cherry agreed.

"But Pearl gets pregnant, and shortly after, Sol is found murdered—we assume by other thugs like him, given how he's beaten—and Tanner is found guilty of running an illegal gambling racket at the club, which closes," Sally went on.

"Sounds right. Right, Josie?"

"So far," I said.

"Pearl goes off to Chicago to live with a great-aunt and have her out-of-wedlock child, which she gives up for adoption to Tanner Sr. and Pamela, who name the child Tanner Jr. and promptly get busy making Maxine," Sally said.

"Yes, and then—" Cherry started.

"I'm on a roll here," Sally said. "And then Pearl meets Millard Oglevee and dates him in Chicago, goes to Bowling Green to become a teacher, and upon graduation marries Millard—becoming the Mrs. Oglevee we all loved to hate—and they move to Paradise when she gets a job there.

"He can't stand the fact she's always so uptight, so he

divorces her, and goes off and makes a new life in St. Louis, living happily ever after, as far as we know. Meanwhile, Tanner Sr. and family have a few tragedies—Pamela commits suicide, and Maxine turns into a needy nut job obsessed with double-crested cormorants—but Tanner Jr., despite his father's deathbed confession about his real mom being Pearl Oglevee, has a decent life and is not too upset at the news of who his real mom was, and doesn't even particularly care if people know, because he figures they won't hold it against him in the upcoming election. People can overlook that, he thinks."

"Well," said Cherry, "it's not like he can help it. Or like he fooled around with some employee. Or did anything illegal."

"So now we know the true story of Mrs. Oglevee's life," Sally said, "and we're supposed to believe that none of this story has anything to do with Maxine coming to Josie's speech yesterday? That Maxine just wanted to get Josie's attention so Josie might take the time to listen to Maxine's concerns about double-crested cormorants and put Maxine in touch with media contacts, but then Maxine just changes her mind and takes off?"

Now Sally sounded disbelieving.

But Cherry shrugged. "Well, everyone says Maxine is a nut job. So that would explain her erratic behavior."

"What about Eileen's murder?" Sally asked.

"Burglary gone bad," said Cherry. "Burglars knew Eileen kept her valuables in her husband's precious fish stuff, so they started whacking walleyes, and Eileen got upset, and the burglar whacked her, too."

"Sol Levine's murder, years ago?"

Cherry had to think about that one. "I think we go with the obvious—Sol was killed by fellow thugs."

"Fine—what about Butt-Hut man following us?"

"He wasn't following us," said Cherry. "Just coincidence."

"The attack on Josie when she left Eileen's?"

"Muggers. Bad timing."

We were all silent for a moment. Then Sally and Cherry looked to me. "What do you think, Josie?" Cherry asked.

I sighed. "I have to admit, we've found out all about Mrs. Oglevee's past. And it makes me understand her better." I paused, thinking how sad it was that she punished herself for her indiscretions by living a life in which she seemed to deny herself—and everyone around her—pleasure. And how hard it must have been, knowing her child lived just a few hours' drive away, and wanting to be close enough to go visit and catch a glimpse of him from time to time, but not being able to contact him.

And then, right before finally embracing life, having a little fun on a cruise, dying . . .

"But what about how Mrs. Oglevee died? What are you going to, well, um, tell her? In your dreams?" Sally asked. "Was she murdered, or did she die of a heart attack?"

I thought about it for a second. "Heart attack."

We all fell silent again.

"Well, this is depressing," said Cherry, perkiness taking over her voice. Sally and I looked at each other. Uh oh. "I'm glad we've resolved everything—even though it would have been so much more interesting if we could have proven that Mrs. Oglevee was murdered. Anyway, this is no way to end the day on Josie's thirtieth birthday! We have to lighten things up!"

I glanced at the clock. It was nearly midnight. "Um, Cherry, really, I'm fine. I loved the surprise celebration at Suzy Fu's yesterday, and this has been an exciting day, and I look forward to the Great Walleye Drop tomorrow, so thank you both. It turned out to be a great trip."

Tears popped into Cherry's eyes, which inspired Sally to roll hers, which, thankfully, Cherry didn't notice. "Oh, Josie," she said, her voice trembling, "I'm so glad you said that. I mean, I did get you two up here because I was in a snit at Dean, but it worked out, right? And Dean and I even made up." She sniffled. "So everything's worked out. Except we haven't sung happy birthday to you yet, not without distractions, at least."

"Really, I'm okay with that—" I started, but Cherry hopped up and rummaged through one of her sacks.

"She says she's okay with that," Sally said, looking concerned. She's tone deaf and gets embarrassed when she sings.

But a few minutes later, Cherry'd put a birthday candle into a minicupcake, and she and Sally again sang happy birthday to me.

I'll admit it—I even had a few tears pop into my eyes, too, listening to Cherry's warbling falsetto and Sally's brave monotone. I was blessed in my friendships—something poor Mrs. Oglevee never got to experience.

Then I stared at my candle. What to wish for? The list I'd made at the library earlier that day popped into my head. How could I pick just one?

So I didn't. I thought about them all, and said a little prayer that I'd make the right decisions no matter what happened in my life, and then blew out the candle.

Sally and Cherry clapped, and I pulled the candle out of the cupcake, unwrapped the treat, and popped it—whole—in my mouth.

Sally and I started cleaning up from our snack fest, but Cherry said, "Wait, there's just one more thing."

We looked at her.

"Now, seriously," she said. "You two are always teasing me about my cheerleading past and my girly-girl ways, but—"

She paused, to dig through yet another suitcase. She finally popped up, with an armful of red pom-poms.

"Oh. My. Lord," Sally said, her eyes wide. "Whatever are you up to?"

I tried to fight it, but I couldn't—a smile was tugging up on my lips.

"It is time," Cherry said, with great seriousness, which only made me smile more, "for the two of you to get in touch with your inner cheerleaders. I brought these along, special, just for Josie's birthday!"

I burst out laughing. Sally moaned. But somehow, within a few minutes, Cherry had us standing in front of her, with strict instructions to echo her chants and movements, which we did to the best of our abilities, waving our pom-poms, and managing to holler as follows:

CHERRY: "Give me a J!"

SALLY and ME: "J!"

CHERRY: "Give me an O!"

SALLY and ME: "O!"

And so on, until we were able to answer Cherry's: "What's it spell?" With: "Josie Rocks!"

And then we collapsed with giggles—even Sally. Although she drew the line at letting Cherry give her a pedicure.

While they were squabbling over that—a sure sign that things were normal with my friends—my cell phone rang, and I flipped it open. Caleb's cell phone number was on the screen. That was a call I was curious enough to take.

"Wow, you really do always answer your cell phone as soon as possible," Caleb said.

I grinned. "Absolutely."

"I just called to ask if you Sea-gals could keep it down over there," Caleb said with mock seriousness. "The rest of the guests here are trying to rest up for the Great Walleye Drop, you know."

"We'll try," I said.

"Oh, and Dean says to tell Cherry he misses her."

"Right."

"And Josie?"

"Yes?"

"Happy birthday."

I touched the heart necklace, still around my neck. "Thanks," I said. And we hung up.

27

" 'Oh Josie, happy birthday; oh, Josie, I miss you—' "

That was Mrs. Oglevee, tromping all over my sleep again. In this dream, I was in bed, and had just woken up—I always hate it when I have dreams in which I'm sleeping and wake up; it's so confusing to recollect later—and there was Mrs. Oglevee, at the foot of my dream-bed, waving huge red pom-poms at me.

I glared at her. "Would you go away? I had a nice celebration with my friends, and I don't need your bitterness to slime it, okay?"

"You were supposed to be finding out if I was murdered or had a heart attack, but as usual, you put off your homework assignments for fun, fun, fun, and—"

"You had a heart attack!" I snapped.

Mrs. Oglevee looked surprised at that. Her pom-poms disappeared, and I saw then that she was dressed to go fishing, complete with tackle vest.

"Really?" she said, sounding a little disappointed, too.

"Yes," I said. "We learned quite a bit about your past—Sol, the Femmes of Iniquity, Tanner Sr., Tanner Jr.—" Mrs. Oglevee looked away, but I still saw a sad, lost expression cross her face, and I softened my tone. "—but nothing to make us think you were murdered."

I waited a second and said, "Though your niece, Eileen, was," I said. "By burglars. Just yesterday. I suppose she hasn't shown up . . . wherever you are, just yet?"

I was always trying to get Mrs. Oglevee to give me some clue as to where she'd ended up in the afterlife—besides in my subconscious—but so far, she'd ignored every effort. She also didn't seem the least concerned about Eileen's being murdered.

"You talked to Eileen?" she asked. "Did she tell you about the letters? I sent so many letters to Rose over the years. Rose rarely wrote back. But I poured my heart out to her." She paused and frowned. "Especially those last few months I wrote her, right before I passed. I can't quite remember what I wrote, but she never wrote back . . ."

"She passed away, right before you did," I said, gently.

Mrs. Oglevee said, "Oh," a deflated, sad sound. She floated around the end of my bed, and sat down on the edge. I scooched up a little. "Well. Our paths . . . haven't crossed."

Then she looked anxious. "That means Rose never saw the last letters I sent."

Well, that would be true. Eileen had said as much.

"I can't remember what I wrote—but it had to be something important," Mrs. Olgevee mused.

That fit, too. After all, Eileen had said that whenever her mother got a letter from Pearl, she seemed a little upset—never saying why, just that Pearl could never send a simple birthday card or note—she always wrote a meaty, in-depth letter—usually about the past, and usually when she was depressed.

"Did Eileen show you the letters?"

I shook my head, reluctant to tell her the truth. "She told me that her mom kept them in a safety-deposit box at the bank."

Mrs. Oglevee laughed gleefully. "That sounds like Rose! Probably didn't want her precious daughter or husband or

friends reading my scandalous memoirs in letter form!"
Then her mood turned abruptly serious again. "But she still
had them, right? She could show you the letters—"

"She was murdered yesterday!" I reminded Mrs. Oglevee.

"Oh, yes, that's right," she said casually. I guess being
dead doesn't seem that big a deal . . . to the already dead.
"Well, ask her kids, then, when they come back to town to
make the arrangements, to see the letters. I wish I could
remember . . ."

Suddenly, swimming around her head were miniature
walleyes. I gasped. Were we under water in this dream? All
at once, I had the sense we were, and I didn't like it at all—
even if it was just a dream.

And the walleyes were snapping at . . . what? At bait? No,
the things were too shiny. Lures? Yes, lures, I reckoned was
the right term—lures that were popping off of the front of
Mrs. Oglevee's fishing vest and trying to swarm me. Lures
shaped as . . .

One sped in front of me, fast, a walleye in slithery pursuit,
and then several more, and I realized what they were: miniature keys. I swatted at them. They were annoying, like key-
shaped, underwater gnats.

"I am not going to ask the children of a woman who's just
been murdered if I could possibly see their grandmother's
letters from their great-aunt," I said.

"Hmm, you worked that out nicely," Mrs. Oglevee said,
but she crossed her arms and glared at me. "As usual,
though, you're afraid to do that last 10 percent of the work
any project requires to be top-notch . . ."

"It's not fear," I said, swatting away. "It's common decency.
Besides, you could be more help, you know. You're the one
who isn't sure if you were murdered or had a heart attack."

"I am not in the habit of giving away all the answers to
my students," Mrs. Oglevee said, her fishing outfit suddenly
turning into a flowered shirtwaist dress, one I remembered
her wearing often to school. "I gave you plenty of hints on
the way up here!"

I looked away, gazing past the darting walleyes and keys into fog—which didn't really fit with the sense we were underwater, but then, dreams don't have to be logical.

What had she told me? She'd referred to Commodore Oliver Hazard Perry. What had she taught us about him that could be relevant? Sally had remembered his famous quote—"We have met the enemy and they are ours . . ." which he penned to send to his general, after victory in the Battle of Lake Erie . . . which, though part of the War of 1812, took place in 1813. And a fact which, I remembered now, always amused me as a kid . . .

"We have met the enemy and they are ours . . ." Perry had meant his troops had defeated the British squadron, but another way to look at "ours" would be ownership, or being part of someone's family or group.

In a sense, the young Mrs. Oglevee—back when she was the wild Pearl Armbruster—could say both Tanner Sr. and Tanner Jr. were "hers—" her lover and her son. Were they also her enemies?

And there was something else . . . yes! Then I remembered.

Perry had penned his famous statement on the back of an old envelope.

Envelopes. Letters.

I looked back at Mrs. Oglevee. "Eileen told me she threw the letters away," I said quietly.

"What?" Mrs. Oglevee bellowed, so loudly that I clapped my hands over my ears, and the miniature walleyes and keys froze for a second, before disappearing completely. "And you believed that? You must have talked to her on the phone. Eileen has always been a pack rat. Her house is crammed with stuff! She never throws a thing away—and no matter what she says, she wouldn't throw anything away that had been precious to her mom. Not even letters from her hated old Aunt Pearl."

Doubt started turning in my head.

Eileen had looked away, seemed uncomfortable, when

she talked about throwing away the letters. She had seemed to cherish her mom—and all those collectibles she'd inherited. Would she have thrown away something so precious to her mom?

Or just kept them, as her mom had, in a safety-deposit box—or a box, perhaps, in the attic?

And, from the news, the walleye collectibles in her house had been torn up, as if someone had been looking for something. But the only thing cited as being stolen was jewelry from the box on her bedroom dresser.

Could you really store letters, or anything of value, inside a stuffed fish? I didn't think so. The fish would be stuffed with . . . whatever people stuffed fish with to preserve them. But, perhaps, you could . . . if it was something small. Something like a key.

What if, I thought, my heart suddenly racing, there was something in the letters that Mrs. Oglevee sent—that Rose never read—that revealed something about the truth of her death? Or something that would be far more embarrassing to Tanner Jr.—and more threatening to his campaigns—than the simple fact that his birth mother was Mrs. Oglevee?

What if my visit to Eileen inspired her to look at those letters—and for some reason confront Tanner with their contents?

I frowned. But he'd been so relaxed at his party. He hadn't seemed nervous at all.

Which could mean he already had found the letters at the house—and had destroyed them.

Or thought he could get to them—before anyone else did—if they were still in a safety-deposit box, somewhere.

After all, he was Eileen's attorney. So he could get into her safety-deposit box, right, to get to the will, before her kids returned home?

"I think," I said to Mrs. Oglevee, "that if Eileen did keep the letters, then whoever is after them, must have already found them—or the key to get where they are."

"Are you sure?" Mrs. Oglevee asked. "Think again about what Eileen said about my letters."

"She said that her mom had kept them in a safety-deposit box, and that after Rose died, she'd destroyed them," I repeated, slowly trying to reason out what Mrs. Oglevee wanted me to think of. "But if she couldn't bring herself to destroy them . . . but also didn't want to be tempted to read them . . . she wouldn't keep the key to the safety box in her house or within easy reach, either. Whoever searched the house knew she'd hide valuables with her walleye collectibles—that's why they looked at all of those things, and tore them apart . . ." And then suddenly it hit me.

It was a fishy case of hiding something by leaving it in the open.

"The key. She put the key with the 'good luck' lures—what did she call them? Spinners and jigs, I think. Yeah. She would put the key with the lures, because it would blend right in," I said. "And as a, well, key figure in getting the Great Walleye Drop started, she could go see Wylie, any time, and in the meantime, Wylie is kept locked safely away . . ."

Mrs. Oglevee looked proud—and just a little exasperated—that I'd finally figured this out.

"Eileen was pretty wily after all," she said, grinning. "Don't you think?"

28

I waited until 7:52 a.m.—the exact moment on the morning of New Year's Eve—when I could stand waiting no longer, and woke up Cherry and Sally, who moaned and groaned at the cruelty of being awoken so early.

I didn't blame them for being annoyed, but truth be told, ever since my dream-encounter with Mrs. Oglevee, I'd tossed and turned, trying to convince myself to just accept the simple explanations that Tanner and Maxine had given the night before.

Sure, they seemed in spots as believable as a one-product-cleans-all ad, but then again, my latest what-if theory seemed a little far-fetched, too.

Which Cherry and Sally grumpily told me when I finally got them awake after threatening them with cold, wet washcloths.

But, to their credit, they listened to my theory. And to my worry that I would always wonder if I was right if I didn't try to find Eileen's key on Wylie's good-luck lure. And to my other worry, that I wouldn't be able to get rid of Mrs. Oglevee from my dream life once and for all if I couldn't say, with full conviction, "It was a heart attack!"

And to my impassioned plea for their help in getting that lure.

They agreed to help me, mostly because Plan A for doing so was very simple. A good thing. At that moment, it was also my only plan.

Shortly after breakfast—again, at the Port-O'-Call Diner, which seemed to be the only place open near the town square, we walked around a little bit, and found several restaurants and coffee shops closed for the season.

We also wandered past the newspaper office (closed for the holiday), post office (open), Great Lakes Popcorn Company (open later), the old movie theatre (now the office for Davis Brothers Plumbing, with IF YOU'VE GOT GUNK, WE'LL GET IT UNSTUCK on the marquee, which led to some debate about whether or not the slogan would be improved if "unstuck" were changed to "unstunk,") and the armory, (which had at one time been converted to an arts/crafts shop but which had been put up for sale.)

We all paused a moment at the World War II tank and the eternal flame, both in a tiny park behind the old armory. And we were all glad that those memorials were still well preserved.

Then we hurried over to the Port-O'-Call for breakfast, where I casually asked our waitress if she knew when Wylie-the-fiberglass-walleye would be on display, as I was so eager to get my photo taken with him.

"Oh, any time, between ten and noon," she said, and told us to look for Wylie on the east end of the town square.

Sure enough, there he was—all twenty feet and six hundred glorious pounds of him—in the back of a heavy-duty flatbed truck. The crane was the kind used to hoist beams for buildings.

Wylie and his crane were surrounded by snow fencing, held in place by four portable posts.

And men—bundled up for long watches—were at each post.

"Why are they guarding Wylie?" Sally asked. "It's not like anyone could steal a six hundred-pound fish and mount it on his wall."

That had been my thinking, which is why Plan A was me sidling up next to Wylie for a photo while no one except the photographer was watching. Sally was supposed to be the photographer, and Cherry was supposed to distract the men by jabbering at them about something—anything. I was simply going to nab the good-luck lure collection, look for the key, take it if it was there, and return the lure to Wylie's fiberglass lips. Or mouth. Or whatever you call a fish's bait-hole.

That, I could see, wasn't going to work.

"Maybe they're worried about someone—" Cherry started.

"—spraying Wylie with graffiti!" I finished, before she could give us away.

"What a sad world, in which someone would spray graffiti on a fiberglass walleye," Caleb said, a mite sardonically.

"Truly," Dean said, sounding outraged at the very thought.

"Can you imagine? I mean what if someone sprayed— Perch Rules!" Caleb said. I swatted his arm, and glanced at Dean.

But he didn't seem to catch that Caleb was teasing him. "Or, Cormorants Rule," Dean said. "Do you think there's been some Wylie threat from Maxine and her environmentalist cronies . . ."

Sally, Cherry, and I ambled toward Wylie.

"Now what?" Sally whispered.

"We get the picture, anyway," I muttered. "Your camera's digital, right?"

"Yeah," Sally said. "A Christmas gift from my ex-in-laws." In some ways, she was closer to her ex-in-laws than she was to her own family of origin.

"Take just a regular one of me. Then I'll try to hold out the lure, and you zoom in and take lots of close-ups. We'll study them later. Make excuses about how this is a new camera—a gift—and you have to take lots of pictures. That will give me time to study the lure," I said.

"What do I do?" Cherry asked.

"Chat up the Wylie guards. Find out why they're guarding Wylie and if the big fish is ever left alone," I said.

"Then what?" Sally asked.

"We go shopping—just us three," I said.

"Oooh, yay!" Cherry said, a little too loudly. "It's taken you until you're thirty, but you finally want to go shopping! For clothes, right? Not for books, like usual?"

"Neither," I said. "I just need us to get away for a bit so we can come up with a Plan B—if I find a key on the lure."

It turned out that Wylie's guards were very nice, letting us take plenty of time with me right by Wylie—and the lure—and plenty of pictures.

It also turned out that, sadly, Dean was right—there'd been phone call threats on poor Wylie, one of the guards told us, threatening his lovely greenish-yellow scales with mutilation.

My heart clenched when, mixed in with the shiny spinners and jigs, I saw the key, small and brass, just right for a safety-deposit box. The key and lures were secured to an O-ring—piercing the big fish's lower lip (Wylie, the original Goth walleye) by a simple asymmetrical clip that would snap open on the side with just a little thumb pressure. The wide end of the clip held the lures—and the key—and the narrower end went through the ring on Wylie.

I recognized the clip—I'd used similar ones in strapping old washers and dryers onto dollies for moving out of my laundromat—and wasn't surprised such clips would be useful in boating and fishing as well. I only needed a few seconds to get the clip off, then get the key off, and then return the clip—but they had to be seconds when no one was paying attention.

That was going to be the tricky part.

But after the photo op, Sally, Cherry, and I took off in Sally's truck. We'd told Caleb and Dean we had to go shopping for new clothes for the Great Walleye Drop festivities (Caleb: "But won't we all be bundled up in coats and gloves, anyway?" Dean: "Don't ask, brother. Cherry can find any reason to shop.")

We headed generally west, toward Toledo, and brainstormed until we came up with a Plan B.

Which, sadly, was not as simple as Plan A.

But which, to Cherry's delight, ended up involving shopping. As well as calling Wylie—that is, Henry Steinbrunner—and convincing him to help us.

Without, of course, telling him what we were really up to.

"So, what do you think of my new boots?" Cherry asked Dean.

He looked down, as Cherry coyly turned around, modeling the spike-heeled, faux fur (hot pink with leopard spots) boots that she'd bought on our Plan B shopping trip. Along with matching scarf, gloves, and hat.

Cherry had argued that she, at least, had to buy something on our shopping trip other than our Plan B items, or Dean and Caleb would definitely know something was up.

Sally and I had agreed, but argued that boots that were not spike-heeled would be a better choice, just in case things went wrong and we had to run. We should have known that Cherry would not be able to resist hot-pink, leopard-spotted boots.

In the town square, Dean was admiring Cherry's boots—or at least the calves they encased—lustily. Cherry was sad that Dean had told her he would have to leave right after the Great Walleye Drop, in order to get back in time for his New Year's Day shift. But, to her credit, she didn't suggest she and Dean skip the festivities and go back to the Perry Inn, leaving Sally and me to pull off Plan B.

If you could call what we were witnessing "festivities."

It was almost 9:30 in the evening. The main street through town square had been blocked off. The air was redolent with the scent of frying funnel cakes—from one food truck—and Italian sausage—from the only other food truck—but not of fish.

In fact, we couldn't find one place that was serving anything walleye.

Well, the Great Lakes Popcorn Company had "Wild Walleye" popcorn, which was popcorn seasoned with Cajun spices. We'd all opted to share a box of caramel-flavored popcorn, though.

Few people were out in the town square, or in the tent that featured a carnival "fishing" game for kids (sponsored by the local high school's Junior Optimists club, with all proceeds going to the local Habitat for Humanity, so we all chipped in five bucks each), and a table where Great Walleye Drop Christmas ornaments were for sale—metal ornaments shaped like walleye (Sally, Cherry, and I each bought one of those), and another table where glow-in-the-dark necklaces were for sale (proceeds to the local alumni association of Ohio State University.)

The university's fight song was playing from a portable stereo. Sally and Cherry gave me nervous looks. I tried to smile, reassuringly, although I was pretty nervous myself, and suggested we check out the T-shirt shop.

The shop, open late just for this event, was packed with folks flipping through T-shirts with amusing—but bawdy—sayings. Unfortunately, one of the first T-shirts Sally found was one that referred to Ann Arbor (the location of University of Michigan) as a naughty girl, in not-very-nice terms.

Cherry and Sally gave me more nervous looks.

"It's a little after ten," I said, checking my watch. "We'd better get a move on if we want to be close to the stage."

"Why would we want to do that?" Caleb said. The nice lady selling the walleye ornaments had told us that the on-stage entertainment didn't start until 10:30. Caleb was all for hanging out in the Cut Bait, and watching the Great Walleye Drop from the window. Or, at most, running out around 11:58, then running back in at 12:02.

"Because of the Elvis impersonator," Cherry said. "I just love Elvis impersonators!"

Dean looked at her, confused. "You do?"

"I do," said Cherry.

"Me, too," I said.

"Really?" said Caleb, also looking confused.

"Really."

"Me, too. Yeah, the tall chick without a date on this shindig," said Sally, "I love Elvis impersonators, too!"

As it turned out, the Great Walleye Drop Elvis impersonator (Las Vegas version, but with gold-studded white gloves and scarf, in consideration of the location), who was really Gary Kruetcher, was really a good singer. Every now and then he forgot he was impersonating Elvis, and slid into his own style, and then he was even better. So it wasn't too hard to scream and yell maniacally whenever he came to the part of the stage where we stood. He even kneeled down a few times and gave us hankies, which, of course, had not a bit of sweat on them, since it was twenty-some degrees, although he obligingly patted his brow.

Wylie the Walleye Mascot—Henry Steinbrunner—in his walleye fish suit—danced onstage, too, but didn't say anything.

The master of ceremonies—none other than Tanner Van-Wort Jr.—announced that sadly, Wylie had a bit of laryngitis and wouldn't be able to sing along this year.

I felt relief at that announcement—Wylie was going along with Plan B instead of bailing out—but nervous that soon I'd be on stage with Tanner Jr. The crowd started to grow. I took a few moments to glance around at the faces.

And I was touched. These were the faces of hard-working people. It had been easy, earlier, to laugh to myself at the idea of lowering a big fiberglass fish on New Year's Eve—but maybe the people here, who relied on sportfishing as a major part of their economy, needed a good-luck ritual, if only to make them think positively about the upcoming season.

But I wasn't sure why so many people had referred to the event as "wild." There was a lot of smoking in the crowd. Very little drinking. No rabble-rousing.

Everyone applauded nicely when the fishing captain of the year was named.

Everyone went along with Tanner leading the crowd in the "Lake Erie wave," just like sports stadium "waves," only from the front of the crowd to the back, and then to the front again.

Everyone cheered dutifully when Tanner pointed out the Toledo News's TV van and camera crew at the edge of the crowd.

Truth be told, the only people who got a little wild were the five of us. Maybe we just weren't as used to the cold as the northern crowd, and it got to us, but it seemed to make sense to dance to "All Shook Up."

Just as it made sense to lock arms and sway as we sang along to "American Trilogy," Elvis's remix of "Dixie," "Battle Hymn of the Republic," and "Hush Little Baby," which Tanner Jr. said we should all sing along to in memory of Eileen.

It should have been a serious moment, but it actually sent me into giggling fits. It just seemed a little surreal to be only a few hundred yards away from Lake Erie on New Year's Eve, crooning "Look away, look away, look away Dixieland," along with an Elvis impersonator, performing below a dangling six hundred-pound Walleye, and onstage with a man dressed as a fish, and another man who'd turned out to be the love child of my old, feared school teacher and who, I thought, might have something to do after all with Eileen's death.

But my giggling fit ceased when Wylie patted his left shoulder. We'd worked that out as his sign to his handler that he had to visit the facilities.

As Wylie and his handler left the stage, I said to Caleb, "I'll be back in a little bit."

He frowned. "But it's fifteen minutes until midnight."

"Sorry," I said. "I—I have to go to the bathroom." I hurried away, through the crowd.

Three minutes later, I was in the men's room at the Cut Bait, standing on top of a toilet seat, thankful that men's rooms never seem to be occupied. No one noticed me going into the Sea-Guy's room. Everyone was gathered by the window, waiting to see the big fish come down.

I heard a little cheer, and calls of "Hey, Wylie."

Then the door opened, and shut again.

"Josie?" Henry's voice was barely intelligible through the costume mouth hole. Nice to know, in case I needed to speak.

I hopped off the toilet seat, opened the door and popped out. Henry already had the walleye head off.

"I could get in so much trouble for this," he said.

I pulled a stuffed envelope out of my coat pocket. He started to grab for the envelope, but I pulled back.

"A deal's a deal," I said. "I get to be on stage for the lowering of Wylie—as Wylie the mascot—and you get three hundred dollars."

He looked at me and shook his head, but started unzipping the costume's front. "I don't get it . . . this is your big thirtieth birthday fantasy?"

"Yep," I said, trying to look eager as I stared at the fish head.

Oh Lord, I thought, help me out. I'm not exactly claustrophobic—but I don't really like closed spaces, either. I'd dressed up once as the Easter Bunny for the children's Easter Egg hunt at my church—and swore I'd never do it again.

Why did I have to remember that—now?

But I was closest in height and size to Wylie, so I was the one who had to do this.

Sally and Cherry just had to divert the crowd—without getting killed.

"Now, listen," said Henry, "you had better not tell anyone

about this, ever. My name would be lower than cormorant poop around here if anyone knew—"

"Don't worry," I said. "Sally, Cherry, and I will never tell a soul. Just help me get in the walleye costume. We don't have much time."

I handed him the envelope, and smiled, trying to look thrilled.

Ten minutes later, I was onstage—dressed as Wylie the Walleye. The fact I was about two inches shorter than Henry must not have been noticeable with me in the costume, and in the dark, because my escort just said, "C'mon, gotta hurry if you're going to be back onstage in time."

Navigating up the steps to the stage was trickier than I'd anticipated—partly because of the fishing boots that were part of the costume, and partly because I was trying not to hyperventilate in the fish head.

But then I was onstage. "Elvis" was asking me to dance along with him to one last tune—"Jailhouse Rock," which surely we'd all be humming if we were caught—and somehow, I managed to do the twist, and glance down through the screened eyeholes at Sally, Cherry, Dean, and Caleb. I felt a pang as Caleb looked around the crowd, acting worried, watching for me to return.

Then the song was over, and Tanner Jr. clapped me on the back, and I stumbled just a step.

"Wylie, you ready for the big count down?" Tanner said enthusiastically into his microphone. "We have just thirty seconds!"

I nodded, trying to put eagerness into the gesture.

"Everyone, you ready?"

The crowd roared—finally showing a little wildness.

And then we were counting down.

"Ten . . . nine . . . eight . . ."

The crane started lowering Wylie the fiberglass fish— very slowly.

"Seven . . . six . . . five . . ."

I shuffled so that I was standing close to where Wylie would come down.

"Four . . . three . . ."

Wylie was getting closer—slowly—but my heart fell, fast. At the rate he was lowering, I wasn't sure I'd be able to reach that good-luck talisman of lures.

"Two . . . one . . . *Happy New Year!*"

Wylie, the fiberglass fish, was as low as he was going to go, his fishy lips and the lure, dangling head-high, not three feet from me.

The crowd was cheering.

A fireworks display—launched from a boat not far offshore in Lake Erie—began.

And Cherry and Sally went to work. They ripped off their coats, scrambled on the stage before Dean and Caleb could stop them, and revealed, for the whole crowd to see—their chests.

Not naked, of course. That wouldn't have created as much a stir as what they were wearing.

Which were navy blue sweatshirts, decorated with gold "*M*'s" for University of Michigan.

Earlier that day, we discovered that there wasn't a single University of Michigan sweatshirt at the Toledo-area mall we visited. So we'd crafted our own—from the sweatshirts and sparkly gold fabric paint.

And as Cherry and Sally hollered, "Michigan rocks in the new year!" and Tanner yelled "get those nuts off of my stage," and Dean and Caleb jumped up to do just that, I turned my back to the crowd, unscrewed the clip of lures, grabbed half of them—along with the key—and clipped the rest back on, then turned back around.

I didn't think anyone noticed. Everyone was staring at Cherry and Sally, and yelling at them, while Caleb said, "Sorry, sorry, they had too much to drink," even though that wasn't true. In fact, the four of them didn't seem to notice me as they hurried down the steps, off the stage.

I counted to three, and walked down the steps, too, and right up to my handler, and thumped my shoulder with my fist clenched around the lures and the key.

"What, again?" he said, staring off angrily in the direction Cherry, Sally, Caleb, and Dean had run.

I put my hand to my stomach, and bent forward, as if I needed to throw up.

That got his attention. We hurried back to the Cut Bait, and the men's room.

29

"What in the hell were Sally and Cherry thinking?" Caleb asked incredulously.

"I don't know," I said, with a guilty pang at my white lie.

Caleb and I were back in my motel room. The lures—including the key—were zipped safely in my coat pocket. I'd managed to get ahead of my handler, unzip the front of the suit as we walked, shove the key and lures in my coat pocket and zip it up, and then re-zip the walleye suit, just as we walked in the Cut Bait.

Then—after more reassurances to Henry that of course none of us would mention this incident—I turned the suit over to Henry. I waited a few minutes after the rightful Wylie had exited the men's room, and then through the crowd, abuzz with chatter about "those crazy Michigan fans."

I headed back to the Perry Inn, where, sure enough, I found a tearful Cherry apologizing to Dean, who was not at all amused at Sally's and her antics, while Sally tried not to laugh, and Caleb just looked confused. All Sally and Cherry would say was that they thought it would be funny.

I claimed no knowledge of their prank (this white lie was part of our plan, because we knew Caleb and Dean wouldn't believe I'd pull such a stunt, another reason I was the one who had to dress up as Wylie) and commented on how Sally and Cherry always had been ones to pull such crazy stunts (which was true), and said they must have bought the sweatshirt supplies while I'd been browsing the bookstore (also true.)

Finally, Dean gave Cherry a long hug and a demure kiss and told her of course he loved her, anyway, and then headed back to Paradise, so he'd be in time for his 7:00 a.m. work roll call.

Cherry and Sally decided to go out for "just one drink," which worried me, but Sally promised she'd keep an eye on Cherry, who said she needed to calm her nerves, since she was afraid Dean was really upset with her. Sally left her truck keys on the dresser, telling Cherry the walk would do her some good.

I think she was thinking if Cherry didn't have a ride home, and had to walk, she'd be less likely to overdo the drowning of her sorrows.

That left Caleb and me . . . alone. In the motel room.

Which made me a little nervous. And excited, too.

"Well," Caleb was saying, "you do have some crazy friends."

I laughed. "Yeah. Don't know where they get their ideas."

Caleb suddenly looked serious. "Missed seeing you at the stroke of midnight. I wanted to give you a New Year's kiss."

I smiled at him. "You still could," I said.

He moved from the chair next to me on the edge of the bed.

"Ten," he said, and gave me a tiny kiss on the forehead. "Nine," he murmured and softly kissed my left temple. Oh my . . . By the time he got to "one," he was finally at my lips, and that kiss was not in any way tiny or soft.

In fact, it launched us back on the bed, and he was starting to countdown the unbuttoning of my blouse, when my cell phone rang. I sat up suddenly, and accidentally whacked my forehead into Caleb's jaw.

"Sorry," I said, and hopped off the bed. I grabbed my backpack from off the floor, and then remembered I'd transferred my cell phone to the zipped pocket of my coat, because I didn't want to take my backpack purse to the Great Walleye Drop. Hard to wear that gracefully with a walleye suit—especially if you're supposed to be a man.

"Josie," Caleb was saying, while rubbing his jaw, "it's nearly one a.m. Surely—"

"I always answer my cell phone," I said, digging past the lures and the key to the cell phone. I pulled it out, flipped it open, too distracted by making sure the lures and key were safely still in my coat pocket to check the caller's number. As I answered, I re-zipped my pocket.

I listened for a second, and then pressed my eyes shut, and said. "Happy New Year to you, too, Randy. You're a little late and a little drunk, though, so good night!"

I snapped the phone shut, and put it on the nightstand. Then I rejoined Caleb. "Now," I said, "where were we?"

He smiled down at me, and gave me a soft, little kiss on the forehead. My heart sank. Uh oh. We were right back where we'd started.

"I like you, Josie," he said. "A lot. And I'd like to explore what that means, for both of us, but I'm thinking maybe this isn't the trip to do it on. See you in the morning."

He stood up and walked out, shutting the door gently, and I stayed on the water bed, staring up at a stain on the ceiling.

Was it in the shape of a walleye?

Okay, it was a silly thought. But I was also suddenly teary-eyed—a combination of wishing Caleb would stay, not sure I was ready for him to just yet, and exhaustion from the night's caper—and was willing to think anything to keep myself from melting down.

I drifted awake, realized both that I'd fallen asleep fully clothed and that I hadn't dreamed about Mrs. Oglevee. I fuzzily thought of looking at the clock, but drifted back to sleep . . .

Until my cell phone rang again. I jolted up, answered it.

"Josie? It's Mary. I'm sorry to call so late—well, early, in the morning. But I'm afraid Guy has had a diabetic reaction. He's at Masonville City Hospital—"

"Oh Lord," I moaned. "Okay, listen, I'll be right down."

"Now, Josie, I just wanted you to know. No need to panic—"

But I hung up, assessed the situation.

Glance at clock: 2:00 a.m.

Sally and Cherry not there. Still out partying.

I'd leave a note—no, I'd just call Sally's cell phone once I got on the road, she'd understand . . .

Thank God, I thought, I was fully dressed. I grabbed on my coat, snagged Sally's keys from the dresser, saw a note had been slid under the door and ignored it, and stepped outside.

And then, just as I stepped out, I stopped.

Mary's voice had sounded a little low. And Mary had gotten wrong the name of the regional hospital. She wouldn't do that, I thought, my hands clenching the keys . . .

But the thought came a little too late—just before a sharp crack on my head.

I groaned, feeling nauseous. What was wrong with this sloshing water bed? I was rocking around like I was on a boat.

I opened my eyes, slowly, my head pounding, struggling to sit up, but then I realized my hands were bound in front of me. My ankles were bound.

And I *was* on a boat—with Sally and Cherry, who were bound together, as well as to the built-in dinette table. I was lying in the aisle. The carpet smelled of mildew and fish.

Maxine sat at the wheel, but she wasn't running the boat. She was swiveled in the captain's chair, a battery-powered camper's lamp at her feet. It cast an eerie, greenish glow around the cabin.

We were being towed, I realized, hearing the sound of a motor not far ahead of us.

"Hi, Josie," she said.

I moved my bound hands toward my coat pocket—not that I could get into my pocket.

"Don't bother," she said. "Even if you could get in your pocket, you won't find the key or lures. Got those already."

"You pretended to be Mary," I said.

"Of course. How else to, well, lure you out of the motel room?" She laughed at her little joke. "I asked your pals, there, the best way, and Sally told me. Quickly. A little too quickly—should have noticed that. If you'd have hesitated just a little sooner, we wouldn't have snared you. She 'fessed up soon enough that she'd given me the wrong name of the hospital, hoping you'd catch it, after I asked her a few times why you hesitated like you were going to turn and run back in the motel room."

I looked at Sally. Even in the dim, greenish lighting I could see that her left eye was already swelling shut. She looked defiant—even though she was gagged. Cherry was, too, and she looked terrified.

I looked back at Maxine. "You knocked me out?"

"No, that was Martin," she said. She laughed, seeing the recognition on my face. "Yes, the guy who had the room next to yours—until you got him kicked out. And the guy who tried to knock you out when you left poor Eileen's. I'm surprised he didn't succeed. He's usually good at knocking people out—worked on me, when I stepped out of the Mason County Library for a smoking break. He managed to do it fast, and get me in the back floor of his car and throw a blanket over me. Then he waited, and has been following you—more-or-less—ever since. As a never-to-be-employed again ex-fishing captain, he does whatever my brother wants."

"I—I don't understand," I said, although I understood perfectly well that Sally, Cherry, and I were in grave danger. "I thought you were—"

"Save the questions. I'll just tell you what I'm sure you want to know. We don't have much time. Martin is towing us in this boat—my boat, which is in need of repair, as my neighbor Dell told me he already told Cherry and her sweetheart—yes, Dell repeated the whole conversation to me, word for word, because Dell is like that. We can only go so far before it's too icy for the commercial fishing boat, and then we need to get it back to the company fleet, and back up on blocks, before dawn.

"You already know much of the truth. Pearl Armbruster was my brother's—my half brother's—birth mother. Dad confessed that on his deathbed, and some other things, too. One was that he and Pearl had a confrontation with Sol. Pearl was going to leave Sol, and dad was going to leave mom—divorce was scandalous in those days, but Pearl was pregnant with my brother.

"Sol reacted with anger, hitting Pearl. She'd put up with abuse from him in the past, but this time, she wanted to protect the child she was carrying, so she hit him—again and again. And dad joined in. Who knows who landed the final, fatal blow? In any case, he was dead, and they dumped his body in the woods. The police were happy to assume that Sol had been beaten up by someone he cheated, and there wasn't much of an investigation.

"After that, although they loved each other, they just couldn't be together, and Pearl didn't think she could raise a child as a single mother. So she gave up Tanner to my parents, who raised them as theirs—and then had me."

I was fascinated, even though I was scared, but as I listened to Maxine—who spoke in a tired monologue—I kept looking around the cabin, hoping to find something that could help Sally, Cherry, and me.

"Fast-forward to ten years ago. Pearl contacted my father, telling him she wanted to see him before she went on her dream cruise. He showed up at her house late at night, and she turned on him. I guess a lifetime of regret and bitterness had turned her love to hate. She told him she had already sent a letter to someone close to her—that had to be Rose—confessing what they'd done. She didn't know that her sister had died the month before. Anyway, Pearl was planning to disappear in Europe, after sending letters about what they'd done to everyone he knew—unless he gave her a half million, I guess to make her new life there much more comfortable."

Maxine gave a derisive laugh. "Was she nuts? Dad had money—but not money like that."

I saw it, then—the tackle box. If the plan was that Maxine would leave us here, then after she and Martin left, I could simply get to the box, and somehow nudge it open, and get out a fishing knife. There had to be a knife in the tackle box, right?

"In any case, Pearl's request made dad angry. He confessed to us that he grabbed a heavy skillet, and ran at her with it, but before he could hit her with it, she collapsed. He'd scared her into a heart attack.

"He left her there and learned later she'd been found, and her death ruled a heart attack, but of course he blamed himself. And a few years later, as he was dying, he wanted us to know the truth—to protect ourselves in case Pearl really had sent that confessional letter to Rose, and Eileen had read it.

"But Eileen either never did, or was such a friend of our family, that she wasn't going to use it against us," Maxine concluded. "So, there's the whole story."

"Not quite," I said. "You came to see me. You gave me a note that claimed you were Pearl's daughter, that she'd been murdered."

"Like I said yesterday evening—well, really two days ago, now—I made the claim about being Pearl's daughter to get your attention. And Pearl, in a sense, was murdered. My father literally scared her to death, by his own account."

The fact that Mrs. Oglevee was older, probably had high blood pressure, and had lived a tension-filled life, and was stressed by anticipating the Europe trip and her confrontation with her old lover had all been major factors, too—but I decided not to point that out.

"And, like I said, I thought you were close to her, due to the article about the speech, and that you'd listen sympathetically. I'd planned to tell you everything I'd just told you—except Martin nabbed me before I got the chance."

I looked at Sally and Cherry. They were both staring at me wide-eyed. I gave them a look that I hoped flashed: we will get out of this. Somehow.

"And what was I supposed to do when you told me?" I asked.

"Be outraged on behalf of your old friend and teacher," Maxine said. "Go with me to your media contacts to spread the news—because no one would take me seriously, alone."

"But—why? Why would you want to do this, now?"

"My brother is about to run for Congress," Maxine said. "And I have no doubts he'll win. And if he does, he plans to support legislation to make the local killing of cormorants, and oiling of cormorant eggs, legal." For the first time, there was passion, and anger, in her voice. "If news like this came out, he wouldn't win, though. Being an illegitimate child is something most voters would overlook. Knowing his father was party to murder—twice—and hiding that fact for eight years? No. If I could prevent his election, and give his opponent the chance to win, well, then the cormorants might have a chance."

"But you changed your mind," I said, still confused. I dared another glance at the tackle box. It wasn't locked. I looked at Cherry and Sally, tried to convey: *We'll be okay.*

Maxine shrugged. "Tanner had you followed, knew you'd been to Eileen's house. Martin didn't have orders to hit you that night, but he did, hoping to see if Eileen had given you anything of interest. Trying to score brownie points. Meanwhile, I'd been kept tied up—just like the three of you—in a rarely used storage room at the company. Tied me up, just like the three of you now. I finally told him that, apparently, Pearl left a will with her attorney—I'm guessing she set it up thinking she'd get the half million from my father, and that she'd have a fake certificate of death sent to the attorney as she disappeared in Europe—that dictated that when her estate reached a certain amount, the bequest would go to the library.

"And that two letters would be sent. One to me—telling me to ask Eileen about a letter sent to her. And, it follows, one to Eileen. Those letters were sent just a month ago. I tried to talk to Eileen, but she told me she knew nothing about any letter from her aunt, that I was just as crazy as her aunt had been. I could tell she was lying. Eileen's always been terrible at hiding her true thoughts.

"After I told this to Tanner, he told me we would go to Eileen together, and insist she share the letter, and that if I helped him convince her to do so, he'd back off on the cormorant-killing legislation as part of his campaign platform. I agreed. We went to Eileen's not long after you left. She said all her letter said was that Pearl knew she hadn't cared for her, and that Rose had kept her letters private, and that Eileen probably had never read the letters—but that she should. Then Eileen tried to tell us that after her mother died, she got rid of the safety-deposit box and of the letters, unread.

"Something in Tanner's manner scared her. He became furious with her. He hit her, hard, and she fell, hitting her head against the sharp corner of the living room table. Then he grabbed a lamp, and hit her again. She died before I could stop him."

"Another murder in the passion of the moment that you're willing to cover up?" I said. "Because of a deal you cut with your brother . . . to possibly protect cormorants? Another congressperson could propose the very same type of legislation your brother wanted—"

"Yes! To protect cormorants!" Maxine snapped, and I realized I needed to shut up. She'd built a whole identity around protecting these birds. It was who she was. The only way she had to relate to her father. And she didn't want her brother to so vehemently oppose her on this. She was willing to hurt us to protect the birds . . . and, so, to protect her own identity.

"Tanner is Eileen's attorney and executor. He knew if he could get the key, he could get in her safety-deposit box before her kids return to town. He knows where she banks, so it wouldn't be difficult—if he had the key. But he tore the place up, looking for it, and couldn't find it—until tonight."

Maxine patted her coat pocket. "From your pocket, to mine," she said.

"But how did you know—"

Before I could finish the question, Maxine was over by Cherry. She pulled off the gag, harshly.

Cherry immediately started sobbing. "Oh, Josie, I'm so sorry . . ."

Sally gave her a hard look, and I knew if she could have, she'd have kicked her. I pressed my eyes shut. They didn't need to tell me—I knew what had happened. Cherry, despite her best intentions, despite Sally's efforts to keep her company, had started talking about our caper and how it upset Dean and how she was just trying to help . . .

. . . the very kind of thing I'd said in the past, right before I mucked things up.

"Martin was at the Cut Bait tonight," Maxine said, smiling.

I looked at Maxine. "What are you going to do to us?"

Maxine looked away, a flicker of guilt crossing her face. "Leave you out here. Ride back to shore with Martin. If you're lucky, hypothermia will set in before this boat sinks." She looked back at me, her face rigid. "Don't think Martin will have second thoughts—he's paid too well. Don't think I will, either. I'm doing this for Tanner—his insurance that I won't tell what happened at Eileen's. I don't have it in me to directly kill you, so I'll just let the ice storm and sinking boat do that."

"But—"

"No. Don't try to convince me Tanner will change his

mind about backing off of the legislation. We're both in too deep now."

She glanced at the tackle box. "Don't want to leave this in here. Knowing you, you'd try some heroics to save yourself and your friends. It's going overboard!"

My heart fell. She was right; part of my mind had been thinking, if I could just butt-scoot to that box, flip open its lid, maybe I'd find a fishing knife and could somehow maneuver to cut the ropes. Maxine tried to pick up the box, but it was too heavy, so she shoved it to outside the cabin, on the side that seemed to be sinking.

Maxine came back in. She pulled Sally's gag off, too, and Sally immediately started yelling curses at her.

"Sally, no," I said, shaking my head. If we could just talk, maybe we'd work out a plan to save ourselves.

Sally piped down, and Maxine chortled. "Let her scream if she wants. No one's going to hear any of you, anyway. Besides, the more you scream and talk, the more energy you use up. Ice storm coming. This is where we leave you off."

She started to walk out of the cabin, and then came back in with a wrench—probably from the tackle box. Which meant, maybe, she'd left it unlatched . . .

"Nothing to tie you to, Josie," she said, "At least not fast, and Martin and I need to get out of here."

Then she lifted the wrench and brought it down on my head.

30

When I finally came to, the first thing I heard was Sally and Cherry screaming my name. My first question was how long had I been out—maybe fifteen minutes, they said. My next question was why was the cabin dark; the battery-powered camper's lamp had still been on when Maxine had knocked me out. Sally said Maxine had turned out the lamp but hadn't bothered to take it with her.

That woman really wanted our last moments to be cold and miserable. But I wasn't going to give up without a struggle.

I tried chewing through the rope around my wrists while Cherry and Sally quibbled. I quickly gave up on chewing—we'd sink before I'd gnaw my way through.

Our boat rammed into something hard—huge ice chunk? I was hoping for pier or land. I told Cherry to stop humming the *Titanic* movie theme, and tried to think.

The tackle box . . . just outside the cabin. Maybe if I could butt-scoot to it, I could find a knife inside, cut myself free, cut Sally and Cherry free, and somehow the three of us would figure out a way to get help.

Sally and Cherry talked. I thought about telling them to

be quiet, to preserve their energy, but then I realized if chatting kept them calm, that was good.

The next thud sent me spinning across the floor. I started butt-scooting again and finally got to the cabin door. I worked my way out, gasping at the first hit of icy rain. Somehow, I found the tackle box, used my bound hands to lever the lid open, and used my teeth to pull the glove off my right hand so I could more easily feel around for a knife.

I yelped when the knife stabbed into the side of my hand. Calm, calm, I told myself. I awkwardly maneuvered the knife with the tips of my fingers, moving slowly and carefully although I felt panicked. But if I lost the knife, we were doomed for sure.

Finally, I angled the knife's blade up in the tackle box—using the top fold-out compartment and the inside of the box to hold the knife more or less steady. Then I turned my hands so that the rope on the top of my right wrist was against the sharp edge and started sawing slowly, with a back and forth motion.

But just as the rope gave way, the boat lurched again, and the motion made me lurch, too, so that the knife stabbed the top of my left wrist. Still, I grabbed the knife with my right hand, knowing I had to have that knife to save us.

I heard Cherry's voice, tried to respond, but then a rush of warmth and light-headedness took over . . . I heard Mrs. Oglevee yelling at me to wake back up, grab some rags inside the cabin, stop the bleeding . . . how did she know about rags in the cabin? . . . never mind that . . . I had to wake back up. Try. I had a lot to live for, and so did Sally and Cherry.

A cold, sudden slap of lake water woke me up. The boat was listing dangerously now.

I was still clutching the knife with my good hand. Calm, I told myself, as I cut the rope binding my ankles. I crawled back into the cabin and knocked into something. It took me a few seconds to realize it was the battery-powered camper's lamp.

Finally, I got it on, and felt a rush of relief at its greenish glow. Then I spotted, under the captain's chair, the box of rags. I got to the box, grabbed a rag, wrapped it around my wrist and made my way over to Cherry and Sally.

"Sally, I'm cutting you free first, then you undo Cherry, then both of you come help me find a radio," I said.

I started working on the ropes around Sally's wrists.

"What if there isn't a radio?" Cherry said.

"Houseboats always have radios," Sally said. "Look at the helm—by the steering wheel."

"What if Maxine took the radio?" Cherry said.

"Then we figure out Plan B," I said.

Cherry groaned.

"Steady, Sally," I said. "I'm going to slip the blade under the rope here." I pointed to where I'd been cutting from the top. "And then I want you to pull down in one fast movement."

"Got it," Sally said. We did just as I said. I handed her the knife, and she got to work on the rope around her ankles.

I stumbled back to the helm. I could feel that one side of the boat—the left side, from my perspective, since I didn't know actual nautical terms—was distinctly lower than the other. How long did we have before the wind and the sinking made the boat capsize? Half an hour? Less?

Finally, I found it—a tiny handheld orange radio. And I had no idea how to use it . . .

"Just find the On switch! It's probably battery powered," Sally called.

I did what she said, trying to focus, but my earlier head wounds and the cut in the top of my wrist were making me dizzy.

Then the radio cackled to life.

"The National Weather Service has issued an ice storm warning for all of northern Ohio . . ."

I glared at the radio, found the channel selector. The radio was on channel 1.

"There's a channel for emergency transmissions," Sally

called, "but I don't know what it is! Just keep flipping to each channel, keep trying!"

I flipped to channel 2. "Mayday, Mayday," I hollered at the radio. But that didn't seem to be the right channel.

Now both Sally and Cherry were free. Cherry stumbled over to me. "Oh God, Josie, keep t-trying," she said.

Channel three. "Mayday, Mayday . . ."

"I'm getting the life jackets," Sally said. "Keep trying, Josie!"

But I passed out again, somewhere around channel 6.

Mrs. Oglevee and I were sitting in a small fishing boat, facing each other. It was a spring day, and we were on a lake, no shoreline within sight. Just us, the boat, the water. At least the water was calm, the breeze warm, and the sky sunny.

"So," Mrs. Oglevee said, "I had a heart attack, but as a result of Tanner threatening me at a very stressful moment. I might have had it, anyway, without Tanner, or perhaps his threat was enough to cause it. I guess there's no way to know that . . . unless I ever see Tanner again."

I was startled. Had I been telling her all about what Sally, Cherry, and I learned from Maxine? I reckoned so.

"I'm not sure I really want to see Tanner again," Mrs. Oglevee said. She sighed. "But I would like to see Rose. Perhaps on my travels."

I noticed, then, that she was dressed in a tan coatdress and a matching hat. At her feet was a small toiletries case.

"You're going somewhere?" I asked.

Mrs. Oglevee smiled. "You kept your promise. You found out how I died," she said. "So now I have to keep mine." She leaned forward and looked side to side, and then whispered, "They're very strict about that kind of thing here."

She sat up again, primly, and I was even more startled to realize that this—the outfit and pose—was exactly how she probably dressed and looked as she waited, with her sister, to get on that bus to New York.

Only now, her face was lined with sadness and time.

"It's up to you, Josie," she said. "I can stay . . . or go. Your choice."

I stared at her for a long moment. This was it. I could banish Mrs. Oglevee from my dreams. Never have to deal with her popping up in the middle of a good sleep to nag me.

The lake and sky started fading from blue to a steely white.

"Wait!" I said. "I . . . I don't know! What do you want? I mean, I know it's my decision, but . . ."

But Mrs. Oglevee offered no advice. She just gazed at me, smiling, apparently at peace with either decision. The whiteness edged onto our fishing boat, around Mrs. Oglevee . . .

"Josie?" I heard, as if from a great distance. Someone else speaking. Not Mrs. Oglevee. Not here.

Now the lake and sky were gone, and Mrs. Oglevee was melting into the nothingness . . .

"Stay!" I yelled. "Stay!"

I came to in Magruder Hospital in Port Clinton, Ohio.

The first few hours after that were confusing, but eventually I was able to get the information I needed to put together what happened after I passed out.

By the time I was out of the hospital, it even made sense.

Sally and Cherry kept trying the radio channels, until finally hitting on channel 16, which is, it turns out, the calling and emergency channel for VHF radios (the type we found on the boat.)

We weren't too far out from shore—ice floes prevented Martin from towing us out much farther—and the fact the boat ended up wedged between two ice floes was really what saved us—they slowed the sinking of the boat.

"Miraculous," our rescuers—members of the Marblehead Coast Guard Station—said later. They picked up our distress call almost as soon as it came in and sent in rescue helicopters.

Cherry says I was in and out during the rescue, but I don't remember any of it.

Of course, the story has been told so many times at Bar-None, that pretty soon I'm going to think I remember it.

We were all treated for hypothermia, and I was kept an extra day for concussion. Sally and Cherry stayed at the Perry Inn, though, until I was released.

And by the time I was out, the Port Clinton police had heard our story, and tracked down Martin, Maxine, and Tanner. Tanner, of course, tried to deny everything. But Maxine and Martin quickly confessed. When Eileen's safety-deposit box—she'd kept her mom's box—was finally opened, and the letters found, our story was confirmed. The final letter from Pearl to Rose—unopened for years—confessed Pearl and Tanner Sr.'s murder of Sol Levine.

Maxine, Tanner, and Martin were all taken to jail, pending trial for attempted murder. Eventually, we'd have to go testify against them, but for the time being, we were glad to be back home in Paradise.

Pretty soon, though, even the regulars at Toadfern's Laundromat, and Cherry's Chat N Curl, and Sally's Bar-None were tired of our Great Walleye Drop tale of bravado—although the town buzz about Mrs. Oglevee as an exotic dancer and murderess would continue for a long time.

On the evening of January 6, Cherry, Caleb, Dean, and I were at Sally's bar, enjoying some barbequed chicken wings and beers all around.

Dean, who was horrified that he'd almost lost Cherry, had forgiven her for her shenanigans at the Great Walleye Drop—and Sally and me for having talked her into them.

"Wanna dance, sugar cakes?" he asked her.

"Sure, sweetie pie," she said.

And off they went to the dance floor. Since Cherry's hot-pink faux-leopard fur boots had been destroyed on the boat, she'd gotten a new pair. *Purple* faux-leopard fur boots. With spike heels. And they actually looked good with her purple faux-leather miniskirt.

"Only Cherry," Caleb said, chortling.

I laughed. "To friends," I said, and tapped my beer mug against Caleb's.

Then his look turned serious. "I left you a note that night," Caleb said, "under the motel door."

I glanced down in my beer mug. "I'm sorry I never saw it."

"I can tell you what it said."

I looked up. "Okay."

"I just wrote that I couldn't sleep, so I decided I might as well be like Dean, and drive through the night. But that I find you . . ." He reached across the table and took my hand. ". . . very appealing. And I'd like to go out more with you—just the two of us. But that you can answer your cell phone, any time, and I won't mind . . . as long as you do one thing."

"What's that?" I asked. If it was about turning it off from time to time . . .

"Could you change your ring tone?"

I laughed. "Okay. We can pick one together, if you like."

"Later," Caleb said. "Want to dance?"

I was about to say sure, but then I heard a whoop from the dance floor. It was Dean.

"I just whispered in this little lady's ear, would she marry me, and you know what she said? She said yes! I'm the luckiest man alive!"

"God help the poor guy," Sally said. She'd just come over to our table with another pitcher of beer.

"Guess we'd better congratulate the lucky couple," Caleb said, standing up. He waited for me.

"Go on," Sally said, shooing him along. "I want to ask Josie something. We'll be over in a moment."

He held his ground and lifted an eyebrow at her.

"Woman talk," she said.

He turned and headed for the dance floor.

"Works every time," I said.

She sat down across from me, leaned forward, and whispered, "I just wanted to know . . . have you heard from . . . you know?"

I knew just who she meant. I hadn't told her or Cherry about the fishing-boat dream, and I didn't think I would, not in detail, anyway.

But I smiled at Sally. "Not for a while. I think she finally went on her vacation. But I'm real sure," I said—and was surprised at how glad I was to say it—"that she'll be back."

After all, back in Port Clinton's library, I'd made some New Year's goals . . . and I was sure Mrs. Oglevee would have a firm opinion on every single one.

PARADISE ADVERTISER-GAZETTE

Josie's Stain Busters

by Josie Toadfern
Stain-Removal Expert and Owner of Toadfern's Laundromat
(824 Main Street, Paradise, Ohio)

Where do you get your coffee? I usually just brew mine, myself, or if I'm feeling fancy, I pick up a go-cup at the Beans-Gone-Wild Café at the Pump-N-Save in Masonville.

Truth be told, no matter where you get your coffee—at a fancy place where a "venti-vanilla-latte-half-caf-skinny" costs even more than a gallon of gas—or, well, at the gas station, where you can just get a "large with crème," a coffee stain is a coffee stain . . . and coffee stains are always pesky.

To remove: rinse as soon as possible with cold water, from the back of the stain. Then treat with my favorite standby, a mix of ⅓ white vinegar and ⅔ water. If your coffee included milk and/or sugar, follow the vinegar/water solution with enzymatic pre-wash. Let the treatments soak in for at least 10 minutes before laundering as usual.

A great way to remove coffee stains from cups is to sprinkle baking soda inside the cup, and gently scrub with a sponge.

Here are some other tips I recently found useful:

Makeup (from towels or clothing): baby wipes are good for pre-treating stains, but I also like using a grease-cutting dish detergent. Then wash as usual.

Candle wax: freeze the cloth and peel off as much of the wax as possible. Then, put the stained side down on paper towels, and press the clean side with a warm iron to melt the wax into the tissue. Then launder as usual.

If something smells fishy or smokey . . . Great odor removers in the wash are: white vinegar, borax (my favorite!), and baking soda.

I do want to forewarn my readers though about mixing things willy nilly. Why do you think these stain tips work? Because of chemistry, that's why! (Which is also sometimes why they don't work . . . for example, if you let the stain go too long without treating. You just have to carefully test each tip.) But I've heard some of my customers say (and even read tips on the Internet) that, for example, treating coffee stains with chlorine bleach, even on colored clothing, is okay.

No, no, no! There's no one-solution-for-everything (although I have to say, white vinegar comes mighty close). And you have to know what you're doing when mixing things. For example, NEVER mix chlorine bleach with anything acidic, such as vinegar, or ammonia. Harmful—even deadly—fumes ensue! In fact, just do me a favor, and don't mix chlorine bleach with anything ever.

To be extra safe, do what I do. Have one of your soaking buckets JUST for using chlorine beach mixed with hot water to soak pure whites (such as athletic socks—you don't want to use chlorine bleach on fragile fabrics). Label that bucket—you can get a decent plastic one for just two bucks (less than that venti-vanilla-latte-half-caf-skinny will cost you)—with a laundry marker: BLEACH ONLY. That way, you don't have to worry, as you're pouring bleach in a bucket, did I thoroughly rinse that bucket clean of other cleaning products, or not?

Until next month, may your whites never yellow and your colors never fade. But if they do, hop on over and see me at Toadfern's Laundromat—Always a Leap Ahead of Dirt!

Investigate the Hottest New Mysteries!

Sign up for the FREE HarperCollins monthly mystery newsletter,

The Scene of the Crime,

and get to know your favorite authors, win free books, and be the first to learn about the best new mysteries going on sale.

To register, simply go to www.HarperCollins.com, visit our mystery channel page, and at the bottom of the page, enter your email address where it states "Sign up for our mystery newsletter." Then you can tap into monthly Hot Reads, check out our award nominees, sneak a peek at upcoming titles, and discover the best whodunits each and every month.

Get to know the magnificent mystery authors of HarperCollins and sign up today!